My Best Friend, Maybe

ALSO BY CAELA CARTER

Me, Him, Them, and It

My Best Friend, Maybe

CAELA CARTER

BLOOMSBURY
NEW YORK   LONDON   NEW DELHI   SYDNEY

First published in the United States of America in June 2014
by Bloomsbury Children's Books
www.bloomsbury.com

Bloomsbury is a registered trademark of Bloomsbury Publishing Plc

For information about permission to reproduce selections from this book, write to
Permissions, Bloomsbury Children's Books, 1385 Broadway, New York, New York 10018
Bloomsbury books may be purchased for business or promotional use. For information
on bulk purchases please contact Macmillan Corporate and Premium Sales Department at
specialmarkets@macmillan.com

Library of Congress Cataloging-in-Publication Data
Carter, Caela.
My best friend, maybe / Caela Carter.
pages   cm
Summary: Colette's life is near perfect, if boring, so when her ex–best friend, Sadie, asks
her to come on vacation to the Greek Islands for a family wedding, Colette agrees but is
surprised to learn Sadie's true reason for the invitation.
ISBN 978-1-59990-970-7 (hardcover) • ISBN 978-1-61963-235-6 (e-book)
[1. Best friends—Fiction. 2. Friendship—Fiction. 3. Voyages and travels—
Fiction. 4. Weddings—Fiction. 5. Lesbians—Fiction. 6. Greece—Fiction.]
I. Title.
PZ7.C24273My 2014   [Fic]—dc23   2013038530

Book design by Regina Roff
Typeset by Westchester Book Composition
Printed and bound in the U.S.A. by Thomson-Shore Inc., Dexter, Michigan
2 4 6 8 10 9 7 5 3 1

All papers used by Bloomsbury Publishing, Inc., are natural, recyclable products
made from wood grown in well-managed forests. The manufacturing processes
conform to the environmental regulations of the country of origin.

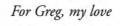

For Greg, my love

My
Best Friend,
Maybe

Ἔκπληξη
(Surprise)

"So, you wanna go?"

That's how she asks me. Like she's talking about a party. Or a chick flick. Or lounging around in her basement during a thunderstorm making ants-on-a-log by scraping the peanut butter out of the middle of peanut-butter crackers because everyone knows that's the best kind.

It's been three years since we last did that, or anything, together.

I raise my eyebrows.

"It's on my mom if you do, the whole eight days. We'll fly into Athens from Newark," Sadie is saying, and I'm wondering if this is real or some bizarre dream. "Then we have to transfer planes for Santorini. That's where my cousin's getting married. Then we'll take a boat to Crete for the party with his family. He's Greek." She adds the last two words like they explain everything. Like my biggest confusion in this jumbled invitation is why Andrea is getting married in Greece.

I slump back in my chair to put a few more inches between us, and I watch her push her white-blond hair out of her eyes. It's streaked with red these days—a new look that blossomed for our junior AP exams last week.

"Charlie's bringing his girlfriend. I don't know about Sam," she's saying.

Her brothers. Who used to feel like my own brothers. It's been ages since I've seen any of them. *Do they miss me? Does her mom?*

"I thought about asking someone else . . ." Sadie trails off.

After a second she says, "I ended up buying you a ticket. So let me know either way, Colette. Okay?"

She actually bought me a ticket?

I shake my head to clear the fog. She takes that as a no, and for a moment I see disappointment clash with triumph across her delicate features.

Then I open my mouth. "Sure."

Sadie's dark-blue eyes grow huge in shock, and I force my own not to mirror them.

"Sure?" she asks, her casual attitude flickering. "That's all?"

"Yup, sure." I slam shut my French notebook and shove it into my backpack. Technically the bell hasn't rung signaling that we can pack up and talk, but everyone has finished their finals. Madame isn't even in the room. She walked out twenty minutes ago. I was the only one with a book open when Sadie plopped down on my desk, her beautiful and intimidating face looming over me as she started babbling about a trip to her cousin's wedding in a few days.

She didn't even say *hello*.

She didn't even look like *sorry*.

"Don't you have questions? Don't you need to think it over?" She leans into me, an amused lilt to her voice, and I remember how she always got most aggressive right before she lost a board game or a race in the pool.

I shake my head, not taking my eyes off my backpack. Of course I have questions. A million questions foaming in my lungs, but they aren't the ones she thinks I'll ask. And to ask them is to lose.

The tension is as thick as the heat in the classroom, the morning sun knifing through the window and drawing a harsh edge across Sadie's profile so that half her face is cast in shadow.

"You aren't going to ask your parents? Run it by Mark?"

♡♡♡ 3

Now I look at her.

"What's the problem?" I say, still not sure whose words I'm speaking. I want to say *Why, Sadie? Why now? If you're going to break the silence and invite me somewhere, why couldn't you ask me to hang out at the mall or go swimming?*

Why is everything so big and complicated with you?

She shrugs, but she's staring at me.

"What?" I say. "Do you think you have a monopoly on spontaneity and adventure?"

She raises her eyebrows, her face caught between emotions again: this time, amusement and mortification.

"Okay, I'll see you in Greece, Coley." She pats my brown hair like I'm a little kid. But she always used to do that. But then again, we always were little kids.

Coley. It's still repeating in my ears when the bell rings. No one has called me that in years. Three years.

Ω

"Come on, Coley, wake up!" Sadie said.

The words had barely wiggled their way through my hazy sleepiness before something soft but sharp crashed into my body, forcing me out of my slumber.

Ten-year-old Sadie stood next to my bottom bunk in our tiny beach bedroom. She was holding my purple Speedo, air-dried from our swim the previous evening, right after my family first arrived in Ocean City. She was already dressed in her own red racing suit. She smiled at me and whipped my suit across my middle once more for good measure. My four-year-old twin brothers breathed deeply in the bunks next to ours. "The sun is out," she whispered. "Let's go!"

I smiled and rolled out of the bed, grabbing for my suit. I knew my parents wouldn't let us go down to the beach without them—the shore was a few blocks away and Dad was always saying how dangerous the ocean was—but I didn't argue. I was still nervous about how it would feel to have Sadie on this vacation. This was the first time she'd been invited on my family's beach week, and in the year we'd gone from nine to ten, I'd begun to realize all of the ways Sadie and I were different. Sadie's house was big and extravagantly decorated; her family vacations were to places like France and Hawaii, places that required an airplane. What would she think of this typical beach vacation? What would she think of my mother's skirted bathing suits, my father's corny jokes? Would she get annoyed by Peter's constant whining? Would she be embarrassed by the tiny apartment we rented each year? The outdoor shower? The small room we had to share with my brothers?

But the thing about Sadie is, except for the ways we're

different, we're exactly the same. Or that's the way it used to be. Two brothers (but hers are older), skin so tanned it looked like we'd rolled in the mud pits by the bay, a love of peanut butter, and an ache to be in water whenever we were forced onto dry land.

In the water, all of the differences washed away.

Wearing our suits, we tiptoed down the short hallway and into the little yellow-tiled kitchen of our beach apartment. My mom was sitting at the kitchen table in her faded pink robe, a coffee mug in one hand, her book of morning meditations in the other.

"Good morning, girls!" she whispered. "Looks like you're all set to go."

"Can we?" Sadie asked as my mom handed each of us a granola bar. "Can we put our feet in, at least? The lifeguards are already on duty." Sadie was always the brave one.

My mom glanced at her watch and, to my surprise, seemed to consider the request.

"You won't go in past your knees until we get down there?" she asked.

"Oh, no, Mrs. Jacobs," Sadie said through a mouthful of granola. "We'll just play trip tag until you get there. Colette has been 'It' since last summer. I have to give her some chance to catch me."

I nodded enthusiastically beside my best friend. I loved trip tag. It was better played in deep water, but we could play it in the shallow part. It was a game we'd invented with Sadie's brothers the summer before. When you were It, you had to dive for someone else's ankle and yank it so that he or she tilted into the water. If the tripee got her hair wet, she became the next It until we played again. And Sadie was right—I'd been It for a good nine months now.

"We'll be safe until you get there, Mom," I promised.

Mom chuckled. "Well, I hope you'll be safe even after we get there," she said. And I knew we had won.

Minutes later we were sprinting down the few short blocks between us and the water, flip-flops clapping against the pavement, towels streaking behind us. By the time my parents finally got to the beach, I was no longer It.

That's how things went all week. Trip tag in the early morning. Jumping waves, body surfing, and making up imaginary games in the ocean all day. It was the best week of summer. My long hair turned to straw and my brown eyes were constantly ringed with an edge of red from hours and hours spent in salt water. Being in the ocean with Sadie was like being in another world, one without rules or gravity.

My dad called us mermaids, but I knew we were more than that. We were fish. We were best friends.

Sadie was mine and I was hers. I knew it the way I knew my backbone held me up.

I was wrong.

Ω

I dart out of the classroom the minute the bell finally buzzes. I need to beat Sadie out of here. I need to get out the door without looking in her eyes, without her seeing that I'm confused. Maybe terrified.

I dodge the start-of-summer celebrations in the hallway, hurrying through crowds of students to get to my locker. Was it a real invitation or a challenge? The tight knot of our friendship had been loosened by time and then frayed by all the ways she ignored me, all the times when we passed in the hall and I didn't even get a small wave. It's over. I've dealt with it. I've moved on.

Why did I say I would go?

I stop dead when I see my locker, and a train of squealing freshman girls crashes into my back. I wasn't even thinking that he'd be there.

It's a Friday, and even if it is only noon, it's technically the end of the school day, so of course Mark is leaning against my locker with a pink paper cone in his hands. I try not to roll my eyes as I resume walking down the hallway. It's peonies this week. It was just peonies, like, three weeks ago.

I used to love the Flower Routine. Back when we first started going out at the beginning of my sophomore year, it was so exciting to have this hot junior standing by my locker every Friday morning with a different bouquet. I counted the weeks we'd been dating by numbering the displays in my head: 1. White roses. 2. Purple orchids. 3. Pink carnations. 4. Red roses . . .

As a senior Mark has been able to leave the campus during his free periods, so he switched it up about halfway through the year and started bringing me flowers at the end of the day instead of the beginning. Living dangerously! The first Friday morning that he wasn't leaning on my locker, I was shocked at the relief I felt seeing its empty surface. Maybe we were done with the charade. Maybe we could be a real couple now. Maybe he'd start acting the way guys are supposed to: like he was into me—my lips, my hair, my chest—more than our relationship. But there he was at the end of the day, with sunflowers. That was a new one.

I'm not supposed to want those other things anyway. I have to be the girl who wants flowers.

"Here you go, beautiful," he chirps when I get to my locker. "Happy week-versary."

I make myself smell the purple buds. I make myself say "Thank you."

He puts his hands on my shoulders, and I bend my neck

back to look at him before he can give me a kiss. His chestnut hair falls across his forehead, into his hazel eyes. His smile makes his cheeks puff out and rearranges his freckles. I love how I never know quite where to look for them. His one front tooth is slightly crooked, something I'd never be able to see if I wasn't standing this close to him. It makes me think about running my tongue over it. It makes me imagine crushing my body into his, jamming him against the locker and feeling his pectoral muscles stiffen as he squeezes me tighter.

He brushes his lips lightly against mine. That's all I'm supposed to want.

"So, what's new?" he asks.

I blink hard to make the body-crushing fantasy go away. It fades but it's always there, buzzing on the edges of my being like a siren.

"I was talking to Sadie Pepper," I say.

His eyes go wide. "Seriously?"

Yes, seriously. She was my best friend.

I nod, then put the flowers down so I can finish cleaning out my locker.

"What did she want?" he asks carefully, and my heart melts. He tries so hard to never say anything bad about anyone. He won't admit he hates Sadie, even though I know he does. Even though he hates her for hurting me. He's so good.

"She wants me to go on her family vacation this summer. To Greece. For her cousin's wedding." I see him wince despite the fact that I left out the part about this Sadie-trip starting only one day before Mark and I are supposed to leave for Costa Rica for our service trip. The one we've been planning all year. The one that I raised thousands of dollars to go on. The one that took months of pleading and persuading and petitioning my parents before Mom granted permission.

I crouch, concentrating on cleaning the few remaining notebooks out of the bottom of my locker, stacking them neatly to put into my backpack. But everything should go in the trash at this point. Another school year mastered. Another check in the box indicating another 365 days of doing everything right. Perfectly.

"Really?" he asks, picking up the peonies from where I left them next to my knee.

I suck in air. He's staring at the flowers, chewing his bottom lip. Scared. Adorable. Maybe we'll get to make out again after his graduation tomorrow.

"I'm not going."

"'Course not," he says, but I feel his relief. He squeezes my shoulder and slides down to the floor, his back against the lockers, his long sweeper-legs sprawled out in front of him.

"Why would you give up the summer with me right before

I leave for college? Why would you give up Costa Rica for Greece?" He smiles a goofy smile. "Who does Sadie Pepper think she is?" He chuckles.

My best friend, I answer in my head. *Maybe.*

"That girl," Mark concludes, shaking his head.

I miss her.

It never does any good to tell him that.

"I know, right?" I say, rolling my eyes.

Maybe she misses me. Maybe she still thinks about the milk shake, the promise.

Guilt bites at my heart. I try not to lie to him. Unless it's about flowers.

Τελειότητα
(Perfection)

During the three-mile drive from school to the town pool, all Mark wants to talk about is Costa Rica. Fund-raising meetings this week. He's only a few hundred dollars away from financing his trip. Of course, I've been budget-ready for weeks. Six days until we leave. We'll need sunblock and bug spray and pencils . . . He goes on and on.

At least he's not talking about his graduation tomorrow, or complaining about the raging college parties that haunt his future, or freaking out about how to live a pure, straight-edged life at Princeton next year.

Yesterday I would have relished talking about Costa Rica.

"I can't believe we're finally going," he's saying. "We've

been talking about doing something huge like this since we first got together, you know? Almost two years."

I watch the houses fly by the passenger-side window. *Sadie.*

"Do you think we can make an actual difference there?" He bites his lip. "Do you ever worry it'll be just like the trip we took with your church to Appalachia?"

I don't want to go. But I'm not sure if I mean Greece or Costa Rica.

I shrug. "It doesn't matter."

"See!" Mark says, banging the steering wheel. "That right there!"

"Huh?" I twist to look at him, jolted out of my own head.

"That's what makes you so good at this stuff. You're flexible. You're there to lead and be of service. You're so in tune, Colette." He puts his right hand on my knee (exactly on my knee, no higher). "You're brave and selfless. I'm so lucky to have you."

I smile at him, a wobbly smile.

Ω

We spend the afternoon at the pool with the rest of our high school and basically the entire town. We sit in the shade on top of the hill and play cards, Mark, me, and the other youth group kids.

I wish Louisa, my real best friend, would hurry up and get here already so I could unload the Sadie-gossip on someone. But she won't be around until after her Japanese tutoring.

The pool's grounds are sprawling, a sloping blanket of green grass surrounding a blue L-shaped jewel. The shouts of the younger kids in the water echo off the sky and bounce down to us, making me ache to join them. Everything smells like chlorine mixed with freshly cut grass. I love the smell of chlorine. I crave it when I haven't been swimming for too long.

I wish I were swimming right now, but it's been complicated to swim socially since I got to high school. The girls from our school all flit around the concrete edges in bikinis and rarely get in the water. If they do, they float. Boring. And girls like me don't wear bikinis: I'm not supposed to want to show off the way swim team has chiseled my abs. Kids like me camp out under the trees—boys in nothing but cargo shorts, girls in tank tops and cutoffs. The group shifts throughout the summer, some of us disappearing for service trips and family vacations and summer jobs at the cafés in town, or teaching vacation Bible school. But there's always a crowd to be found under these trees, playing cards, laughing quietly, being polite. Acting like loving all of God's children means liking each member of youth group equally.

When Louisa is here I sometimes hang out with the self-professed nerds at the snack bar tables. Up there it doesn't matter if you're in a bikini or shorts or a space suit. No one notices. Sometimes they play cards, but other times they just gossip or talk about books or politics. Sometimes they read, and some of them even venture down to go swimming.

Sometimes I like hanging out at the snack bar better than hanging out with the youth group and Mark. Sometimes that makes me feel awful.

Mark creams me in a game of Spit. He puts his hand on my shoulder to console me, his fingertips soft pads against my bare skin. I lean into him and he pulls away as a few of the non–youth group guys from Mark's soccer team plop down on our blanket.

I sit back and scan the crowds for my mystery ex-bestie.

"You going to Sally's party tonight?" I hear James, one of the soccer dudes, ask.

Mark nudges me and I shrug at him, barely hearing, focused on searching for Sadie in the crowd below. There's no point in going to parties with him anyway.

"I don't know, man," Mark says. "I'm sick of watching our classmates get wasted, you know?"

From this high on the hill, I can almost see the entire campus—the young mothers crowded around the baby pool, the elementary school kids dotting the big pool with splashes and neon-colored bathing suits, the high schoolers who lie on towels closest to the water, trading smiles and fashion magazines. I look for Sadie in the towel-lying crowd but I spot a flash of blond-and-red walking across the far sidewalk. There she is, in a black one-piece. She stands next to a guard chair as a redheaded guy climbs down; then she climbs up.

Oh, my gosh. She's working here this summer.

In middle school both of us were on the swim team. The summer after eighth grade we took lifeguarding lessons together so that we could work with each other the next summer. We were so proud of ourselves when we managed to drag up, back-board, and save the instructor's three-hundred-pound husband from a pretend drowning. But by the next summer we weren't talking. I filled out a job application at the ice cream parlor instead.

I watch her scanning the pool for accidents. I wonder if she knows I'm up on this hill. I wonder if it's as easy for her to find me as it is for me to find her.

I'm still watching Sadie when my phone buzzes with a text from Louisa: "Meet me at the snack bar."

I wave at Mark and make my way over there, my bare feet hopping over towels and purses laid out to mark the territory for a family or a group of friends. The grass wiggles between my toes, itchy and tickle-y and begging my feet to jump into the pool.

Louisa is at a table leaning over her Japanese flash cards and her iPhone.

"Welcome, earthling," I say, giving her our standard dorky greeting.

She smiles at me. "One more day," she says. She presses a finger onto the screen of her phone.

I sit across from her. She's in cutoff shorts and a black bathing-suit top that's definitely a two-piece but not quite revealing enough to be a bikini. The sunlight reflects off the caramel skin of her shoulders as they hunch over the cards.

"One more day," I repeat. "You're totally going to get in." I watch her pink sparkly fingernails as she jams her pointer finger into her phone again.

I was hoping that I could tell Louisa what happened with Sadie today. She would be the one person in my life who wouldn't get mad at me for what I said back. Who could possibly have some practical advice to get me out of this Grecian mess.

She's the only person in my life in any way ... different ... from everyone else. She doesn't go to church and she curses occasionally and, unlike most of this white-bread town, she's Japanese. But her polite attitude toward adults and her valedictorian status in our class keep her close enough to Perfect for Mom's approval. There's no way Mom knows how fun she is. How loud our laughter gets when we're watching sci-fi movies or her old DVDs of *The Twilight Zone*, how we imitate our teachers' voices behind their backs, and how she knows about my crush on the swimmer Ryan Lochte. For my birthday she gave me a poster of him smiling at me and wearing only board shorts and Olympic medals.

But when I see her slumped over her Japanese study materials like this, I know I can't say anything. It wouldn't be right to start talking about myself on her day. She's had a one-track mind all year: get into this exclusive boarding program in Japan for her senior year. Study abroad, in another country, in a foreign language, in her parents' homeland, and still be the valedictorian of our class when she returns for graduation. Beat her sister—who will be giving the valedictory address tomorrow night at Mark's graduation—once and for all.

When she's thinking in Japanese, I try to support her. I don't want to distract her from her goals with any silly Sadie-drama.

Instead, I remind her all the time that she's already beaten Jasmine in so many ways. More friends. Prettier. More extracurriculars. Funnier. Way funnier. It's never enough for Louisa. I'm not the one who needs to notice. I'm not her parents.

"I'm not going to get in!" she declares, and she shoves her choppy black bangs away from her heart-shaped face in frustration. "You need to stop saying that I will, Colette. Thousands of kids applied. From every English-speaking country in the world. There's no way I'm going to get in."

I reach across the table to pat her hand. "None of them could have worked as hard as you," I say. "I know you're going to get in. I'm so excited for you." I say it like I mean it. And I should mean it, I know. It's what my best friend wants. But whenever we have these conversations I feel like crossing my fingers behind my back because I can't make myself want her to be in Japan for an entire year. Our senior year.

She hits her phone again.

"What are you doing?" I ask.

She holds up her phone, and all I see is a mess of Japanese characters.

"I thought they're supposed to let you know tomorrow," I say.

"Tomorrow happens earlier in Japan," she says. She punches refresh again.

I drum my fingers on the table.

"Look, I'm sorry," she says. She glances at me, her brown

eyes darting back and forth in her skull. "This is too boring even for me. Let's go play cards with Mark. I need a distraction."

Ω

When we leave in the early evening, Sadie is on break. She's swimming laps in the pool, the blue water mixing with the colors in her hair.

Of course Sadie would figure out the only way to swim in a one-piece at the town pool and not be a social enigma. Of course. Sadie figures out everything.

We're almost to the exit gate when I hear her voice echo across the water: "Coley!"

I turn. No one else does.

I walk over to where she's bobbing at the edge of the pool. Mark vanishes through the gate without seeing me. Good.

"What suit are you wearing?" She scissor-kicks to bounce herself out of the water and lunges for the bottom of my tank, yanking it to try to see underneath.

I jump back, shaking the water that she splashed off my arms as if I don't want it there.

"I'm not wearing one."

She throws her head back and laughs, almost friendly. But then she says, "Looks like you're going to need to do some shopping before our little trip."

I pause. She's challenging me. Her face is hard as concrete. There's no invitation there now.

This is stupid.

"Okay, Sadie," I say, rolling my eyes. "See you."

"Coley!" she calls after me. But this time I leave.

Ω

The last time Sadie and I spoke was the first day of our sophomore year. I mean, really spoke. Quick hi's in the hallway and teacher-mandated conversations in French don't count.

I was in the first-floor bathroom scrubbing my hands before lunch, and she walked out of the stall behind me. For a moment we both froze and locked eyes in the mirror. Her skin was still ruddy from whatever she'd done all summer, and her hair was plain blond, for once, but so sunned it was almost white.

My own skin was burnt enough to hide the way I blushed when I realized I'd been staring at her.

It was weird to see her like that, in front of me and behind me like a Coley sandwich. It was strange to have the reality of her surrounding me when I'd been missing her so badly all summer. Now it was the day after the last day of summer and, after a year of barely acknowledging one another, we hadn't seen each other once for almost three months. It was a gaping hole in my life. I didn't know if I was missing Sadie or my entire childhood.

I went back to washing my hands when I saw her start walking toward me.

"Hey, Colette," Sadie said, hoisting herself onto the sink next to mine without checking to see if there was any water on the counter that would wet her jeans.

I wondered if she used my full name to hurt me.

"Hey," I said.

"How's your mom?"

I blinked at her reflection. What a weird question.

"She's fine. How's yours?"

Then Sadie smiled the same way she used to when we were sharing some inside joke, but it felt unfair now because I was on the outside of the joke and I thought she should at least have a different facial expression for excluding me than the one she'd used to include me.

"Same as always," she said. "How was your summer?"

Boring. Predictable. Lonely.

"Great," I said.

"Me, too." She left without washing her hands.

(Boredom)

At dinner that night I nod politely to Mom's cheery questions about how I think I did on my finals and whether my report card will be a delight as usual. Adam talks about Little League and Peter talks about swim team and the summer musical. Mom talks about book club. Dad chews. I smile, nod, shrug.

I can't tell them about Sadie. I can't say a word about her without my mom telling me how worried she is about "my old friend," how I'm safer without Sadie and the rest of "those strange Peppers."

I can't tell them that I might like the idea of trading perfection and service and college-resume bonus points for a simple vacation. A little adventure. A little drama. A summer with Sadie.

"So, Mark graduates tomorrow. How are you feeling about that?" Mom asks.

The question sends lightning bolts through my veins.

I shrug again, shake my head slightly like it's too hard to think about.

"You're really going to miss him, aren't you?"

Yes, but . . .

More things I can't tell my parents.

Dad pats my hand, but he doesn't say anything. He never does, anymore.

Mom says, "At least you have an entire summer together. And a trip. We're so proud of you for choosing such an upstanding and God-fearing young man."

And predictable. And chaste.

I love Mark.

It's not like Sadie actually wants me to go. She wants to prove her point, that her way is better than mine. That she's more fun and that she can swim in social situations and dye her hair any color and flirt with every boy in the class and laugh like she's five years old. It's better to go on the service trip to do something good than go to Greece just to prove Sadie wrong.

I'll find another adventure, outside of Sadie.

My parents are looking at me. I'd like to be honest with them, so I say, "I'm starting to have some doubts about this trip."

Mom's tan eyes go wide. "But you've been looking forward to it for so long. You've raised all the money and gone to all the meetings to prepare. And you worked so hard to convince us that it would be okay for you to go away with Mark and his church instead of going back to Appalachia with ours."

"What's wrong?" Dad says, pouring Peter more milk.

I shrug.

"I told you, Colette. I warned you that you might be more comfortable sticking with your own youth group. Different isn't always what it's cracked up to be," Mom says. "Remember that there's only one right path and when you start looking for change you risk straying."

I roll my eyes.

"Colette!" Mom says.

"I'm only going on a different service project. Not snorting cocaine."

"Colette!" Mom says louder.

I sigh. "I'm only looking to do things a little bit differently. To make my own choices. Maybe have some fun."

Why am I still fighting this fight? It started last summer—me insisting that I wanted to do something different, go to Costa Rica with Mark to build houses. Now it doesn't feel big enough, different enough. But somehow I'm still fighting for it.

I'm always trying to be honest with my parents but I always end up lying.

"Fun is overrated. You can't make your decisions based on fun," Mom says.

Dad nods.

But he used to crack jokes and play Nintendo and cheer at Mets games. He used to have fun sometimes. I remember.

I sigh bigger this time, blowing out all of my boredom, frustration, angst. "I know," I say. "I'm sorry. I'm off today. It's . . . it's harder than I want to admit to think about life without Mark."

I settle for a lie because it's easier, even if it is wrong. And somehow, even though she knows everything, Mom doesn't notice.

She nods. "That's understandable. But watch your words. Especially in front of your brothers."

I look at them across the table. Peter wiggles in his chair and twirls his spaghetti dramatically. Adam smiles at me, wide enough that I can see the gap in his molars from where he got hit with a baseball last summer. They're trying to be perfect.

Just like me.

It's sad.

Ω

After dinner, I pull my bike out from the back of the garage, pump new air into the tires, fasten my helmet, and shove off into the evening. Twilight sparkles around me, stars' pinpoints over my head and summer moisture buzzing on my face and arms.

I could drive to her house, of course. I could climb into the hand-me-down Camry Mom lends me and be there in, like, five minutes. But that feels wrong. If I'm going to face her, I want it to be like it was three years ago.

She won't be home anyway. It's the last day of school: she's surely at some party drinking beer and laughing with all the girls she found to replace me. Some adorable boy is probably hanging on her every word, waiting to pull her into a closet and shove his tongue down her throat.

I don't want that.

The road to her house hums under my tires, winding and hilly and familiar. It takes me to her.

And then I'm there. It's the same—mint-green siding,

multicolored curtains in every window, and all of the lights on like the house itself is laughing.

The yard smells like honeysuckle and dandelions, like childhood summer evenings after a long day in the sun and chlorine, like making up fairies to play with in the yard while we wait for Edie to grill some veggie burgers or order some sushi.

What happened to make this familiar place feel like a distant fantasy?

Then I'm ringing the doorbell. The part of my brain that forced out the "sure" during my French final today propels my hand forward until my index finger manages to slam on the button.

The door swings open and classical music and cinnamon waft out. Edie stands on the porch, an older, plumper version of Sadie without the red in her so-blond hair. Her eyes are such a dark blue they're almost purple. Her smile is so wide it glows. Everything about her got bigger since I last saw her.

Her face falls when she sees me on the stoop. Her mouth twists into something close to a scowl. "Colette!" She sounds startled.

I didn't realize until now that I was expecting her to hug me, now that I'm standing on this stoop without her fleshy biceps around my upper arms. She always hugged me whenever she saw me, almost every day. She probably hugged me more in those years than my own mother did. Now she stares, angry. Of course she's angry.

"Hi, Mrs. Pepper," I say, finally.

She sighs like I'm exhausting her. "Oh, Colette. You know you call me Edie."

I nod. My mom always hated that.

She looks me up and down. "We've missed you around here." She says it like it's a question.

I don't know what to say. I don't know how she feels about me anymore. I don't know what Sadie told her.

"I guess you'll want to scoot on upstairs. Sadie's in her room." She pauses. I'm still frozen on the stoop. "You know the way."

I nod. "Thank you."

It feels so awful to have her angry with me, even though I'm almost positive that I've done nothing wrong.

The stairs are lined with even more photos than there used to be—Sadie and her two brothers who don't look like they're hers. Sam and Charlie were both adopted from Haiti and have pronounced cheekbones, soulful eyes, and skin so dark it reflects the lights in each photo. But I've known them since I was too young to notice that. Sadie's head pops up in the middle of each set of frames—the three of them as naked toddlers, smiling kindergartners, awkward middle school-ers. Then come the pictures I haven't seen yet. Sadie on her first day of high school, Charlie's and then Sam's graduation photos. My parents always say that Edie has odd ideas about parenting and creating a family, but except for the faces inside the frames, her stairwell looks a lot like ours.

Top of the stairs, to the right, past the bathroom, end of the hallway. Knock on the door I always used to walk right through. I can't believe she's home.

"I knew you'd do this," she says as soon as she sees me in the hallway.

Her room is behind her, red and gold and glittery, the same as it used to be. I feel like I took a time machine here. That's what I wanted it to feel like. But the time machine failed: I'm not laughing.

"I knew you'd punk out," Sadie is saying.

"You haven't even let me say anything." I hate the whiny vibrations on the top of my voice.

She nods like, "Then speak." She says these words so clearly through her eyes but she still hasn't made them say "sorry."

"I'm not punking out." *Yet.* "I wanted to ask a question."

"Right, knew you would," Sadie says, turning and walking into her room. "Well, my mom has you covered so it's not like your folks have to fork over for anything. And Mom'll be there the whole time so we're properly chaperoned. And we'll have Wi-Fi, so you don't have to be cut off from your precious boyfriend." She turns around and stares at me from five feet away. I'm still in the doorway.

"That's not the question," I say.

"We'll type up a full itinerary and we'll be safe," Sadie says.

"That's not the question."

"What then?" Sadie plops down on her cherry-print bed-spread. "And you can come in, you know."

I stand in the center of her gold carpet and face her. It feels good to be the one towering over her at this moment.

"So, what is it?"

I open my mouth and the words fly through it the way "sure" did in French today. "Why are you inviting me?"

Sadie's face cracks open and she smiles at me with the inside-joke smile and I shift my feet because I'm not sure which side of the joke I'm on this time. But I can't help smil-ing back at her. "I need you," she says with a shrug.

And then my whole world tilts and the room spins out of focus. Because that's not what I came to find out. That doesn't answer if she misses me or if she wants me there or if she has to prove something. That's not an answer at all. But now, I need to go. No Costa Rica. No Mark. No parental objections. Now I need to go.

Sadie invoked the promise. She remembers. And I'm not going to be the one to break it.

"Come here," Sadie says, still smiling. She stands up and for a second I think she's going to hug me but instead she spins me around and clips the top of my hair back. Then she faces me again. "Yeah, like that," she says. "Maybe we should get haircuts before we go. Some new clothes, too."

It's almost exactly what she said at the pool today, but this time it's nice.

She walks over to her dresser and opens a makeup case, then attacks my face with a huge blush brush.

"What are you doing?" I ask.

"Getting you Ready," she says. "We're going to Sally's party."

I nod. I'm still not asking all the questions.

Διασκέδαση (Fun)

The bathroom door swings open as we step into the hall outside Sadie's bedroom. I can't believe I'm going to this party. With Sadie.

Steam pours out the door and then an older, taller, more muscled Pepper brother emerges wearing nothing but a white towel around his waist. It's Sam. My jaw drops but I manage to clench it shut before he notices me.

He's standing surrounded in steam, his black hair cropped close to his skull, his brown eyes smiling as they land on my face, his dark chest dotted with beads of water, the muscles in his arm flexing as he moves a hand in a stunned wave.

Oh, my gosh, Sam is hot.

"Colette!" he almost shouts, a huge smile spreading across his face.

He said my name! I think, like he's a movie star and not a boy who used to drive me crazy playing keep-away with my favorite stuffed elephant when I was eight years old.

"Hi, Sam," I manage.

He's three years older than us, so he'd be . . . twenty. I haven't seen him since he was my age now.

"You're really coming to Greece with us?" he asks slowly.

Sadie grabs my hand. "Told you she was!" she chirps. "Come on, Coley! Let's go." She pulls me down the hallway toward the stairs.

"Bye, Sam," she calls over her shoulder.

I force myself not to look back at him.

Ω

On the mile walk to Sally's house, my body feels enormous. I'm short for a swimmer but right now the two inches I have on Sadie make my head float suspended above my body. My arms swing like a monkey's, almost reaching my knees. My legs are too long to step gracefully. I'm bloated and awkward and I don't know what I'm doing but I keep taking another step, then another, then another into the deep hole of Sadie-drama.

I've been to Sally's parties before. Often the whole high school is at her shindigs. I've gone there with Mark and sat in a corner and talked or played Text Twist on his phone while everyone else lived their normal lives. And that's okay. When Mark isn't there, I hang out with Louisa, playing Kings or I Never and actually sipping beer and hoping no one will tell my straight-edged boyfriend. It's not like I drink enough for it to matter. It's not like I've ever had more than one. But I don't think Mark would understand that.

Neither Mark nor Louisa will be there tonight; they would have texted me about it if they were going. This will be a smaller cool-kids-only party.

What will I do? What will Sadie do?

She's rattling on and on about Greece and I can't believe I have to go there with her. I can't believe she invoked that ancient promise.

But! But! But! The still-tiny, still-fun Coley who lives in the back of my skull is screaming: *But what if she does need me?*

The thought sends fire into my veins, makes my eyes want to explode with tears of relief and worry. What could be wrong? Is it Edie? Her brothers? Andrea? Why would she need me on a family vacation?

But no. I can't ask those questions. It'll hurt too much

when I'm wrong, when her need turns out to be pure manipulation and vindication.

Sadie stops suddenly and says, "Here we are."

But we aren't. We're standing on a sidewalk surrounded by the tiny shops that make up the small one-block expansion we refer to as the "center of town." I look around.

"We're not going to Sally's?" I ask.

"We are," Sadie says. "But I owe you something first. Wait here one minute."

Then she disappears into one of the storefronts, and my heart hammers in my chest because I know what she'll be holding when she comes back. I know what she's about to give me. And I can't believe she remembered.

Ω

After the last home swim meet, the summer before high school, I sat on the bench outside the locker room, my hair dripping onto my T-shirt and my muscles twitching from swimming the butterfly leg of the group medley during the last race. I was waiting for Sadie so we could ride our bikes into town and get peanut-butter milk shakes.

I wrung my hair out to my side, hummed a song, and told my brain not to worry about all the ways that things had been weird for the past few months. I was outside the locker room because I didn't feel like hearing any more of Sadie's inside jokes with Lynn. Their giggling had gotten on my nerves. On that bench, I was feeling good and a little nostalgic. It had been my last meet at the town pool—after eight years, summer swim team was over because it didn't extend to high school—and I'd won all four of my races. I had chlorine in my hair, sun on my skin, four new medals clinking in my backpack, and plans with my best friend. Because Sadie and I always got peanut-butter milk shakes after home meets, just the two of us. No matter how weird things were.

Finally, after close to an entire week, I was going to get Sadie to myself for an hour. Not that I didn't like the other girls on the team, but Lynn had gotten so clingy with my best friend. It was hard to be around them without feeling dizzy. At least Lynn was a year younger. She'd be stuck in middle school in the fall and I'd get the real Sadie back. Until then, we had our milk shakes.

So I kicked my feet out and leaned my head back against the wall and smelled the chlorine. Then Sadie burst out of the locker room in a storm of giggles with three other girls. Lynn included. A big girl, a head taller than Sadie with bulging biceps and wide shoulders, she stood with her arm slung around my friend's neck.

"Coley!" Sadie said when she saw me on the bench. "Ready to go? We're gonna hang out at Lynn's house."

My jaw dropped. "But . . . milk shakes . . . ," I managed.

"We'll get them tomorrow," Sadie said. Part of her hair was dyed green. It looked mildewed. She was elbow in elbow with another girl, Sue, on her other side. They were always touching. It was so annoying.

"And Lynn has a pool in her backyard," one of the girls said.

I stared, dumbfounded. We were at a pool. If Sadie didn't feel like drinking a milk shake, we could stay here.

It wasn't like I refused to hang out with these girls. It wasn't like we hadn't spent every day that week hanging out in a group. All I wanted was one afternoon with Sadie to myself. We could go to Lynn's tomorrow.

One of the girls sat down so she could whisper to me, her words tickle-y and uncomfortable in my ear: "Her parents are away for the weekend and her cousin who's watching the house bought all of this beer but he's not there right now either."

I lowered my eyebrows at Sadie, confused. She wanted to drink some nasty old beer? Instead of a thick and sugary milk shake?

"But, we have plans . . ." I trailed off.

"Give me a sec," Sadie said to the group. She dropped Sue's elbow and sat on my other side, swinging her arm around me. "She always has trouble if we change things around," she said over my wet hair. I didn't like her talking about me like that. "Come with us, Coley. It'll be fun."

"We hate beer," I said.

Sadie shrugged. "Maybe this time we won't."

I felt like I might cry and I didn't want to do that in front of these girls or in front of Sadie, even though I had cried in front of Sadie a million times before. But everything was changing. First, things changed at home when chaos in the form of two screaming babies took over my house and the entirety of my parents' attention. Now things were changing with Sadie.

It felt like everything we used to have—swim team, trips to the beach, running through her huge backyard during thunderstorms—had been invaded and rewritten by these girls. By Lynn. Now the milk shakes? I didn't want to give up the milk shakes. I couldn't.

"You guys go ahead. I'll meet you at the bike stand," Sadie said finally. They started to file out and she took her arm off my shoulders to face me.

"Do you really need me to go get milk shakes?" she asked.

I did. I clearly did. But that word "need" sounded so pathetic. I needed her to want to get milk shakes. I needed her to rank all of her friends for me so that I could hear my name at the top of the list. I was afraid I was sinking lower and lower on it, and if I sunk too low on Sadie's friend list, I might sink out of real life.

"No, it's okay," I said. "Have fun."

"Milk shakes tomorrow!" Sadie pronounced, like it didn't even matter that we'd just won our last-ever swim meet at the town pool.

Ω

The cold plastic cup pressed in my palm sends goose bumps up my arm and into my lungs. I stare at the milk shake, shocked.

"You're really coming with me, right?" Sadie says. Her blue eyes are even bluer because of the turquoise shirt she's wearing. Her hair is swept up in a bun on the back of her head so I can't see the red part. She's suddenly thirteen again, and so am I.

I giggle. A milk shake is such a silly thing. A milk shake is nowhere near the equivalent of a trip halfway around the world. A milk shake is nothing. Big Colette knows all of this. But I don't want to ruin the moment for little Coley, for the small part of me that's dancing for joy because she didn't forget.

"I told you I was," I say, wondering if this means I really have to, if a milk shake can possibly have that much power.

Sadie clinks her own plastic cup against mine and it feels so good to giggle with her as we take our first chilly sip.

Then we're on our way again.

As Sally's mansion rises into view, my nerves start to knock against each other. At this party we won't be half-thirteen/half-seventeen. At this party we'll be in high school and I doubt Sadie actually wants me there with all of her new, beautiful, popular friends. Should I tell her that I won't go to Sally's? Should I tell her that if I'm going to go with her, she'd better not ditch me?

My steps have slowed so Sadie is a few strides ahead as we enter Sally's yard. She turns to me and chirps, "Come on, Coley!" She smiles at me like she used to when we were little and playing dolphins in the pool.

Maybe she does want me here.

Then she plows ahead of me onto Sally's lawn.

But maybe not.

I scurry to catch her and I'm about to tell her that if she doesn't want to hang with me at the party, I can leave. But the door swings open and there, just inside, is Mark.

With a beer.

Ω

Sadie and I sat facing each other, cross-legged on her gold bedroom carpet, the brown bottle standing up like a mini-rocket between us.

"You try it first," she said.

I shook my head. "No, you."

The late-afternoon sun gathered heavily through her

windows, darkening the red stripes in her wallpaper so that they reflected brightly into her hair. The Miller Lite bottle was in a puddle of sunshine, the brown surface sparkling.

She smiled and scooted closer to the bottle. And to me. "You have to try first. It's your turn. I'm the one who stole it," she said.

"You just stole it from Charlie," I said. "We can't get in trouble for that." Because Charlie was only sixteen and wasn't supposed to have beer in his room anyway. Sadie stole it out of his gym bag.

We were only nine. And not supposed to have beer at all.

"Come on, Coley." She nudged the bottle so it almost tipped but I managed to catch it with my palm. And then it was in my hand. Warm, almost hot, dangerous and tempting.

Sadie kept talking. "In twelve years we'll be twenty-one and we'll have to drink beer when we dress up and go into New York City together and find the bar where Miley is playing live. And we'll be doing our dance moves and some guy will see us and he'll buy us two of these beers and we'll have to drink them. So we might as well start practicing."

I took a deep breath, swung the bottle to my lips, and sucked in a huge mouthful. It was hot and thick and it tasted worse than vomit. The liquid sloshed over my tongue, back and forth between my molars. My throat closed against it and it grew *thicker, into my cheeks. I tried to hold my breath with my mouth full, tried to force it down without tasting. But my lips opened just as my throat closed, and instead, I sprayed it all over my best friend's red sundress.*

My breath caught. For a moment we stared at each other wide-eyed. I thought she might get mad. Sadie really liked her clothes, not like me who spilled things all the time and didn't care as long as my mother didn't find out.

But then she yanked the bottle out of my hand, took a sip, and spit it on my chest on purpose.

"Gross!" she squealed.

We broke down laughing.

"We're not going to drink beer at the Miley concert," I said.

"No way!" she said as she giggled, wiping her shirt with a tissue. "No. Way. I'm never having a beer again."

She handed a tissue to me.

"Me neither," I said, and we laughed.

That promise we both broke. But Sadie broke it first.

Ω

Mark's eyes go wide when he sees me, and he swings his long arm around to force the brown bottle behind his back.

I feel like I should be mad; instead I'm curious. I'm the one who drinks behind his back.

"H-h-hey," he manages, still looking at me with wide eyes

and bouncing freckles. They are so adorable. I want to touch each one of them with my index finger and giggle. I don't want to be mad.

"What's up?" I whisper, trying not to laugh at the way he's keeping his arm twisted to hide something I might be happy about.

"Oh, you two are so cute," Sadie says. I almost forgot she was there.

She wraps an arm around both of us and I see Mark stiffen. His eyes grow wider.

"Nice to see you, too, Mark. I'll be right back, Coley," she says, and disappears into the crowd.

Mark's friends from the soccer team are standing behind him. He takes another step away from their circle but they're still there, pounding the bottom of their beer bottles into the top of someone else's to make it fizz over so they have to try to suck the foam through the neck as quickly as possible. They yell and hoot and bump into us as my boyfriend and I stare at each other. He moves closer again. I can smell the Pert Plus that keeps his hair so silky.

"I texted you," he says finally. "You didn't respond." His hand is still behind his back.

I crack a smile as I pull my iPhone from my back pocket.

"Oh," I say, showing Mark the black screen. It's dead.

He shifts his feet back and forth and chews his bottom

lip. I keep smiling at him. He's definitely hiding his beer from me.

Then Sadie is there and she hands me a magenta bottle, Hard Berry Lemonade. "You'll like it better than beer," she says with that inside-joke smile. "Trust me."

Then she's gone again.

Mark's eyes travel to my drink.

I shrug and dodge one of the soccer guys. "You have a beer," I say.

Mark pulls the bottle out from behind his back and stares at it like he doesn't know where it came from or maybe like he doesn't quite know who he is.

Finally, I laugh. I clink my bottle against his and take a sip and so does he. The sweet liquid fizzes into my mouth, syrupy and delicious and so much better than beer that it feels dangerous. I clink Mark again. I can't believe he drinks beer. This means he's heaped lie after lie onto our relationship, but I don't care. I'm glad. I'm relieved. It frees me to admit to all the lies that I've piled on myself.

We both laugh and then he puts his long arm lightly over my shoulder. And, we're us again. Well, we're us with drinks.

"So . . . what have you girls been up to, you and . . . Sadie?" he asks carefully.

"Relaaaaax, Maaark." His friend Joe faux-punches his beer-holding arm. "Sadie's a cool chick. It's not like she showed up with another dude."

He shrugs Joe off.

I take another sip. It tastes like the berry-flavored Pop Rocks we used to eat on the boardwalk, almost sickeningly sweet.

Mark leans toward me. Now I can smell his skin, salty and soapy, and I want to rub my face against his, bury my nose in his neck, and . . .

"Let's talk upstairs for a minute," he says. I know he's worried about Sadie, whether I'll be friends with her again and whether I'll ditch him and go to Greece after all. I don't want to go upstairs with him.

But when we start to cross the few feet toward the stairwell and the boys erupt into a deafening chorus of *Ooohs*, I realize that yes, I do.

And then we're in a dark room, standing close, and I know that no matter what he was thinking when he asked me to come up here, there's no way we're about to chat about Sadie. The light is out and the shades are drawn, but just enough street light is sneaking around them for me to see a little bit. The room is tiny and it smells like wood. The bunk beds against the wall remind me of our old beach apartment. There is a border of primary-colored trucks and boats running along the middle of the walls: a little boy's room.

I stop looking around and turn to Mark. He's standing in the middle of the blue carpet, his face cast in shadows but the gray light highlighting the muscles in his right arm, the arm holding the beer.

For the first time all day, I'm not thinking about Sadie or milk shakes or Costa Rica versus Greece or being perfect versus having adventures. I'm thinking about Mark.

I step toward him and clink my bottle against his. We both drink. We're standing so close the energy bouncing between us is visible—silver and electric.

"So," he says, but I move closer. Now our clothes are touching, my skin breaking out in goose bumps beneath the fabric of Sadie's shiny black T-shirt. I clink again.

He smiles. His crooked tooth is so skippin' adorable. He brushes his hair out of his eyes.

"So," he says. This time I kiss him. Hard. He stiffens for a second but when he doesn't pull back, I put my left hand behind his head and rake my fingers through his smooth hair the way I've always wanted to when we're kissing. His mouth opens and our tongues find each other and he inches into me so our entire bodies are touching, his chest flexing against mine, his free palm running the length of my side and then pressing into the small of my back, and *this this this. This* is what I've been wanting. And for once I don't feel wrong about wanting it. *This* is perfect.

Then he pulls his lips away.

He smiles down at me, his arm still tight, keeping me close. "You graduate tomorrow," I say too quickly. It's so stupid how I feel like I always have to have an excuse to make out with him. Like loving each other for years isn't reason enough. But we only make out on special occasions—Christmas and Valentine's Day and when he got into Princeton.

"I know," he says. "I was just looking at you." Then his arm is gone and my heart falls, until he reaches for the bottle in my hand and puts both of our drinks on the edge of the top bunk, and I realize he was just freeing up his other arm to get me even closer.

He crosses back to me, sweeping me up so my feet hover off the floor; my chest crushed into his is the only thing connecting me to the ground. And then we're making out again. And I feel like we're floating, suspended above the carpet, close to the ceiling. Like I'll never come back down to earth.

The other times we made out were not like this. We'd be leaning over the divider in the front of Mark's car or the armrest between our movie seats. This is like our whole bodies are making out, pressed together, wanting more.

He puts me down but our mouths stay together. I pull my hand from his hair to touch his stomach. I feel the ripples of his abs through his soft T-shirt. They're as delicious as I always imagined.

And then I almost gasp through all the kissing because Mark's hand goes to my stomach as well. Leaving his lips on mine, he tilts his hips back so that he can trace his pointer finger across my abdomen and I realize that he's following my lead.

My nerves squeak with all the words my mom would use— "lust" and "danger" and "temptation." But for once I ignore her.

Slowly, very slowly, I move my hand up the fabric of his T-shirt. My palm moves one inch. So does his. Then another, another. It's a game. It should be a game.

We're in high school and teenagers and in love and it should be like this. Fun. Pure, not at all overrated fun.

Finally my fingertips pause at the crease where his abs become his chest and my heart skips a beat when I feel him start to play with the underwire of my bra. This is it. He hasn't been resisting me. He hasn't been un-into-me. He's been following my lead.

I slide my hand up so that his pectoral muscle is in my palm and his hand hesitates over my left breast for just a second before it's on me in the most intimate touch of my life and my entire body erupts with tingles.

Then the moment is over, and that's okay.

He plants a kiss on my cheek and bear-hugs me. "I love you, Colette," he says.

"I love you, Mark," I say, and I kiss him again and mean it, and there's no way I'm going to Greece, no way I'm leaving him this summer after that. Even if I do kind of wish he'd called me *Coley*.

Εγκατάλειψη (Abandonment)

"Colette! Colette!" I hear Louisa squealing my name before Mark and I are even halfway down the stairs. "I got in! I got in!" She's screaming when we reach the bottom. She hugs me and spins me around. "Can you believe I got in?"

"Got in where?" Mark asks.

"You're going? To Japan?" I ask slowly.

She nods, her smile so wide it puffs out her thin cheeks.

My heart slows, almost dissolves, almost drips down my rib cage into my feet. I paste a smile on my face. I have to be happy for her. I can't think about senior year with no Mark and no Louisa.

"This is huge!" I manage to squeal back. "Congratulations!"

She keeps spinning me, the two of us dancing in circles. "I want to hear all about it."

This is the part where I'd normally turn to Mark and awkwardly make arrangements about meeting up with him later, but I can feel a shift between us, puzzle pieces falling into place. "Congrats, Lu," he says, patting her on the shoulder. Then he swigs his beer and disappears into the crowd.

Louisa stops spinning and holds me at arm's length. "Is he drinking? A beer?"

I nod, my mush of a heart so happy and sad and confused as images of what happened upstairs explode in my brain like fireworks right next to the blank surface of a lonely senior year.

"Does this mean you can 'cheers' me on my good news?" she asks, exclamation points dancing in her dark eyes.

"Sure," I say.

We snake our way through the crowds in the hallway, living room, and kitchen to the back deck. There, I grab two magenta not-beers and huddle with Louisa at the bench on the far side. A bunch of youth groupers are playing volleyball in the yard below us and beyond them a group of pretty-girls sit clustered by the stream at the edge of Sally's property. Their noises gather around us—the giggle of tipsy girls, the slap of a palm on the ball's surface, the shouts of the score back and forth.

"Do you realize how huge this is?" Louisa demands.

"To you!" I say. I hold out my bottle and she clinks hers against mine before downing almost half of it in one long gulp.

"Do you realize how many people I beat to get this spot? There were, like, thousands of kids who applied. Thousands! From all over the world. I never thought I'd get to go."

"Yes, you did," I say.

Louisa shakes her head, her straight bangs rearranging themselves on her forehead, her eyes still wide with surprise and adrenaline.

"But all that extra studying," I point out. "And you asked for leave from work."

She nods. "I know. I like to feign confidence sometimes." She giggles. I can count the number of times I've heard her giggle on one hand. "But it happened. I'm going."

I pat her arm. "I'm not surprised," I say. Inside I'm wondering what else this confident, energetic friend of mine feigns. How do I comfort someone who is faking confidence?

She sips again. "I get my class schedule next week. I'm taking classes at . . ." She keeps talking and I try to listen but her words don't make it past my ears and into my brain. They're blocked by my own panic. *Lonely.*

She's drinking and drinking and talking and talking and her words loosen up until she's chatting about her nerves and her fear and the classes she hopes to take and the boys she hopes to kiss. But all that jabbering globs up thick outside my skull and stays there.

Inside, one word pounds on repeat to the beat of the party's hip-hop: *lonely lonely lonely.* No Louisa. No Mark. No Sadie.

We lean close together. The party shifts around us, kids passing through the deck to the yard and back, grabbing drinks and clinking them together, making out, swatting at mosquitoes. I focus on Louisa. I let her talk and watch her drink until, after three bottles, she's swaying a little.

She's leaving. Right after I get back from Costa Rica, she'll be getting on her own plane. She'll be gone for our entire last year in this boring town. She's the only person I could ever tell what just happened with Mark. She's the only person I could ever talk to about Sadie.

But this is Louisa's day and I can't be selfish.

And then she'll leave and I'll never get to talk about myself, the real me who lives somewhere underneath the Perfect crust created by my parents and, even, a little, by Mark.

"When do you go?" I ask when she starts to slur her words together. It strikes me that even though I've been to so many of these parties, I'm not sure I've ever talked to a drunk person. I've watched them from afar, but I've kept myself among people who control themselves.

A slow, contented smile spreads over Louisa's face and for the first time I can see the appeal of consuming multiple beers. Not vomiting and making out with strangers like the party frothing around us, but smiling so easily like Louisa is right now. "Three weeks," she says.

The summer spreads out before me, lonely except for Mark. No smart talk by the pool. No sci-fi marathons with homemade cookies. No loose smiling like that. I suck it all in.

"I hope my Japanese is good enough," she repeats.

"It is," I say again.

Then she leans even farther toward me, her elbows on my knee.

"But can I tell you something, earthling? Something I don't want to say out loud? Can I?"

"Sure." I smile. Out of the corner of my eye, I notice a shadow in the doorway to the kitchen. A steady figure that's been there for a while, almost like it's watching us. It's probably Mark looking to take me home . . . or maybe back upstairs. I wonder if he's also a little drunk, loose-smiling, like Louisa, now that he knows I won't mind. But I also wonder if I would mind.

"Don't repeat this, okay?" she says. "Not even to me, okay?"

I nod and focus on her, ignoring the shadow streaking the deck. He can wait.

"I kind of don't want to go anymore. Does that make sense? It's like I worked so hard for this and I work so hard to be as good as everyone else. As smart as everyone. And now that I've proved it, I kind of want to spend my summer hanging out at the snack bar."

She slouches like it felt really good to say that but now she wants to suck the words back in.

My eyes go wide. I almost tell her how much I get that, and how that's exactly the way I feel about my Costa Rica trip. I want to stop with the goals and the fighting for stuff and the preparing for my future. I want to have fun.

I'm nodding, but then the shadow shifts and I can't help but turn my head to motion for Mark to wait a minute.

Only it isn't Mark. It's Sadie. Standing just inside the glass door. Watching us lean together with a long face, a lonely face. The face that would spread along her features when we were ten and her brothers were refusing to let her play basketball with them.

I turn back around. "I get it," I tell Louisa. *Don't go.*

"Let's go home," she says.

We find Mark. He's drinking a Pepsi and playing volleyball and stone-cold sober. He drives us both home. He drops me off first so all I get is a little peck.

Αποφάσεις
(Decisions)

It's the first day of summer, but I'm back at school the next evening. It's a cold day for late June. I sit on the football bleachers next to Mark's parents and sister and I try not to shiver as the wind cuts through my light blouse and long skirt. Principal Morris drones on in an oh-the-places-you-will-go-type speech, and as the goose bumps crawl up my arms it hits me: my life is changing. Mark will not bring flowers to my locker every Friday in September. He won't take me to every school dance. He maybe won't text me every morning. In fact, he didn't text me this morning. Last week I would have felt some sense of relief and breathing room in the absent text but in the wake of what happened last night, it's making me anxious. We'll probably make out even less. He'll go off to college and I'll be . . . here, without Mark and without Louisa.

(And Sadie? No. No Sadie today. This is Mark's day.)

Principal Morris isn't talking about me, but he kind of is. Things will change. Maybe they're shifting, wiggle room for something else, someone else. Some adventure.

I look around for Louisa, wanting to roll my eyes as our principal spouts yet another cliché into the microphone. I glance past Mark's parents and I catch his mother eyeing me. Like she can see right through me. Like she can open up my scalp and watch the scene that has been playing on repeat in my brain like it's on HDTV: Mark's hand inching up my shirt, grabbing on for just a second. Or the other scene—the one that takes place in the future, the one where we do more.

My cheeks burn crimson and I feel a vague sense of guilt. It hits me for the first time that what we did was wrong, technically wrong. Against the rules. It didn't feel wrong, though. It feels like it can't be. It was too small and quick to be either right or wrong. But it's been feeling so right all day. And I've always been taught it's wrong, wrong to let anyone who isn't my husband touch me like that. Even if everyone acts like Mark is going to be my husband. Like it's a done deal.

As if it's possible for me to imagine having a husband.

I hear Jasmine start her valedictorian speech and I try to

focus as she talks about hard work, goals, and all of the things that have been drilled into me for as long as I can remember. I can't help thinking it sounds boring.

Later, Mark and I sit side by side in his car in my driveway and I can tell something isn't right. We should be kissing, leaning over the barrier to get our mouths as close as possible. I've been imagining more all day: crawling into his lap, into the backseat.

Instead, Mark watches the driveway like he's doing ninety on the freeway. While we sit, still. His freckles don't bounce.

"So . . . congratulations," I say.

He rewards me with a quick smile, a glimpse of the crooked tooth. Then he turns back to the windshield. Does he want me to go inside?

I put my hand on his. He doesn't take it, but he lets it sit there, my palm grasping his knuckles as he clasps the steering wheel.

"Look, Colette." He finally turns to me and I can see worry etching lines in his forehead. I've never seen that before. He's always so self-assured. So laid-back. "I know I owe you . . . an apology. I don't know how to say it."

My eyebrows shoot up.

"God! This is so awkward!" he almost shouts. I've never heard him say "God" like that before either.

"It's okay," I mumble. Even though it's not. Because if he's going to apologize for what I think he's apologizing for, then it's the apology that's not okay.

"No, I need to show more self-control. I hope you know I don't see you . . ." He shifts around like he can't find the words and I lean closer to him, willing him to stop talking, to stop saying the things we hear in church and from our parents, to ignore all of those rewritten instincts and to wrap his arms around me and press his lips to mine and let our nerve endings make our decisions. "You know . . . you're not an object to me. Or whatever."

I burst into laughter.

He looks surprised but he doesn't crack a smile.

"An object? Come on, Mark. It's me. I know you love me," I say. I move to kiss him but he doesn't meet me halfway. "Seriously, everything's fine," I say, straightening up. "You graduated tonight. You should be happy."

He nods, working his lip with his teeth. I want to kiss him. I want to feel his overlapped tooth. I want him to pick me up again, press his body to mine so that my feet have to leave the ground. It felt joyful. It felt fun. It felt like love. How does it merit an apology?

"Still," he mumbles, "I shouldn't have . . . I should have—"

"But." I cut him off. He turns to me and his eyes are so sad

I can't finish my sentence. *But I liked it. But I started it.* My cheeks burn with shame.

"It was, like, thirty seconds," I say, trying a new approach. "Not a big deal."

"Yeah, okay." He looks at me again. A little smile. And when I try to kiss him this time he lets me, but only for a second.

"Wasn't Principal Mo's speech awful?" I say.

"Totally!" He nods, joy on his lips but stress in his eyes.

"'You will climb mountains and run marathons and hear the screams of new life,'" I quote in Principal Morris's low voice. "'You will sail the high seas.' Who is going to sail the high seas?"

Mark laughs. He says, "So, why were you at that party with Sadie anyway?"

It feels like all of the giggles cram their way back into my throat and I choke. "I don't know," I say. "I was at her house."

Then I remember that my bike is still there.

"Why?" he asks.

I shrug. *Honesty*, I think. Mark isn't my parents. I have to be honest with him. "Sometimes I miss her," I say.

He frowns. I don't think I've ever seen him frown. I've seen him frustrated with his sister and I've seen him disappointed about a test grade or a soccer game, but I've never seen him like this. "So here's more of why I'm sorry," he says. "I know it's wrong to be jealous but when I see you with her . . . I don't know the Colette that was friends with her, you know? When you say you miss her . . . I don't get it. I see Sadie screaming in the hallways and dyeing her hair crazy colors and draping herself across all of my teammates and dressing in those crazy outfits . . . She's just so . . . much. I don't get why you liked her, why you liked being friends with her."

For all of the reasons you just said.

"I was friends with her for a long time," I say.

"I know." He sighs. "I shouldn't worry about this. I trust you. But when you talk about missing her and show up with her at Sally's party. When you talk about going to Greece with her. Between all of that and us acting so . . . different . . . last night. And me going to college . . ." He trails off.

He looks so sad, hazel eyes pasted to the driveway, freckles practically drooping. And I know him so well. That was a bunch of disjointed nonsentences he just uttered, but I know exactly what he meant. And I do love him. My heart breaks as I watch his face get longer and longer. I do love him. I must.

So I do what I know I shouldn't. I lean over the barrier myself, drape my arms over his chest, and put my head on his shoulder. "You aren't losing me, Mark. You aren't," I say.

And finally we're kissing. It's not like last night. Not joyful and passionate and as close as possible. Instead it's long and slow and sad-but-relieved and I know, as his tongue inches around my mouth, that Mark and I could go to Appalachia or Costa Rica or Greece or all around the world and he still wouldn't scratch this itch in me. For adventure. Fun. Squealing laughter.

Maybe we are losing each other slowly. Maybe he's only someone passing through my life. Maybe I'm a blip in his.

So I really shouldn't be kissing him like this.

Ω

I wait inside my front door, watching through the sheer white curtains as Mark's headlights back away and hoping my parents didn't hear me come in. I have another two hours until curfew and I want to sneak out again, hoof it to Sadie's to pick up my bike, and tell her that I'm not going, that I'm breaking my promise. That even if she does need me, it's too late to play that card. Other people need me more. People who have been good to me. People who haven't left me reeling for three years.

But Mark's Jeep screeches to a halt at the end of the driveway and then I see her blond head emerge around the side of his car. She's walking my bike. Like she knew exactly what I was going to do. Like she had to beat me to it.

Once she's safely in front of the car, he zooms out of

the driveway and cascades down the street faster than he ever does.

I come out the front door.

"Hey," I call across the yard.

"Oh, hey," she calls back, her voice high and nasal and sarcastic. "I thought I'd, you know, bring you your bike." A familiar pouty tone hangs on her words, one I'd completely forgotten about.

"Thanks," I say. I'm standing in front of her now at the edge of our driveway, the baby-blue bike resting on her thigh like a division line, turning us into a fraction.

She stares at me.

"Do you want to come in?" I ask. I might as well get this over with.

"Ha." She laughs, staccato. "I don't think so."

We aren't best friends. That was her choice.

I yank the bike away from her. "Well, thanks for returning it," I say, and start to wheel it down the driveway.

"It was pretty messed up what you did last night, you know?" she calls to the back of my head. I freeze. The image of Mark's hand on my breast shows up in my brain for a split second, but that can't be what she's talking about.

I turn.

"I can't believe you left me there like that," she says. "I was looking for you for, like, half an hour when I had to go home. I didn't know what happened to you. I missed curfew."

My jaw drops. I hadn't realized it. But she's right—I'm the one who ditched her at the party. "I-I'm sorry . . . ," I stammer.

"Why would you do that, Colette?" she demands, again wielding my full name like a weapon. "You could have at least said good-bye."

I stare at her.

She sticks her hip out, her fist jammed into it. "Were you too embarrassed to be seen with me in front of your perfect friends? Too embarrassed by—" She pauses and searches my face. Then she finishes the sentence. "The red in my hair or the way I don't think a B is a mortal sin?"

That's it. I drop the bike and charge at her. "Sadie, it was one party." I hate that my finger is jabbing the air the way my mother's does when she's correcting my brothers. "I ditched you for one party and I'm sorry if you were lonely or worried or late or whatever." My voice makes each of these adjectives long and high like a snotty girl and even though I kind of hate myself right now it also feels almost fun, to be honest, to let it out, to be so . . . right. "But it was only one party. One. Party. It's nothing compared to—"

"To what?" she demands.

We're face-to-face now, a foot away from each other. The

twilight blurs her features but I can still see the angry sharpness in her blue eyes; the wind whips her hair around like it's angry at me, too.

I almost back off. I almost apologize and go inside. I'll call her tomorrow and say I'm not going. I'll stop dealing with this. Forget that stupid promise.

But even as my brain is planning this retreat, my mouth opens and the words escape so quietly I think the wind will whip them away: "You ditched me everywhere."

"What!" she practically screams.

I shrug. "It was one party," I say. But maybe to her it wasn't. Maybe I don't care.

I start to turn. When her voice comes back it's not pouty or angry anymore. It's curious. "Is that really your version of what happened?" she asks.

When I look at her again, the wind has blown her entire head of hair straight up so that she looks like she's crowned with gold-and-red spikes. And for the first time I realize there might be another side to the story. Another side I need to know.

I nod.

She doesn't explain. She says, "Will you drive me home? Since I had to ride your bike here?"

We're quiet in the car. Whenever I glance right, I can see the wheels in her mind moving, like mine are, working over what I said and what she said, trying to figure out what I think happened to our friendship and what she thinks happened and where the truth lies between those two stories. I stop in her driveway and turn to say good-bye. It's completely dark out now so I can only see flashes of blue in her eyes and blond in her hair. She smiles at me and a pang of missing her whacks my heart like it's a punching bag. I want to laugh with her.

"You realize this is the first time you've driven me any-where? Or the other way around?" she asks, and we're both smiling seven-year-old smiles.

"Oh, yeah," I say. "Wow."

"So," she says. She shifts around and pulls a piece of paper out of her back pocket. "It's your ticket. Or itinerary. What-ever. You know, it's what you need to check in at the airport."

She holds it out to me and it's folded in a way that I can see my full name across the top. She did buy me a ticket.

She waves it, slightly. "Are you still coming?"

I reach out and then it's in my hand.

"Yes," I say. I say it without thinking. I want to go with her. I want to laugh and swim and have a vacation and be a kid again. And I need the answer. I need to know what happened.

But I want to be there for Mark. I want to savor the last of his time before college. I want to feel his hands on me again and again.

Sadie gets out of the car and I watch her approach her front door. It swings open just as she reaches the stoop and a figure waves at me, a shadow outlined by the lights inside the house. Then he smiles.

Sam.

My heart beats faster like it's Ryan Lochte himself standing fifteen feet away and smiling at me. I send back a friendly *beep* and tell my heart to shut up.

This is only Sadie's brother. This is a real person in actual life. I'm not allowed to think about his bright smile or his chiseled chest. I have a boyfriend.

I drive home wondering if it was that boyfriend I lied to tonight, or if it was Sadie.

Μοναξιά
(Loneliness)

The next day, Sunday (my last one as Princess Perfect if I get on that plane in three days), I convince Louisa to come over for brunch after my family gets home from church.

It's a warm day, so Mom spreads out our meal on the back deck. I change into shorts and let Louisa in when she arrives, and the six of us sit around piles of crisp bacon and fresh bagels and a colorful fruit salad.

"It's lovely to have you here, Louisa. I wish you'd been able to join us for our service," Mom says, like I explicitly asked her not to.

Dad shoots her a look. I roll my eyes at my nonchurchgoing friend. Her face glows; she's embarrassed. She shrugs.

Adam and Peter both start talking, two eleven-year-old conversations that run parallel without overlapping.

Peter's black curls bump against his forehead as he announces, "Colette! I got the solo! Will you come see me?"

I smile at him, his bounciness, his enthusiasm. "Of course," I say.

"Don't boast, Peter," Mom says.

"And then"—Adam finishes up whatever conversation he was having by himself and I shift my gaze from one brother to the other—"I caught the line drive."

Dad pats his head. Mom says, "Don't boast, Adam."

"Will you come to one of my games, Colette?" Adam asks. "I'm practically the star of the team, right, Dad?"

I smile. Dad nods.

Mom says, "Adam."

"Will *you* come see the musical?" Peter asks, looking at my friend this time. "It's only seven dollars."

We all giggle and I watch Louisa. "I'll try," she promises my little brother.

It strikes me that the twins are lucky. They'll always have each other; they'll always know who their best friend is.

Louisa cuts her bagel in half, her eyes on her plate. She keeps her mouth shut except to take bites. She keeps track of my brothers' voices, smiling politely when they are trying to be funny and raising her eyebrows when they want to be surprising. But she watches my parents out of the corner of her eye.

How do my parents do this to everyone?

"Louisa," Mom starts when she's had enough of baseball/musical theater, "how did you find the graduation yesterday? Colette hasn't told us a thing about it."

Because I didn't pay any attention.

I shrug.

"It was nice," my friend says. Then she pauses for a bite, probably hoping the questions will skip to me.

"Your sister gave the valedictorian address, didn't she?" Mom says. "You must be very proud of her."

Louisa nods, chewing, and I know that nod is a lie.

"Louisa's doing even better than Jasmine," I say. "She's studying in Japan next year." Louisa's head whips around, her eyes wide. Because to her, the connection is obvious—her trip to Japan proves that her claimed sisterly pride is nonexistent.

But I'm sick of everyone lying to my parents. I'm sick of the corners they back everyone into.

I expect my mom to say something about pride and accomplishments or opportunities or some other cliché, but instead her hand juts out and her palm covers mine. When I turn to meet her eyes, she's a million years younger: the mom of a toddler, when there were no lies, expectations, or commandments and everything was easier. It's like I skinned my knee.

"Colette," she says. "What a year it's going to be for you."

My heart gets wobbly inside my chest, my blood running a little thicker than usual, and I worry I'm going to cry because my mom's right. There are so many people to miss all of a sudden. Mark and Louisa and Sadie. And Dad.

"Colette has lots of friends," Louisa says beside me as I stare at my mother who is morphing into something familiar but forgotten, something nice. And even if Louisa's words are true on paper, and my mom sees slews of youth group kids pass through her house and hears the names of girls on the swim team I travel with and about the parties I get invited to, it seems like she gets it that, in a real way, I don't have a lot of friends. In a real, practical way I have Louisa and Mark. For a second, it seems honest and I imagine telling her that I'm going to Greece with Sadie. For a second, it seems possible that she'd actually understand.

"Then I made the winning run!" Adam screams, breaking our eye contact.

"You did?" Dad says, patting him on the shoulder like he's a grown man already.

"That was great, honey," my mom says, ruffling his hair. "But don't boast."

I wonder why she went to the game and Dad didn't. They always used to go to my swim meets together.

Ω

After brunch, I take Louisa out for a celebratory pedicure. Celebrating my friend's accomplishments—my impending loneliness.

"You know you'll be fine, right?" she says as the bubbles tickle our ankles. And because I don't want her to feel guilty for her dreams coming true, I nod.

"You'll find a new partner in crime if you have to," she goes on. "You've done it before."

I glance at her. Even though she's smiling, I can tell the thought of me passing notes about teachers and watching *The Twilight Zone* until midnight and going for celebratory pedicures with someone else bugs her. My competitive friend. Then I remember the way she talked to me two nights ago, how she almost told me now that she's won, she kind of wants a break. She kind of wants to stay right here.

And I know the clock is ticking. I'm either getting on a plane in three days or four. Going to Europe or Central America. Choosing my new life or my old life.

"I'm not sure I'm going to Costa Rica anymore," I start.

She doesn't give me the surprised face I was expecting. She nods.

"I get it," she says.

"Instead," I say, "I might go to Greece with Sadie."

"Sadie Pepper?" she squeals, and I have to shush her because we're out in public in our small town.

We lean toward each other, whispering through our giggles as the nail techs rub that tickle-y exfoliating brush against the soles of our feet. I tell her everything and she doesn't look hurt or confused or like she doesn't know who I am. She's fascinated and curious; she smiles and urges me on when I tell her about ditching Sadie at the party, about Mark being so weird last night. Even when I tell her about missing Sadie.

She doesn't stop nodding until I say, "But I don't think I can go."

"Why?" she asks.

"I think Mark needs me more. I think I need to be more loyal to him than to Sadie after the past three years."

Louisa shakes her head, sits up straight, and runs her hands through her hair. "Why do we do this to ourselves?" she asks.

I raise my eyebrows to ask her what she means.

"What about you?" she says. "What about doing what you

want? What about being a good person because you're loyal to yourself?"

I nod, slowly.

"But that's not us, is it? Little Miss Perfects." She sighs and looks at me. "Have fun in Costa Rica."

"Louisa?" I say quietly. "Maybe you shouldn't go to Japan."

She snorts and shakes her head and we're quiet for a minute until she changes the subject.

When I go home, I don't say anything. I read my summer-reading book. I play pirates with Adam and Peter. I talk to Mark on the phone. I make the salad and set the table. I eat dinner. I go to bed.

I don't call Sadie. I don't call Edie. I don't call it off.

Ω

In the morning, I somehow find myself alone at the Bridgewater Mall. The wad of cash in my pocket is stolen from my Costa Rica emergency fund. The books in my shopping bag are full of beautiful pictures of Greek beaches and islands. The dresses hanging on my arms are skimpier than anything I've ever tried on. The thoughts running through my head are vain. Totally, completely, entirely vain.

I'm not sure I've ever had this much fun by myself before.

Sadie said there was going to be a wedding. Andrea's wedding. I loved Andrea—she was my babysitter. I need a good dress for her wedding.

If I go. If I can manage to talk to Mark and my parents and get myself to Newark Airport on Wednesday.

I enter the dressing room with six dresses and I try them all on twice. I love how they hug my hips and show off the muscles in my legs. I stand on my tiptoes and step in a circle, craning my neck to see every inch. I'm a teenage girl. I'm supposed to hate the patch of skin that gathers under my armpits and the dumb tan lines on my shoulders, and I do. But more than that, I love the freedom that I can wear whatever I want to this wedding. If I go.

Finally, I decide on the red dress and move on to the shoe department to buy a pair of serious black heels that will highlight my swimmer's calves. I'm there when I get the text from Mark.

"Sorry about Saturday night. Meet me at the pool?"

Ω

I spot him right away, sitting alone on the top of the hill, tearing up a piece of grass to make duck calls. It's too early in the day for the typical crowd to have shown up yet. There are only a few patrons dotting the hill and swimming laps in the pool as the lifeguards scurry around checking the water and cleaning leaves out of the shallow end.

I stand outside the gate, watching my boyfriend, and I wonder why I don't feel like walking forward. For the first time ever, I will myself to think about being pressed against him, about his freckles or his lips or his crooked tooth. But I can't.

The appeal of Greece is stronger than the appeal of Mark.

"Coley!" Sadie calls too loudly from a lifeguard chair clear across the pool's campus.

Mark's head whips up and he finds me at the gate. I see him looking at me, but I'm too far away to read the expression on his face, to see if he's hopeful or sad or angry that Sadie saw me first.

She's ten or so feet away, and I can tell she wants to talk, to chat, something casual. That thing I've been waiting three years for from her. I give her a little wave before I climb the hill.

"Hey," Mark says. He throws the piece of grass he was pulling apart down at his feet. But he doesn't stand or kiss me.

"Hey," I say.

I stare down at him awkwardly for a moment before he shifts over on his towel and I drop beside him.

Put your arm around me. Kiss me.

"What's up?" he says.

Tickle me.

I shrug.

We're silent for a few seconds and then I blurt, "I want to go to Greece." But he's talking at the same time.

"What?" I ask.

"What'd you say?" he says, louder.

"What did you say?" I repeat.

"No, no," he says. "No, you said something about Greece." He leans toward me, his freckles almost vibrating. "Did you say you want to go to Greece?"

I nod.

"With Sadie?"

I nod.

He gulps a huge mouthful of air and for a second I think I'm about to see Mark cry. "Really?" he says.

"What did you say?" I ask.

Now that he's like this, the fantasies come back. He's so close to broken, I want to take his head in my lap and rub the worries out of his scalp. I want to lie down next to him and put my head on his chest until his heart slows down. I want to kiss him like I did Saturday. I want to touch him like that.

"I said I don't want to break up," he says.

I hadn't even thought about breaking up. Not today. Not as a real, practical thing that will have to happen at a specific moment in time. Still, relief floods my system. I put my hand on his far cheek to turn his face to mine and then I kiss him. Even though I feel like I'm supposed to let him take the lead, I don't. I press my lips to his.

He pulls back. "But do you think we might have to?" he asks.

I freeze. This cannot be happening. Even if this has to happen somewhere, someday, somehow, it cannot happen now and it cannot happen here. I'm not ready.

My hand still glued to his cheek, I say slowly, "Have to what?"

He swallows again. "I don't know, Colette. When you say you want to go to Greece, when you drink at Sally's party, when you hang out with Sadie . . . I'm worried I don't know who you are anymore."

"I'm me!" I say, afraid of what he's saying even though I also don't know who I am anymore. "I'm still me. You were drinking at the party, too."

Mark nods. His cheeks turn a little pink beneath his freckles. "I almost always have a drink or two at a party. If you aren't there."

I put my head on his shoulder. It's suddenly too painful

not to be touching him. He puts his cheek to my hair, and I feel my pulse calm down.

"Me, too," I say.

"What else were you hiding from me?" he whispers.

Everything, I think.

"Nothing," I say.

Now he kisses the back of my hand. "Promise?"

Honesty. "Well . . . I hate sitting on this hill."

He looks startled.

"I mean, I hate being here and not swimming. When I'm at the pool, I want to be in the water."

Mark smiles at me curiously, his adorable tooth finally making an appearance. Then he throws his head back and laughs. I join him.

"Tomorrow," he declares, "wear your bathing suit. We're swimming."

He hugs me. His skin on mine feels so good.

"Anything else?" he says.

"I wish we made out more." I'm feeling so good, the words explode out of my throat like it should have been easy to say them the entire time.

Then, his mouth is on mine in a deep kiss. He pulls me up and we jog out of the gate. We run into the park and sit behind the big oak tree, where we kiss and kiss and kiss for hours.

We should have done this years ago.

Finally, he says, "I have to go."

My lips are chapped and my butt is sore against the ground and both of our stomachs are rumbling.

I stand and help him up.

"I love you," I say.

He smiles. "I love you, too."

We walk hand in hand back toward the parking lot. "Colette?" he asks quietly.

"Yeah?"

"So . . ." He hesitates, studying his bare feet. "You're not going to Greece then, right?"

I turn red. I understand he wants to know, but the way he's worded it, like I no longer have a choice, irks me. "I don't think so," I say slowly.

He stops walking and yanks on my hand to get me to face him. "So you still might?"

I shrug.

"Really?" he says. "You still might go to Greece? With Sadie Pepper?"

I shrug again. I hate his voice right now. It's aggressive and demanding.

"After all that? After today?"

"The whole Greece thing . . . it's not about you," I whisper. "It . . . I just . . . miss her."

"Wouldn't you miss me?" he asks.

I feel my heart soften. "Of course," I promise. "I miss you already."

"But you'll ditch me and not go to Costa Rica? After everything we've gone through to get there? You'll go to Greece and end things?"

"End things?" I say.

He sighs. "How can you be my girlfriend if you . . . leave me?"

"So, if I don't go to Costa Rica, it's over?" I ask.

My head is spinning. Minutes ago we were making out under the tree, loving each other. Now we've skidded into a fight and onto the edge of breaking up. I'm wishing he'd broken up with me hours ago, when we first saw each other today. Or better yet, that he'd sent a break-up text while I was at the mall this morning. I don't want the threats and the guilt. If we aren't going to be okay, I want to know it. I can't skirt this edge forever.

He shrugs, looking at his toes. Then he nods, a tiny jerk of his head. His freckles seem to drip off his face and he looks so sad.

My cheeks are hot. My heart is beating fast. "That's not fair," I say.

He shrugs again. "Maybe not . . ." He trails off and I'm begging him silently not to level this ultimatum at me. "But I can't have a girlfriend I don't know."

I stare at him, hard.

Right now I can't recognize him either. He looks so sad, so broken, so utterly un-Mark, but I'm still here.

Would the Mark I love threaten me like this? Would the me that loves Mark abandon him, let him go to Costa Rica alone?

He's frozen and I'm staring at him and I don't know what to do, so I smush my mouth against his so hard my teeth can feel his teeth and I don't know why I'm doing it or why he's kissing me back but when I pull away, he smiles.

I realize I kissed him because I wanted to. Simple as that.

Αγταρσία
(Rebellion)

"Colette!" my mom is screaming when Mark drops me off the next afternoon after several hours at the pool. "Colette!"

I haven't heard her scream like that since the boys were little and Adam pushed Peter off the swings and gave him a concussion.

I find her in the kitchen on the middle floor of our split-level home. "What?" I demand. I almost enjoy the brattiness underneath the word.

She stares at me and I know why. My hair is wet, dripping all over her clean, white floor, because I said "screw it" and went swimming today. By myself. In my one-piece racing suit. At the public pool. I didn't even care if the flitty bikinis stared at me. My lips are swollen from making out with Mark in the parking lot during adult swim. We snuck away to kiss all day, although I wasn't able to get him to touch me *like that* again. When I put my hand on his waist, he backed away.

I still don't know which plane I'm getting on, if all of this making out is a renewed commitment or a passionate good-bye.

"Don't look at me like that," Mom says.

I twist a finger through my wet hair, halfheartedly wringing it out so I don't get too much water in my ears. I don't want to fly with swimmer's ear.

"Would you please explain the phone call I just got from Edie Pepper?"

My heart doesn't skip a beat the way I thought it would. The delicious secret doesn't immediately slosh back into guilt. Instead I think, *Oh. This. This is how it will happen.* And I notice she called her Edie. She always used to call her Mrs. Pepper, no matter how much Edie complained. So maybe Mom does see that some things have changed. Maybe this won't be as bad as her screaming voice is indicating.

Because while I'm thinking all of this, her voice is cascading around the room, words so loud they crash into the cabinets and bounce off the floor. Words like "irresponsible" and "plan" and "college" and "different" and "Christian." Halfway through her speech she starts banging open cabinets and clanking pots onto the stove like all of this yelling I'm forcing her to do is distracting her from the task of making dinner.

What does "Christian" have to do with anything? I wonder. I'm calm, twisting my hair, tapping my flip-flopped foot, trying not to notice the way my wet Speedo is rubbing against the skin on my butt and shoulders.

"On top of that," Mom is saying, "she started rattling off this list of everything you'll need. A dress. A bathing suit. She knows we can't afford some shopping spree. It was like she was trying to convince me not to drop you off at the airport with that crazy family of hers tomorrow." Mom concludes, "*Tomorrow.* I don't think she even wants you there."

Suddenly, I'm not calm. "Sadie?" I ask.

I take a deep breath. I force my heart to slow down. She's my mother and she shouldn't be saying mean things to me.

"Edie. Who knows what that daughter of hers is thinking? But why would she invite you? After all this time? She can't have good motives." Mom pauses to cluck her tongue. "Did you think of that?"

My mom is across the kitchenette, three feet away from me, but it feels like she's towering over me, like her laser eyes are shrinking me to the size of a cockroach.

I don't want to let her do that.

"After all these years, when you girls have barely spoken,

why would your old friend come out of the woodwork and invite you on some lavish vacation?" Mom says. I am shriveling. "I don't think it's as simple as her wanting you there."

Finally, I can't help it. My face crumples, my shoulders fall, my eyes see nothing but the white tiled floor.

"Oh, honey," Mom says. She take three steps and wraps her arms around me, and even though I'm mad it feels good. It's been weeks since she hugged me. "What is it?"

You shouldn't be allowed to say those things to me. You're my mom.

"She needs me," I say.

Mom backs up, holding me an arm's length away. She plants a kiss on my forehead like she does when I'm upset or sick, even though I'm not crying. Yet.

"Do you know why?" Mom asks.

I shake my head.

"Oh, honey," she says again. She holds me to her, wet hair and bathing suit and all. Then she says, "This is why it's so hard to have friends who are different."

I knit my eyebrows together and peer up at her.

"Sadie . . . she doesn't know how to be your friend, not really. If you keep choosing such different friends, you're going to be lonely."

"Different?"

"Louisa. Sadie," she says. "They're . . . You've always been drawn to people who are . . . Aren't things easier with Mark?"

No.

We're silent for a full minute.

"You know you're not going, right?" she asks me, and I know she wants to call this conversation over. I also know that she can do that. She's the mom. She can determine when we're done with this topic and she can keep me from going where I might need to go.

I walk over to the breakfast nook and pull out the little stool. I look at her, standing at the stove and clanging pots and pans. Her back is to me, so I try to say it casually, like it doesn't make my heart hammer, like it's not a big deal. "I miss her, Mom."

It looks like she shudders. She keeps her back to me.

The front door opens and I hear my dad's heavy footsteps in the hall.

"There's a lot about Sadie that you don't know," she says quietly. "You know you're not going, right?" she repeats.

I sigh. "I know," I say. I guess I always did. At least now I don't need to worry about Mark.

"Going where?" Dad asks.

I turn. He's standing there in a suit—matching gray pants and jacket even though it's almost eighty-five degrees outside.

He has on a red tie, his ex-football-player shoulders fill the doorframe, and his head almost touches the top of it. He shifts his weight back and forth and looks at me. I can't tell if he's smiling with his green eyes or trying to stare me down.

At least Mom is predictable. I knew she'd scream. But Dad, he doesn't scream. It feels like he's barely spoken to me since Sadie stopped being my friend. "Hi, Dad," I say, to stall.

And, like that, he smiles.

I want to rush at him, to jump into his arms and nuzzle his neck the way I did every day until I was eight or nine years old. To feel the stubble of his jaw on my forehead and tell him the most exciting part of my day—Sadie and I played dolphins at the pool, Sadie and I found tadpoles in the creek, Sadie and I baked a lemon cake for the boys' birthday. He would say, "That's great, little lady." Then he'd put me down and pat my head and kiss my mother.

Now he hovers in the doorway.

Mom doesn't turn from the stove. She says, "You better tell your father, young lady."

"Little lady" sounds so much better than "young lady."

I sink into my seat and put my head in my hands. I don't want to tell him. I don't want to think about Sadie or Greece or adventures until I have my own life and I can make my own choices.

I feel both of them staring at the back of my head. The energy in the room cracks and pops. Our kitchenette is too tiny for this much energy, for this many people. Maybe if we had a kitchen like Sadie's—with a full wooden table and a ceiling high over my dad's head and granite countertops and pictures we drew in preschool hanging on the fridge—we could have this conversation in it.

When I pick my head up, I see them looking at me like they don't even know me. Somehow when I stopped being all-kid and they stopped being all-parent, our family got lost in translation.

What comes out of my mouth is the one thing they might understand. "Sadie needs me," I say.

Mom turns to look at Dad.

I gave them a reason they can find a way to take pride in. The jigsaw pieces are back in place.

"Oh," my dad says. His eyebrows jump. His eyes are locked on my mom's, and I can feel their personalities zapping back and forth like they're having a conversation in a secret language.

"She invited me to go to Greece with her family this summer," I say. "Tomorrow."

"Sadie?" Dad says. But he doesn't look at me. He looks at Mom.

"I think I need to go," I say again. Because if Mom is going to forbid it, I want to make sure she knows she's forbidding it. "We leave tomorrow," I say again.

"You're not going," my mom says, as if I'm being ridiculous. The firmness of her words does not match the alarm on her face as she stares at my dad.

"Dad?" I say. He never says anything. He definitely never stands up to Mom. But right now I need to know what's going on, what they're arguing about using only their eyes.

"Mom, I'm sorry but you can't do this anymore."

She finally looks at me and even though I'm wandering into rebellious-argument territory, the room feels a little less tense than it did a second ago.

"You can't dismiss a decision I've made, something I've thought hard about, without taking time to think about it. Without asking for the details or hearing my reasons. I'm too grown up. You can't do that anymore without—I have to do this. Maybe you won't understand, but I have to." I hate the whine in my voice. I hate that I sound like a toddler while I'm trying to argue that I'm grown-up. "And I know you're my parents and you can tell me not to go, but I don't think you should. I think you'll regret it."

My mom comes over to me and puts her hand on my wet hair. For a fleeting second, I think I'm about to get permission. Dad stares and stares at her, his eyes heavy and full of something I don't understand.

"We're still the parents," she says softly. "We might have to run that risk."

My heart plummets. "Dad?"

He stares and stares. We freeze and wait, and minutes and hours and days pass as the silent argument snaps between their eyes.

"Your mother's right," he says finally, almost in a whisper. "You're honoring your commitment and going to Costa Rica." Then he walks out, down the back stairs, a scared shell of his old football-hero self.

"Mom?" I say. I'm almost being honest, almost being me more than I have been with her or Dad or Mark or anyone in so many years. "I think maybe I need Sadie, too."

A pained expression crosses her face. She shakes her head, her blond curls swishing back and forth across her perfect pink cheeks. "I think you need to stay away from her." She swallows. "She's—she's hurt you too much."

I feel the space between us rip into a huge, gaping hole.

I go upstairs, slow, sad, but also peaceful. Sad because now I know I'm not going. I'm going to break that promise after all. But peaceful because I gave it my best try. I did everything I could to get there for Sadie and it's not my fault I can't go. Now I don't need to make a decision about Mark and Costa Rica and perfection versus fun. Mom made the decisions for me. And really, not going will be easier.

Ω

"We're taking Edie Pepper out to dinner tonight," Mom said.

Dad raised his eyebrows at her across the dinner table. "I thought it was going to be just the two of us," he said.

I wiggled in my seat, pushing my spaghetti around with my fork.

"We need to get to know her better. Maybe we'll understand everything she does . . . a bit better . . ."

Dad smiled and jiggled a sleeping Peter in his bouncy seat.

"Sadie will spend the night here," Mom said.

"Yay!" I yelled. Adam started screaming in the bassinet where he had been sleeping.

"Indoor voice," Mom reminded me. It felt like those were the only two words she had said to me in the year since my brothers were born.

"Yay," I whispered.

"Sadie? Will spend the night here? Well, I guess seven is a ripe old age to babysit the boys." Dad chuckled with me. He crossed the room to lift Adam up, patting his diapered

bottom while my brother nuzzled his nose into Dad's sweat-shirt.

Mom shook her head. "I called Andrea Pepper, Edie's niece. She's going to babysit."

"Yay!" I yelled again. This time Peter started crying, too.

"Colette!" Mom said. But Dad was the one looking at me.

"Sorry, Daddy," I said, even though he was grinning. I smiled gap-toothed at him. "But Andrea is magical."

He balanced Peter on his other hip and squatted down to look at me.

"I'm beginning to think you consider all Peppers magical," Mom said.

I nodded. "Maybe," I said. I took a bite. If I ate all my food, maybe she'd stop being angry and smile at me again.

For a second Dad looked nervous, but then he managed to swing around and pick up the pepper shaker without putting down either of my cuddly brothers.

"Even this pepper?" he asked, dousing my plate with the black dust.

"Daddy!" I squealed. "Stop, Daddy, stop!"

He stopped but I couldn't stop giggling. He covered my cheek in kisses, nudging my face in between my brothers' two baby-powdered heads.

"I need to get in on this," I heard my mom say. She came up behind us and spread her arms around us all.

♡ ♡ ♡ 95

"So, Andrea and Sadie and Edie will be here in a few minutes," Mom said when the hug was over. "That okay?"

"Sure," Dad said. "We've got to see what these magical Peppers are all about anyway." He winked at me.

Andrea didn't tell us to use indoor voices that night.

Sadie and I started yelling because we had to, obviously, because there was an ogre after us and if he caught us he would soak up all of our magical fairy powers. We were standing on the sofa in the family room, kicking our legs out to keep the ogre in the sea beneath us that looked like my parents' Oriental carpet.

"Back, ogre, back!" Sadie screamed.

"You'll never get through my magical fortress!" I swung my arms in front of me and said, "Oogly boogly!"

"What's that?" Sadie dissolved into screeching giggles.

"The magic words," I said. Obviously.

"Oogly boogly!" Sadie squealed. "Ogre, disappear to the outside!" We were both laughing loudly when we heard Andrea's boots clomp down the stairs. She had just put the boys in their cribs for the night.

I thought she would yell but she only said, "Okay, fairies. Outside. Now."

"But we just threw the ogre out there!" Sadie yelled.

"Shh!" Andrea whispered. "He'll hear you. Follow me and only walk on your tiptoes!" she said.

We nodded solemnly and hopped down off the couch, tiptoeing behind Andrea through the kitchenette and down the stairs to the back hallway.

"We have to crawl through this part," Andrea whispered over her shoulder, and to our delight she dropped to all fours right on the linoleum floor. We crawled after her and out the back door.

She hopped up to her feet and said, "Now. We fight the ogre. Ch-ching!" She pulled a fake sword from her belt loop.

"Ch-ching!" Sadie followed.

"Andrea," I said. "The boys are inside. You can't be in the backyard."

She made her arm extra long in order to put it around my shoulders without hitting me with the pretend sword. "Don't you worry, Colette-Fairy," she said. "My magical fairy-radio device will let me know the instant the ogre is putting your brothers in any kind of danger." She pointed to the baby monitor that she had clipped to her belt.

I nodded. I went on to fight the ogre, but I wondered why Mom didn't know about the belt clip on the monitor, the wonderful two-inch piece of plastic that allowed us to play outside, screaming our lungs out, until it was time for bed.

Later, once Sadie started snoring lightly, I dug my head into the pillow and replayed all of the best parts of our day of laughing, all the scenes of Andrea and Sadie and even Adam and

Peter, until I fell asleep. During sleepovers, when my mom wasn't there to sit on the edge of my bed and pray with me, those memories were my prayers.

I was still awake, smiling at the dark ceiling, when I heard my parents come in with Edie. I heard Andrea say, "They were great."

Then the front door opened and shut again and Edie and Andrea were gone.

"That was . . . interesting," I heard my mom say.

"Well, I like her," my dad said. "I like Sadie, too."

"Oh, so do I," my mom said. Her voice got a little muffled and I strained to hear more. "Odd ideas . . . family . . . small child . . . There are easier best friends out there, you know, honey."

"We'll watch out for our little girl," Dad said. "Make sure the influence is going in the right direction."

Ω

The sun is barely shining behind the blue curtains of my second-floor windows when my bedroom door whacks open.

"What time's your flight?"

"Dad?" I say. I half sit, rubbing my eyes. My black T-shirt falls off my shoulder.

"Sorry. Should have knocked," he says, but for once he

doesn't sound sorry. He sounds like he knows exactly what he's doing. "When is your flight?" he says again.

"Tomorrow morning," I say. "Nine or something."

I lie down and roll away from him. If I can't go to Greece, at least I can sleep in one last day before I'm stuck doing physical labor for two weeks.

"Colette!" he says, too loudly for the early morning. "Today! What time is your flight today?"

Now I shoot awake, sit straight up in the bed, pure adrenaline flowing through my veins. "To Greece?" I ask.

He nods.

"Five," I say. I don't ask why he's asking. I don't ask if I'm going. I look at him standing tall and proud with a wild look in his green eyes.

"Get up," he says. "Get packed." He pulls his wallet out of his back pocket and starts fumbling in it. "Go to the bank and get your passport out of the safe-deposit box," he says. "And get"—he throws a hundred-dollar bill on the foot of my bed—"anything you'll need."

My eyes widen.

"Be ready by two. I'll call Edie," he says.

I nod. My heart flaps in my throat like butterfly wings, making it impossible to talk.

He turns to go. In the doorframe, he spins back around.

"And, little lady?" he says. "Your mom took the twins to their swim meet all the way in Flemington today. So . . . maybe leave a note for your brothers, but let me handle . . . Mom. Okay?"

"Okay, Dad," I manage.

And then I'm up. I don't let myself think about it as I fold my red dress and count out pairs of underwear. I go buy razors at the pharmacy and shift through our safe-deposit box for my passport. I don't turn my phone on because I don't want to hear Sadie tell me I'm not invited after all, or worse, to see Mark's good-morning text. I work on autopilot until my dad is loading my bags into the back of his minivan with heavy thunks. Then I'm sitting next to him, staring, wondering who he is as he's speeding down Highway 78 toward Newark Airport.

He pulls up to the curb outside the international terminal.

When he looks at me, his eyes aren't so wild anymore. They almost look sad. "You ready?"

"What's going on, Dad?" I ask. It hits me that he somehow snuck me out of the house and he's now ready to push me onto an airplane to some distant island, but he still hasn't said anything real.

He shrugs. "Mom's not always right," he says.

But she is.

His eyes fall to his lap. "Neither am I," he says. "Call your mother. Say good-bye."

My hands shake as I finally turn on my phone.

She answers before the first ring. "Don't get on that airplane, Colette," she says. "I don't approve of this."

"You know?" I ask.

"Your father left a note. Colette . . ." She trails off. "You heard me tell you not to go, right?"

"Yes," I say.

"Well, if you go anyway, be safe. Protect your body and your soul. I changed your phone plan so you can only call home, okay? It's too expensive for you to call Louisa and Mark willy-nilly." *Mark.* "But call when you arrive, okay? So we don't have to worry."

"Okay," I say.

My hands aren't shaking anymore. I'm relieved to hear her sound like any-old-mom.

"And, honey?" she says. She says it so softly I think she's about to tell me to have a nice time. Or that she loves me.

"Yeah?"

"I hope you understand soon what a terrible choice you're making."

She hangs up.

I stare at the phone in my palm.

"She okay?" Dad says finally.

I shrug.

We get out of the car and I spot Sadie and her family climbing out of a limo curbed fifty feet away. She jumps up and down as soon as she sees me, her now purple-and-blond hair waving across her face. I can't help smiling. I can see her mouth moving even from here. "You came! You came!"

I give my dad a quick hug, pull out my suitcase, yank up the handle of my rolly bag, and take my first step as the new, imperfect Coley.

"Colette?" Dad says.

I turn around, ready for him to sit me back in the car, to tell me this was all a test that I failed. Instead he holds out his hand and shoves a stack of bills into my fist. "For whatever you need, little lady. Have fun. I—we. We love you."

Then he's gone.

"Coley!" She's running toward me so quickly that I only have a second to open my phone and click on my good-morning text from Mark.

"One more day! I love you!" the message says.

My heart beats faster and salt water threatens to escape from behind my eyeballs and I know he deserves so much better than this, so much more explanation, so much more of me. And me, too. I know I deserve a better good-bye than I'm going to be able to give him. But I only have ten seconds before she reaches me, before it's time, before the bell rings on my perfect life and I dive into drama with Sadie.

I type the seven letters i-m s-o-r-r-y. Then I press Send. Here we go.

Υποσχέσεις
(Promises)

Later I find myself in the middle of a dark, rumbling airplane. I don't believe it, but here I am. Away from church and my family and Mark.

And I'm terrified. The minute we sat down on the plane, Sadie turned to me and said, "We should try to sleep." Then she stuck her headphones in her ears and closed her eyes and I pulled out the guidebook to read for the thousandth time about the volcano and the caldera and the beaches and the vineyards and the cave-like houses on Santorini.

I'm going to see them all.

As many times as I read the descriptions of this island, as many times as I see the pictures, I can't imagine what anything actually looks like. The entire island rests on a caldera—a volcanic crater. At the top is a cliff with houses and businesses and hotels and stuff built right into it where people work and sleep and live. A red beach is a beach with red sand and a red rock wall behind it. A black beach is the same, but only black. How are these things possible?

Sadie sighs in her sleep as I turn the same four pages back and forth in my *Greek Islands* tour book. I glance around. The plane is the biggest one I've ever been on, with seven seats across and two aisles running from front to back. I nabbed the window seat and Sadie sits next to me, the aisle next to her. Behind us are her eldest brother, Charlie, and his girlfriend, Mary Anne, who has very pale skin and a pink hoop in her nose. Behind them, Sadie's other brother, Sam, sits next to an old man. Edie is up in first class.

It feels like the entire plane is asleep except for me.

I check my watch. In three hours we'll land in Athens, where we'll switch for a plane to Santorini. In Athens it will be morning.

I put down the guidebook and lean my head against the window.

I'm not sure if I actually fall asleep or if exhaustion and the whir of the airplane lull me into a kind of daze, but at some point I feel the plane start to shake with sudden turbulence and I jolt upright.

"Sorry!" Sadie whispers urgently. "I didn't mean to scare you. I was just seeing if you were awake."

Her cheeks grow pink and her blue eyes squint with embarrassment and I realize that the turbulence was actually Sadie shaking me.

"No," I say, smiling. "You weren't checking. You were waking me up." *Like you've done a million times during a million sleepovers.*

When she smiles back at me it's nervous and joyful at the same time and I wonder if I've just given her my version of the inside-joke smile.

"Can I look at your book?" she asks.

I shrug and she pulls it off my lap.

"What are you most excited to see?" she asks. She's speaking in the tiniest voice so that even if everyone on this plane were awake, only I would be able to hear her.

"I don't know," I say. "I don't understand what anything is going to look like, really. I guess I'm excited not to know what to expect." For once.

She nods and closes her eyes again. For a second I think that's going to be it, that's all I'm going to get even after she shook me awake, in the middle of this dark airplane where we are somehow both in private and surrounded by people, both sitting still and propelling forward, both inside and flying through the clouds.

Her eyes pop open again and her pupils are huge. She studies me. "I didn't think you were coming. After . . . everything."

I don't say anything.

"Look, Coley," she says, but she keeps her eyes glued to the back of the seat in front of her. "Let's not do this. Let's not act like strangers when we're there."

"Okay," I say.

"Let's be like we used to be, okay? Let's laugh and have fun and forget about it."

"Okay," I say. And I smile. I like this idea so much I almost agree that simply. But this might be one of my only chances. I don't know when I'll get Sadie alone and open like this, huge-pupiled Sadie who looks almost as scared as I usually feel in her presence. I don't know when she'll show up again. So I ask, "Forget about what?"

She sighs and her face gets a little harder. "Forget about what happened."

"What happened?" I push.

She throws up her hands and rakes them through her blond-and-purple hair, exasperated with me. I feel a little part of me shrink, like she's whittling away at my personality, making me disappear bit by bit. I won't let that happen. Not here. Not again.

"Jesus, Coley," she says, somehow managing to whisper and yell at the same time. "Who knows what happened? Everything happened and nothing happened and suddenly you didn't like me anymore."

No, you didn't like me anymore. You're the one who chose Lynn and a million other girls over me. You're the one who left me dripping on that bench without a milk shake. I stayed.

She continues. "We changed, I guess."

No, you. You changed. I'm still on the swim team and I still have the same hair color. I stayed the same.

"But who cares?" she concludes. "What matters is that you're here for me now. When I need you. What matters is that we kept our promises."

I did. I kept them all. All you did was buy me a lousy milk shake.

"So let's try to have fun, okay?"

I take a deep breath. "Why do you need me? Now?"

She looks at me for a second, considering. If she wants us to magically morph back into our old version of friendship, she has to answer me.

She opens her mouth like she's about to answer.

But then the lights in the cabin come on and the flight attendants start talking about fixing seat backs and tray tables.

Instead she leans toward me and cups her hands around my ear. "You'll figure that part out. I promise," she says.

I think about pushing harder but now it's bright in here and everyone is starting to shift and stretch and my courage is gone.

Ω

"I need you to promise me something," Sadie said.

We were treading water in the deep end of the town pool and I almost dropped under. That word "need" had been haunting me ever since the whole milk shake–ditching incident a few days before. Yesterday, Sadie and I had finally gotten those milk shakes and it had seemed like everything was back to normal. Almost, anyway. Until she left before dinner.

"Can you promise me something, Coley?" she said again.

I didn't like how serious her voice sounded. I tried to answer casually. "Sure," I said.

I dove underwater, reaching for her ankles, but she caught my hand in her own and dragged me back up. "No," she said. "I'm serious."

The fantasies I'd been having all morning about a regular

fun day at the pool were chased out of my head. It was one of our last pool days. We'd go to the beach the next week. Then we'd have only a few days before we started high school. It felt like the world was tilting too quickly in all new directions. "Okay," I said, serious, for her.

"Will you promise not to hate me, even if I do something you don't like?"

I squinted at her. What would she do that I wouldn't like? It was so ridiculous I couldn't help giggling.

"I'm serious, Coley," she reprimanded.

"Okay," I said. "I promise."

"Will you promise to keep my secrets even if we aren't friends?" she said.

Now my heart fell to the bottom of the pool.

"Why?" I whispered. I knew I had to be quiet. Sadie was crazy to have this conversation in water, where our voices could reflect and whatever secret she was talking about could be carried miles away.

"And will you promise . . ." Sadie swallowed. Her dark-blue eyes looked extra wet and redder than chlorine could make them. "If I need you, if I tell you I need you, will you promise to be there?" she asked.

I reached out toward her but the small waves created by people in the pool who were having a normal fun day pushed my hands away before I could make contact. "Of course," I said.

"Even if . . . we aren't friends anymore?"

"Why are you saying that?" I said, too loudly.

Sadie didn't notice. She shook her head. "I have to tell you something. But please promise. First, please promise."

"What do you have to tell me?" I asked. It came out choppy. "What secrets do I need to keep?"

"Promise me first, please. Promise me this and I'll promise . . . unlimited peanut-butter milk shakes whenever it happens."

Whenever what happens? I was in great shape from swim team, but we'd been treading water for a while and my arms and legs were getting tired. So I said it. "I promise," I said. "I do."

Sadie's eyes were full of so many things I didn't understand. We were right there in the same water but I felt like we were on different planets.

"I'm not going to the beach with you this summer," she said. "I can't."

"Why?" I said.

"I can't tell you, Coley," Sadie said.

I was crying now. My heart was broken on the bottom of the pool. The earth beneath the water was shifting to become a place I couldn't recognize.

"Why?" I said again. "What did I do?"

"You didn't do anything," Sadie said, choking back her own sob.

"Then why?" I said again.

She took a stroke away from me. "Please don't ask. Please stop asking. Please just . . . keep my secrets." She took a few more strokes.

She said over her shoulder, "I'll call you when you get back."

But she didn't.

Ω

At the Santorini airport, once we've gathered our bags and used the bathroom, we all pile into a van that was sent specially to pick us up. I know it was because the driver was standing outside with a sign that read THE PEPPER FAMILY.

Sadie and Edie sit in the front; Sam climbs in next to me in the middle; Charlie and Mary Anne snuggle together in the back. It's weird that this suddenly feels like a family of adults. The last time I was with the Pepper family we were all kids. Now Sam is twenty and Charlie is twenty-four. Will my family still be doing beach weeks when Adam and Peter and I are all grown up?

We're driving to the city of Oia, pronounced "Ee-ah," at the northern tip of the island. Our driver is talking on and on about how great it is and I strain to hear. I'm both impressed with how much English he knows and embarrassed that it's so difficult to understand him through his thick accent and over the hum of the uneven road. He says something about wine and the red beach and the volcano. My head starts to bob back and forth with exhaustion. The clock on the dashboard says 13:45 so it's after one o'clock here. The sun is shining brightly into the minivan but it feels like midnight and I realize that I basically didn't sleep for a whole night. The last time I did that was at a seventh-grade sleepover . . . with Sadie. I'm so tired it's hard to make myself look around, but I do—at the pin-straight rows of tiny bushes clustered up against the land, the rocky cliffs on each side of the winding road, the four-wheelers and motorbikes that come barreling at us from both directions. It's a collage out the window: cactus next to palm trees, rocks and dust and soil. Part desert, part farmland, part resort. Who knew God made places like this?

"Okay, family meeting!" Edie announces when the driver stops talking.

He makes a sudden sharp turn that rattles me awake. And that's when I see it: the sea. It appears so suddenly over the cliff to our left that it takes me by surprise. It's a deep blue, almost sapphire, marred only by occasional whitecaps and sailboats. It's nothing like the murky green of the Jersey shore.

Even from thousands of feet above, I can almost see to the bottom.

I get to swim in it. In that water. In all my reading of websites and guidebooks I didn't stop to think about how the very water would be different.

We make another sudden turn, and the sea, the part of it I just saw anyway, is behind us. But I know that because we're on a tiny island, it's also in front of us and to our sides as well, hugging us. I can't see it now, though, because we're surrounded by white buildings that look like they're made of clay. I hear Sadie say, "Seriously, Mom?" and I realize I missed whatever this family meeting was about. If I was even supposed to know. If I'm even part of this family anymore.

"Seriously," Edie says. "Your decisions are so perplexing to me, I have to keep a tight eye on you. You'll stay with me, and Colette will have her own room." Edie glares at me out of the corner of her eye, and I bite my lip, wishing I could disappear. She looks almost hateful. I was stupidly expecting her to be the same hugging, laughing big woman I remembered from childhood. But of course she's mad at me. She's the kind of mom who would be more concerned with protecting Sadie than finding out the truth. So, if I get my own room, some privacy, a sanctuary, I'll take it.

Sam waggles an eyebrow at me, just one. I don't know how

he does that but it makes me smile. When he smiles back, it transforms his whole face the way flicking a light switch can turn a room from sad to exciting in an instant.

The sea pops back into view behind Sam's smile. I do my best to keep listening to Edie while I stare at it, wondering what it will be like to dip my toe in, to dive in, to freestyle and butterfly and backstroke in.

"Now, everyone. There's a dinner tonight that Ivan's family is hosting at a restaurant near our hotel. We all need to be there and we all need to have energy. Be ready to go by eight thirty, and in the meantime, if you need a nap, take it. Aunt Kat sent along these itineraries for everyone. So make sure you know where to be at the right time, okay?"

Edie passes out half sheets of paper and I take a second to read it over before my eyes go back to the sea again.

Day 1
    Arrival
    Free time
    8:30 p.m. Dinner
Day 2
    Free morning
    2:30 p.m. Wine tour (thanks to Andrea's aunt Martina
        and uncle Jorge)

6:00 p.m. Free time

Dinner on your own

Day 3

Free morning

1:30 p.m. Catamaran ride (thanks to Andrea's aunt Edie)

Dinner on your own

Day 4

1:00 p.m. Wedding

6:30 p.m. Dinner and dancing

Day 5

Free day

Day 6

10:00 a.m. Depart for Crete

"What's a catamaran?" Sam pipes up. He waggles that eyebrow around his ebony forehead again. He's looking right at me, and I feel my cheeks warm up. I hope he doesn't think I've been staring at him this whole time. I hope he knows I've been looking at the sea.

"It's a boat or something. Anyway, they say it's not to be missed. Andrea and Ivan and Aunt Kat and Uncle Drew will be busy getting ready for the wedding, which is the next day, but I had to host something so I booked this catamaran-tour thing for us and for Ivan's family and the other guests."

"Mom?" Sadie says in a tiny voice.

"You'll be okay," Edie answers. She pats her daughter's hand.

The glittering sea disappears behind buildings again but this time I'm not disappointed. They're whitewashed and blue-roofed and they seem to grow out of the sea themselves. The road gets narrow and the pavement turns to dirt and sand, and suddenly the driver pops out of the van before it even stops moving. The road has dead-ended in a white-dirt parking lot full of people walking in every direction.

At our driver's instruction, we leave our bags to be picked up by the hotel staff and follow him through a narrow walkway lined with souvenir shops and pharmacies. Every sign is printed in both Greek and English. There are signs with arrows pointing to restaurants and tourist information and travel agencies and car rentals. We have to snake single file past huge tour groups that are led by people carrying giant posters. I hear chatting and shouting and cheering in a million languages before we even walk the skinny hundred-foot path.

And then: *bang*. We step out onto a wide walkway made entirely of slabs of white marble and the sea spreads before us, glittering in every shade of blue. Between the sea and the walkway is the caldera, with a maze of staircases and hotel rooms and swimming pools all carved carefully into a massive cliff.

Sadie and I run across the walkway and lean over, trying to see as many of the roofs and stairs and doorways as we can. There's no beach here, just an entire neighborhood perched precariously above a thousand-foot drop into the shining blue sea. My breath catches.

"Oh, you ain't seen nothing yet," Sam says, coming up behind us.

"Are we staying here?" Sadie screeches.

I sense him nodding. "I was here last summer, visiting Andrea and Ivan," he explains. "It's like nothing you've ever seen. Like nothing you can imagine."

"It's beautiful," I breathe. I turn to smile at him and his face lights up again—his lips spread into a huge toothy grin, his dark eyes widen like he can't see enough, his dimples sink deep into his cheeks. Even his forehead seems to smile.

Has he always smiled this way? Did I just not bother noticing all those years ago?

Ω

Then I'm in my room. Really, my cave. It's a hole sunk into the side of the cliff. After walking up and down and up and down a series of stairs carved into the caldera, you climb three final ones and suddenly there's a gate. You cross a little balcony and open the door and voilà: you're in a cave. My cave.

It's a dome-shaped room, with two little windows and the door at the front; it looks the way I would picture the inside of Winnie the Pooh's tree. The walls and floor and ceiling are painted white and gray and they're part of the rock of the cliff. There's a TV in the front corner and a wooden cushioned bench on the wall across from it. There's a big bed in the back corner, with a small throw rug in front of it, then a door that goes through to the darker-gray cave-bathroom. I open the two windows that look out onto my little balcony and when the sun and the salt of the sea spill in, I decide I'm not closing them for the entire five days we're here.

I don't know how long I spend walking around in a circle. Through the cave-room and into the cave-bathroom and out onto the cliff-balcony and back into the cave-room. *People actually lived like this*, I think. *People do live like this.* It's so different from my house, from my perfectly square room that floats two stories above the earth and has windows on all the walls and cushy beige carpeting. It's impossible that I was in that room less than twenty-four hours ago. That I'm only a plane ride away from that room. I have to be farther. A planet away. A lifetime away.

I know Edie said to take a nap but I can't. As soon as I walk out onto the balcony, I watch the sea spread out around me, hugging the island and presenting the volcano, which feels like it's right outside my front door. Then I remember I live in a cave and I go in to walk the cold floor some more.

If I can't nap, I should do something productive. Something boring that might make me sleepy. I open my suitcase to unpack a little and there, right on top of my pile of neatly folded clothes, is my black racing suit. I try to picture myself wearing it on that catamaran thing, or racing through the sea in this unflattering piece of black fabric.

I should have a bikini.

I can't believe I just thought that.

I can't have a bikini.

It's not just that it's not a bikini, I think as I peel off my jeans and T-shirt. It's not just that it's modest. I snap the straps over my shoulders and yank the fabric down to cover my butt. This is the kind of suit I've been wearing since I was a little girl. This is not made for lounging; it's made for racing.

I close my eyes and use my hands to lead me into the bathroom. I yank the fabric with my fingertips to make sure it's all in place. Then I open my eyes.

Ugh.

I shake my brown hair out of its ponytail. I raise my hands over my head, then put them on my hips. I turn to look at myself from each side. I perch on the side of the counter and watch the ripples appear in my stomach. I put my hair up. I take it down again. I go out of the bathroom and watch myself come in again.

No matter what I do, my midsection looks like a gift box wrapped in shiny black paper. The *X* on my back, the elastic just below my collarbone, the fabric that comes over my hips: I don't look like an adult in this suit.

I spin around a final time, and that's what I'm doing when there's a knock on the door.

Shoot! She's here. My cheeks burn. How long have I been standing in this bathroom checking myself out? How did I get so vain?

"Hold on!" I call. I tie my hair up in a messy bun on top of my head and quickly wrap my body in a towel.

Sadie doesn't answer.

"Coming, Sadie!" I yell through the door once I cross the room.

"It's Sam," his voice answers, low and smooth.

My heart stops.

"I was just, um, changing." My face is on fire now. I hope that he doesn't start picturing me half-dressed.

"Cool," he calls, his voice much quieter than mine. I wonder if he's speaking more softly or if it's the door muffling his voice. "Just came to see if you wanted to go down to the pool. Everyone else is napping."

"Sure," I say. *Why did I say that?*

"Great," he calls back. "I'll be right here when you're ready."

"Okay," I say. Then I stand there. I'll be the only person at the pool in this kind of suit, but I don't have another option. The rest of my suits are brightly colored and even less mature-looking. So it's not like I have to do anything to get ready.

I count to one hundred, step into a pair of athletic shorts, and walk out the door to go to the pool with Sam.

His bare shoulder blades glisten with sweat as I follow him up and down stone mini-staircases. The sun beats on us and I feel perspiration bead on my own nose and forehead.

We aren't saying anything. I'm telling myself that this is a good thing. That at least Sam is not mad at me, even if Edie is. That Sadie's brother being another friendly face on this trip will make it easier. I just wish that friendly face weren't so cute.

He turns. "Here it is," he says.

The pool is at an edge in the cliff and the water flows off the side of it as if the pool is connected to the sea. It's the kind of pool for sitting around, for ordering a lemonade and sipping it and getting a tan. It's not the kind of pool for playing cards, let alone swimming. And right now I am the only person in this kind of bathing suit because we're the only two people here.

"C'mon," Sam says. He drops his towel, runs across the concrete, and cannonballs into the water.

And for a split second I have a thought I never, ever have: *I don't want to take off my shorts.* I'm embarrassed to be exposed in my bathing suit, as modest as it is.

But then Sam says, "I'll race you across," and at once I'm in the water, kicking his butt to the other side of the pool. It feels normal. It feels great. We play tag, the regular kind, in the deep end. We debate who has the more perfect handstand in the shallow end. We race from wall to wall, and I win, again. We don't talk about Sadie.

After a little while, Sam says he's tired, so we climb out and spread across two of the lounge chairs on the deck. And I'm nervous. It's easy to act normal when I'm in the water. Now that we're on land, I'm not sure what we'll talk about.

A waiter in white pants and a white-collared shirt with the hotel's insignia stitched on it approaches Sam from the opposite side. "Is there anything I can get for you, Mr. Pepper? Ms. Jacobs?"

I blink, wondering how he knows our names. This is not the kind of vacation my family would take, no matter how old we all are.

"We'll each have a Greek coffee," Sam says. "Thanks."

When the waiter walks away he turns to me. "Trust me.

They are delicious. And they'll keep you going no matter how many naps you miss. You'll need that kick tonight."

The Greek coffee is frozen and it tastes more like coffee ice cream than regular coffee. We sip.

"When I was here last summer, we stayed in different hotels every night," Sam says. "Part of Andrea's travel agency deals."

"Are they all like this?" I ask, grateful to have a subject other than why we haven't seen each other since Sam was my age.

He laughs. "Well, they aren't all this nice," he says. "But, you know, . . . creative? Like how you don't know where you'll end up no matter what set of stairs you take?"

"Uh-huh," I say.

"Yeah. They're all like that. Isn't it incredible?"

I nod, and my nerves disappear while Sam tells me more. I imagine him traveling with Andrea, and something about the picture feels slippery. I guess I've never thought about the fact that she's Sam's cousin, too. That Sam fits into the entire family, not just Sadie-Edie-Charlie-Sam. I don't know why that seems strange.

I ask him question after question about snorkeling and medieval castles and Santorini cities and Greek food and anything I can think of to keep him talking and to banish Sadie from my brain. For now. While I can.

As our skin dries, beads of water form on his stomach and my arms, until the sun bakes them away. I watch a drop of water travel from the side of his jaw and plummet onto his dark defined chest, and for a second I wonder what it would be like if Sam hugged me really tight. But I shake my head to clear that thought.

I can't have thoughts like that.

I wonder what Sam is really like. My whole life—at home, at school, at church—I've felt like I'm the different one, but here, sitting next to me, is someone who knows what it's like to be different. He's different from his own family.

Οικογένεια (Family)

Later, at eight fifteen, I wait in my room. I'm in my mint-green dress. It's a church dress, but it's the only one I have, besides the new red one that I'm saving for the wedding. And it's not that bad—hits just below the knee, buttons up in a businesslike way, and has a wide-lapel collar. I left three buttons undone. For church I only leave two.

I lie sprawled out on my bed, my feet kicking the bottom of the mattress, my skirt spreading out from my hips, my freshly shaven legs enjoying the smooth fabric of my bedspread beneath them. And I wait. I know there's some dinner and I'm supposed to be ready at eight thirty, but I don't know where I'm going or how I'll get there or who will come and get me.

Despite the coffee, my eyelids are already heavy. So I let them close.

Mark.

Mark, smiling with crooked tooth and bouncing freckles. My Mark. My Mark who I accidentally dumped. Mark, sitting shirtless on a towel playing cards at the town pool, kicking a winning goal at his soccer game and leaping in celebration with his buddies, leaning against my locker with sunflowers. Mark, squeezing me as tight as possible in Sally's little brother's room. Mark, cupping my cheek like it was a goodbye in the middle of our last make-out session.

Why did we keep so many things from each other? Why didn't I tell him about Sadie being fun? About drinking beer at parties? About getting bored with being perfect?

Then, I'm not only seeing him. It's Pert Plus and salty skin in my nose. Muscles and silky body hair under my palms. The roughness of his stubble against my cheek. The taste of his tongue. The music of his laughter.

If I'd been honest with him from the start, would we still be together?

I'm on the brink of crying when there's finally a knock on my cave door.

I cross the cold floor and swing it open. The twilight surrounds Sadie, stars dancing over her head and shoulders, fresh air moving past her silhouette and into my room.

"That's what you're wearing?" She wrinkles her nose in disgust.

I look down. The mint-green stands out in stark contrast to my tanning skin. The black belt hugs my waist at just the right spot. It looks okay.

I shrug.

"Wait here," she says. She darts across my balcony and starts up the side set of stairs.

"Oh, hi!" I call, sarcastically.

She spins, her own hot-pink minidress flying dangerously up her tan leg. She rolls her eyes at me but she's smiling. "I'll be right back, Coley," she says. Like now she remembers I'm a real person.

When she returns, it's not with any of the teeny-skirted, crazy-low-cut dresses I've been dreading. Instead it's a deep gold, almost mustard-colored, lace dress with a fitted top and a slightly poofy skirt. Under the lace is a layer of nude-colored fabric.

Sadie turns her head while I slip into it and when I face the mirror I can't believe how good I look. How does she know these things?

She comes up behind me to finish zipping the back. The top of it reaches all the way to my collarbone. It's cut like a fitted tank top but it flares at the waist. It reaches almost to my knees. Somehow it's both more modest and more sexy than the mint-green one I was just wearing.

Sadie rakes her fingers through my hair and clips up the top like she did for Sally's party.

She spins me so I'm facing her. "There," she says, smiling a smile I've never seen before. She pats my cheek. "You're ready."

We haven't stood close like this in so long, only inches between us. She smells like cherries, her own hair in a messy bun and her eye makeup extending her blue eyes.

Suddenly I'm missing her. Almost as much as I was missing Mark a few minutes ago. But this is stupid. Sadie is right in front of me.

"Ready for what?" I ask when she steps away from me.

Sadie sighs, her face caught for an instant between dread and excitement. "That, I don't know," she says.

We walk back over the marble walkway and down yet another set of stairs to a huge patio. The patio *is* the restaurant, I realize. The entire business doesn't need an inside. There are tables set up across it, lined with brown-paper tablecloths, and the flat surface juts out over the cliff so that it appears to be hovering above the sea. I can't wait to get into that sea.

There's a small cluster of people by the far edge of the patio and the rest of the space is empty. I follow Sadie toward the crowd and recognize Andrea talking to Charlie and Mary

Anne and Sam. She looks so much older, her blond hair pulled into a French twist, her plump body in a rose sundress. She was our babysitter a million years ago. It hits me for the first time when I see her profile across the patio, outlined by the black night sea: Andrea is getting married. I'm here for a wedding. I'm not here for myself or my friendship with Sadie or an adventure; I'm here for Andrea's wedding. I'm here for the wedding of a woman I haven't spoken to in over three years.

I chew my cheek.

When we're about ten feet away, she looks up. Her face spreads into a huge smile and she calls, "Colette! Is that you?"

Sadie smiles. "I told you I'd have a surprise for you."

Andrea hugs her cousin and stares at me over her shoulder, shaking her head. "I had no idea you'd be at my wedding," she says, happy.

Neither did I.

Sadie bites her bottom lip.

"Come here," Andrea says to me. She hugs me and it brings back skinned knees and unfair snubs from Sadie's older brothers. "It's so good to see you," she says.

Why won't Edie hug me like this?

"You, too," I say, and I mean it. I guess I didn't realize how many people I was giving up when Sadie slipped away.

Three feet away, Edie watches her niece and me. I swear

her eyes fall, sad, to the patio beneath her feet. She shakes her head. Even though it's not my fault, I feel awful that she hates me now.

Andrea leads us around the deck, introducing us to Ivan and his parents.

I smile and answer questions about how old I am and where I'm from and what I'm interested in studying. I let my face act the way it's been trained to act around adults, while my mind spins and searches and wonders what I'm doing at this family party.

"Is that it?" Sadie asks once Ivan's and his parents have wandered away.

Andrea gives Sadie a big squeeze. "Yup, you got it down pat? This is the easy one. You should get to know all of these wedding guests so you guys have some people to talk to at the party in Crete next week."

My eyes go wide. "These are all of the wedding guests?" I ask.

It feels like we've only met, like, fifteen people. At my cousin's wedding last summer there were over a hundred people. At the wedding I went to with Mark there were over two hundred. This is the smallest wedding I've ever heard of.

Still, I should have held my tongue. For a moment I'm afraid I've offended Andrea but then she laughs a big, openmouthed laugh. "We couldn't expect everyone to travel across the sea like you two, could we? So that's everyone except—" She pauses for a second to wave cheerfully toward the entrance stairs. "There they are. Now that's everyone."

Sadie and I turn and watch a dark-haired family—a woman, a man, and a girl who looks about our age—walking down the stairs.

"These are all the wedding guests? This is it?" I ask Sadie. She keeps her eyes on the family. I spin around to count the number of people on the deck—Edie, Sadie's aunt and uncle, Charlie, Mary Anne, Sam, Ivan's mom and dad, Ivan's sister, brother-in-law, and two nephews. Plus the three who just entered. Seventeen. Seventeen guests at this wedding.

"Sadie?" I say. She still doesn't turn her head. "Sadie?"

Seventeen. There are only seventeen people coming to this wedding.

"Sadie," I say, jabbing her upper arm with my pointer finger.

She whips her head around and the length of her sad face scares the demanding tone out of my voice. "What am I doing here? Why am I one of the seventeen people at this wedding?" I say it, but too quietly.

"Come on," she says. She puts her fingertips lightly on my elbow and leads me over to Charlie and Mary Anne, who are standing by the bar. I order another Greek coffee and listen to Sadie laughing too loudly at Mary Anne's story about whatever they did this afternoon.

I lean my elbows on the bar while I watch the bartender add cream to ice before even putting in any coffee.

This is too weird.

Suddenly I feel the heat of a large body standing next to me. "You're hooked, aren't you?"

I look up and there's Sam, laughter in his deep eyes.

I shrug. "I'm tired," I say. Even though, really, I'm confused.

He laughs and I turn back to my coffee. I wonder if I can ask Sam what I'm doing here. I wonder if he knows.

"It's so beautiful," he says, pointing out at the sea. I turn to look while he keeps talking. "You never want to sleep when you're in Greece. You look out at the sky at night, at the stars, at the black sea, and you hear the music drifting on the wind, the waves crashing into the rocks beneath your feet. You can't sleep when it's this beautiful. But then the sun comes up and you remember it was even better in the daylight. When I was here last year, I stayed tired the whole time."

I turn to smile at him.

"Hey, is that Sadie's dress?" he asks.

"Oh. My. God. You share clothes? How cute is that?" The

voice is as sharp as a blade and it cuts into the middle of our little group, making everyone stand up straighter and turn to look at the speaker. It's the dark-haired girl who just entered. She's tall and scowling and beautiful and intimidating. Everything about her that could be is thick: her long black hair, her perfectly curled eyelashes, her curvy figure. She wears a skintight black dress that makes her breasts and butt seem to launch out from the rest of her body. Up close, she looks much older than us.

And she's looking at me as if I smell like the Dumpsters behind the gym at school.

She sticks her left hand on her hip and extends her right palm. "I'm Rose," she says. Her voice has a hint of a Spanish accent, which reminds me how little I know about the world. "You must be Coley."

My eyes go wide. I can't believe she called me that. But I manage to shake her large hand.

She turns back to Sadie and says "cute" in a way that makes me feel like an ant or a speck on the end of someone's nose. Sadie shrinks along with me.

"Hi, Rose," Sam tries, but she's already walking away.

"Who was that?" I ask.

Sadie keeps her mouth shut. She watches the girl cross the patio.

"Andrea's other cousin," Sam says slowly. "On her mom's side . . . you know? Rose."

"I do?" I look to Sadie for an explanation. She's tiny, standing between her two brothers, who both seem to puff out their chests to make up for the way she's shrinking.

"Sadie?" I say.

"Let's go," she says. She yanks my arm, pulling me toward the stairway exit.

"What?" I say.

"Let's go. We'll get room service. Andrea will understand," she says toward her brothers.

Sam says, "Sadie, you really have to—"

"I will." She cuts him off. "Come on." She pulls me away. I leave my sweating, ice-cold coffee on the bar and follow her toward the stairs. She moves so quickly I trip back and forth on my high heels. We're only halfway up when Rose's thick voice rings out behind us.

"She isn't even, is she?" Rose calls, laughing. I turn and see her standing on the bottom step and for a second she looks sad. But then she makes herself large and mean again.

Sadie keeps walking.

Rose laughs a horrible fake laugh. "Good luck, Sadie," she calls. "Good luck."

Sadie follows me onto my balcony. I turn around to ask her

what this is all about but before I can say anything I'm startled once again by the view. She's surrounded by a canvas of black interrupted only by stars sparkling and blue gemstones—swimming pools on the cliffs in the distance. "Room service?" she asks before I can say anything.

"Sadie . . ." I trail off. I want to demand some answers but I'm not even sure what to ask her. She looks tiny, so wide-eyed and sad, in stark contrast to the beauty behind her. Finally I say, "Sure."

"Good. I'm starving!" She plows ahead of me into my cave. I watch her through the door for a few moments as she leans over the room service menu, contemplating. I know I should say something. After all this time I deserve to know what she needs from me, what I'm doing here. But with Sadie it's never about what I deserve.

I think of Mark again. Tomorrow he'll be somewhere in Costa Rica pounding a nail with a hammer and missing me. Is he missing me? Did I get what I deserved with him?

Sadie turns around. "Coley? Aren't you coming?"

I tilt my head at her, trying to ask the questions with my eyes that I'm not going to ask out loud. She sighs. "I'll tell you everything when I'm not so tired. I didn't know . . . I thought that . . . I'll tell you about everything. I promise," she says in a voice so small and pathetic it makes me feel like the one in control. "I'm really glad you're here, Coley. I'm really glad you can forgive me."

I nod.

"Can we have fun tonight?" she asks.

I did come here to have fun.

So I try not to wonder what she thought and what she didn't and what I'm doing here while we order lamb kebabs and Greek salads and we sit facing each other at the little table on the balcony, waiting. Sadie pulls a deck of cards out of her purse. I don't know why I'm not tired. I've never been awake for this long at a time. But I know I'd never sleep with all of the questions running through my head. About Sadie. About Dad. About the Peppers. About Mark. About me.

She divides the deck into two piles.

"Remember how Spit was our game?" she says, handing me my half of the cards.

I tap the edges of my pile until it's a neat, perfect square. She leaves hers a shapeless blob.

"Uh-huh," I say. Because I do remember endless hours of this game with Sadie the summer after fourth grade, when Andrea taught it to us. On rainy days, we would play game after game sitting criss-cross-applesauce on Sadie's gold carpet while the gray sky split with lightning outside her windows.

But that's not what Spit is to me anymore. It's Mark and

the hill at the town pool. It's his hand on my shoulder after each game whether I win or lose.

"I still play this game," I say quietly when we start flipping cards. *I'm the one who stayed.* I don't have to say it out loud for Sadie to hear my thoughts.

Sadie pauses, a hand and a card halfway to the table. She looks hurt but I won't let her.

"We're supposed to act like it didn't happen," she reminds me.

Flip-flap. Flip-flap. The cards pound quickly on the table.

Like what didn't happen?

Flip-flap. Flip-flap.

I've always loved the speed of this game. Flip so fast you can't think about anything but the cards.

Then the table beneath them becomes a bed of green grass and the dark sky brightens to pale blue and the buzzing silence is replaced by distant yelps and screams of little kids and Sadie becomes Mark.

I blink and then it's over.

I don't want to miss Mark. I don't want to miss Sadie.

I shake my head at her. We're only halfway through the first round but I stop flipping. "Where's the darn food? I can't play this anymore."

I think about going to bed and letting Sadie eat my dinner

out on my balcony but my stomach is gurgling with hunger. I haven't eaten since we were on the airplane and that was hours ago. My internal clock is too messed up for me to figure out how long it's been since I ate or slept.

"I guess it's more fun to play with Mark than with me, huh?" Sadie says.

I'm so sick of this hurt act. I'm sick of her assuming that whatever this need of hers is, it's worse than anything I'm going through. So I spit it out: "Mark dumped me."

She freezes, her eyes steady on my face. I'm ready for her to say something else, to make fun of the way he was quiet or awkward or the way we barely ever kissed in the hallway for the full two years we were dating, but she doesn't say anything.

Finally I glance at her. She doesn't look sad or pathetic anymore. She doesn't look smug and superior. Half of her face is shocked and the other is . . . guilty?

"Why?" she says.

I sigh. "Or maybe I broke up with him. I don't know. It was confusing."

"Does he know about me?" she asks quickly.

I nod.

Sadie starts to clean up the cards. "Was it because of that? Because of me?" she asks.

I almost deny it. I want to be annoyed with her for being

vain enough to think she could break us up. But I can't because she's kind of right.

"Maybe," I say.

The air rushes out of her like a river. "Then you'll get back together. When you get home you'll get back together. He's freaked out but he won't end it because of something this temporary. Believe me."

I shrug. Will he try to get back together? The thought is both relieving and exhausting.

"Do you love him?" Sadie asks, her eyes on the cards.

I pause. "Yeah. Or, I did, at least."

Sadie nods. "I'm sorry, Coley. Broken hearts are the worst."

I raise my eyebrows, ready to ask her how she knows about broken hearts. But then our food is here. The waiter scrambles around us, laying everything out so that the knives and forks are parallel on the napkins and the salad is between our two plates and the sodas we ordered are fizzing by our right hands. It's nice, all this attention to detail, but I want him to go away so I can ask Sadie.

Finally he does.

"So who was he?" I ask. I study Sadie salting her salad.

"Who was who?" she says.

"Who was he? The guy who broke your heart?"

She looks up sharply, her eyes piercing and confused, trying to drill into my brain and read my mind.

"It was last summer," Sadie says slowly. She puts the salt down.

"Who was he?" I ask. "Do I know him?"

I must know him. Why else would she act so weird? It must be something strange like she had some big crush on Mark and he turned her down or she stole a boyfriend from one of her new bikini-friends. Something big and scandalous like that.

She shakes her head. "No . . . you wouldn't. It was a different school."

I nod.

"But it was awful, Coley. It was completely awful. I couldn't get out of bed. I couldn't swim. I missed . . . you. I missed you so much."

I swallow back a sob.

"I'm not going to let it be that awful for you, okay?" she says. "If it's meant to be, if you love each other, you'll get back together. But either way, I'm going to make sure you have fun. I'll be there for you."

I nod. It's nice to feel the universe clicking back into its rightful order: I'm the one who needs Sadie; she's the one in charge.

She reaches over all the food to pat my hand and I pick up the kebab to take my first bite. The flavors explode across my palate, spices and juices and freshness running through my teeth and over my tongue and down my throat.

"This is amazing," I say.

Sadie takes a bite and nods furiously in agreement.

"Hey, Coley?" she says.

I look up from my plate, stuffing another forkful into my mouth.

"Hm?"

"When was your first kiss?" Sadie asks. "I never got to hear about it."

I smile, remembering Greg, the boy who kissed me in the basement of the church during a youth group social a few months before Mark asked me out.

And that's how we spend the rest of the night, trading the secrets we should have shared a long time ago. First kisses and parent fights and brother issues and junior prom dates and college dreams. When she leaves, I fall into my bed, exhausted.

Ανωριμότητα
(Immaturity)

I've barely closed my eyes before the Beatles' "Octopus's Garden" starts blaring electronically out of the pocket of my suitcase.

Gosh darn it! I think, bolting upright in the bed.

I was supposed to call to say we arrived safely. I know it's Mom because of the new family-only phone plan. (Translation: Mark has no way to contact me.)

I fumble in the bag, then bring the phone to my ear.

"I'm sorry. I forgot to call," I say, attempting to disarm my mother before she can start shouting. "I'm fine, though, totally fine."

"I was so worried." But the voice that comes through the

phone isn't alarmed or hectic or angry or female. It's sad. It's hushed. And it's Dad.

He keeps talking. "I'm sorry to wake you, little lady, but I just got home from work and I was starting to make the salads for the boys' dinner when I saw that you still hadn't called. Mom's note says that you probably forgot, that you're probably having so much fun you didn't remember to check in—"

Jeez. She can give me a guilt trip even internationally.

"—but I needed to know that you're okay. I kept seeing images of your airplane exploding on the Santorini runway or your car diving off the cliffs."

I chew my cheek, not knowing what to say. This might be our longest conversation since Sadie and I were friends.

"What time is it there?" I ask finally.

"Five fifteen," he says. "It must be just after midnight in Greece. Are you used to the time difference?"

I chuckle. "No, Dad. I haven't even been here twelve hours."

He pauses. "Yeah, well . . . it feels like longer. I've been thinking about you."

I smile. I can't believe this conversation is still going. Now that it costs over a dollar a minute to talk to me he wants to drag it out. But it's nice to hear his whispering voice. I lie back on the pillow and imagine the house around my father as he starts dinner for my brothers.

"Why isn't Mom making dinner?" I ask. Dad isn't usually home this early. And I can count on one hand the number of times he's made us dinner.

"Oh. She's . . ." Dad pauses. "She's eating over at Aunt Liza's tonight. No big deal," he says. Then, "So, how's it going? Are you gonna run off like Andrea and marry a Greek?"

I giggle again. "I don't know yet, Dad. I haven't met enough of them."

"What have you been doing?" he asks. "What's it like?"

I try to tell him about my cave-bedroom and the cliff pool and the Greek coffee. I'm not doing any of it justice.

"That sounds great, little lady," he says.

"Will you tell Mom I'm okay?" I ask. "And that I'm sorry I forgot to call."

"Okay," he says. I think he's going to say good-bye but then he says, "Colette?"

"Yeah, Dad?"

"Remember who you are, okay?"

I roll my eyes. "Okay, Dad," I say.

"And remember you can call us. If you need something, if you're sad or confused, you can always call us." He pauses and I wonder if he's hung up but then he says, "Or me. You can just call me, too."

"Okay, Dad," I say. "Have a good supper."

He chuckles. "Sweet dreams, Colette. Sweet dreams."

Ω

One morning, the third summer Sadie was with us in Ocean City, I woke up alone in the little double-bunk-bedded bedroom of the beach apartment we rented. That was weird. Every other beach-week morning for the past three summers I'd been woken up by Sadie wielding my bathing suit like a whip. I crawled out of my bottom bed and climbed a few rungs on the ladder up to her bunk. My brothers were deep-sleep-breathing behind me, but Sadie's bed was empty except for the wadded-up pink sheets against the wall.

That's when I heard the singing. Sadie's and my mother's voices mingling together like a French braid and floating down the short hallway from the kitchen: ". . . the sound, that saved a wretch like me. I once was lost . . ."

"Amazing Grace." That was a church song. I didn't think Sadie knew any church songs.

I tiptoed into the hallway, the dark wood floor cold beneath my bare feet and the breeze from the open bathroom window making goose-bump patterns along my arms and legs. The smell of bacon and pancakes climbed to my nose and made my stomach growl but I was too curious to notice. Finally, I peered around the doorjamb into the shoebox-size kitchen with its seventies-era burnt-orange cabinets and yellow tiled floor.

"Now you pour it," Mom was saying. She and Sadie stood with their backs to the door, two blond heads bent over the skillet on the stove. Mom had her arms around Sadie, steadying her hands while she poured the batter.

"Any pattern? Like a palm tree? I can make a palm-tree pancake?"

"Sure!" Mom said.

They moved together, two bodies in faded pink robes with belts tied tight at the waist . . . wait! Now that was weird. Was Sadie in my mom's old robe?

Their hands worked together as they flipped the pancake.

"Perfect!" Mom exclaimed. Then she turned toward Sadie, and I could see a wide, proud smile slice her profile. Bigger even than the one I'd managed to pull out of her with my straight-A seventh-grade report card a few weeks before.

That was enough. It was too strange to watch anymore.

"Morning," I mumbled, rubbing my eyes and padding into the kitchen so it would look like I didn't see any of the weirdness.

Mom turned away from Sadie's smiling face.

"Morning, honey," she said. She took the two steps over to me and kissed me on the forehead before she and Sadie started pouring the next pancake.

All I got was a kiss on the forehead.

Ω

I'm sure I've barely been asleep for a few hours before the sunlight streaming through the open windows in the front of my cave insists that I not only wake up but get up, out of the bed, and go outside to dance in it to see and hear and smell Santorini-in-the-morning. The view from my balcony takes my breath away once again. The cliffs spread on either side of my little cave, with more caves and staircases and hotels and swimming pools all painted white or gray or blue. The sky is pure aquamarine without a single cloud, only the blaring sun painting white-hot lines across it and reflecting golden on the sea thousands of feet below us. On the level just beneath my balcony, breakfast is being served. The clinking of utensils and the salty, sweet, bitter smells of bacon and pastries and coffee rise up to meet the sights before me. I remember what Sam said last night and I think he has to be right: it's impossible to sleep long enough on an island this beautiful. All of this beauty makes me wonder why God decided we ever have to sleep in the first place.

"Coley's awake!"

I hear the words shouted below me, words that bring back a million sleepovers and summer vacations and campouts. I look over my balcony to wave at Sadie, and then I'm embarrassed that I'm still in my pj's with my hair unbrushed and my face unwashed because she's sitting at a table with Sam and Charlie and Mary Anne. They all smile and wave back up at me.

Sadie says, "Go put your suit on and then come down here for breakfast. We're gonna hike down to the sea for a swim as soon as we're done eating."

She doesn't have to tell me twice.

Ω

Two hours later I'm sucking in the salt air and peering down the mountain of stairs at the sea. Even though we've already been hiking this staircase for an hour, the water seems impossibly far away. The stairs wind back and forth, scaling the entire monstrosity of the cliff under the city of Oia. Each stair is flat and three feet long and the succession of them seems to coil on forever. Stone edges rise up on either side of the staircase, making it impossible for us to see a few paces beyond where we stand. But the five of us keep stepping down them because we've been promised that if we descend far enough we'll reach a little fish market, and beyond that a beach for swimming.

"One hundred!" Sam announces. He's been counting the stairs since we started. When I crane my head back toward the town it looks like we've barely gone anywhere and when I glance down to the sea it looks like we'll never get there. But all that's on today's schedule is the wine tour. Charlie and Mary Anne are both twenty-four so they'll probably have to rush back for that, but Sam and Sadie and I are underage so we'll have all day to relax in the blue before we have to hike back.

Sadie's been marching by my side and sharing a funny eyebrow wiggle with me every time Charlie calls Mary Anne "babe." We've been giggling at nothing, so her brothers think we're telling secrets. We've reverted to being children, and that makes it easier to be best friends.

"One hundred and twelve," Sam mumbles. He's turning the next corner ahead of us. Then he shouts, "Watch out!" and jumps to the side, almost whamming into the stone edges.

When we get around the corner, we see that the steps are nearly black with manure and we can hear the donkey handlers shouting in the distance. Sam is walking on the edge of the stairs now, tiptoeing around the freshest piles of waste and dodging the sharpest rocks that jut out to meet his hip or shoulder. The pungent smell hits us like a wall and Mary Anne retches behind us.

"One hundred and thirty-one," Sam mumbles.

Sadie shrugs at me and we follow behind him, first Sadie, then me, taking his exact path like an old game of Follow the Leader. Charlie and Mary Anne come behind us, silent, ignoring our giggles.

When we round the next corner Sam stops and the rest of us almost slam into him. "It's worse," he says.

"Shit, man," Charlie says, surveying the site. The donkeys are all lined up on the right side of the path and the stairs beneath them are covered in layer after flattened layer of donkey doo-doo.

"You got that right," Sam says, looking up at his brother with a smile. "It's shit, man."

Sadie, Sam, and I laugh.

I glance up to the town and then down to the sea. After an hour's hike we're finally a little more than halfway there. Soon we will be jumping into the glittering water. Then all we'll smell is salt and all we'll feel is clean. Right now, there's sweat pouring down the back of my neck. I don't know why we stopped.

But we stand there, a frozen line. The sun beats down on us, burning my hair and my face and baking the excrement before us, steaming it to make it smell as much as possible. The donkeys smell almost worse than the stuff beneath them.

They are muzzled and they twitch their ears and tails to bat at flies and they stare at us with sad eyes. I have a sudden fear that the one closest to us will decide to kick backward and pound his hoof into Sam's chest. We need to keep moving. If we can only get down there, we can stay all day in the cool water.

"We're giving up," Charlie announces. "As soon as we get down, we'll have to turn around and climb back up to make it in time for the wine tour. And now I think I'll need another shower first."

"C'mon, man," Sam says. "Don't leave me alone with these two giggling fools." Sadie and I giggle at that. "We'll jump in and then you'll be all clean."

"What about the way back up?" Charlie points out.

Sam sighs and glances at his watch. Sadie tries to shove past him but he says, "We better not." She looks up at him. "It's one o'clock already and we have to be ready for the tour by two thirty."

"But we're not going on the tour," I say.

Sadie looks at me curiously. "We're not? We don't have to? Did Mom say something to you?"

I tilt my head at her. "No . . ."

She stares at me. I can feel Sam and Charlie and Mary Anne staring, too.

I say, "But we're . . . seventeen . . ."

They all laugh, and I know that even if I weren't so flushed from the heat my cheeks would be bright red.

"And you've been acting like you're eleven!" Sam says with a teasing smile. He and Charlie start laughing good-naturedly, and begin to move back up the mountain, with Sadie following. For a second I stand still in the middle of the donkeys and the poop and the hot sun, being pulled by the ocean like one pole of a magnet and by my best friend like another. "You still gotta go," Sam calls down to me. "It's not about drinking. It's a wine *tour*. Andrea wants us to see the actual land of the island, learn about the culture and history, blah blah blah. This island is like seventy percent wineries, so they can call any boring excursion a wine tour."

Sadie turns around. When I catch up to her she says, "I'd rather go swimming than drink wine, too. I'd rather go swimming than do anything." She laughs.

"Like old times," I say.

"We'll get there tomorrow." She tilts her head backward to indicate the sea. "I promise."

Another promise.

When we've hiked back to the hotel and showered, we have just enough time to grab something to eat before we have to leave for the tour. Sadie, Sam, and I cram into a booth at a crepe place that feels like it's in a basement because it's dark and we had to go down stairs from the main road to get into it, but the windows at the other end of it show that it's also thousands of feet above the sea. Santorini is a place of contradictions. You go on a wine tour to get history lessons. You're on an island but you never get to swim. And you sit next to the person who has hurt you the most in the world but you smile.

After we each order peanut-butter-banana crepes, Sam leans across the table toward us and starts speaking in a hushed whisper. "So last night, Uncle Drew decides to give a toast . . ."

We nod.

"In Greek. Apparently he's been studying it so that he can communicate with Ivan's family and all that. Of course, he didn't bother to find out that they speak perfect English. Anyway, Ivan was standing next to us so he kept whispering the actual translation of what Uncle Drew was saying."

"Yeah?" Sadie says, wrapped up in the story already.

"And it made no sense at all. His opening line was something like 'We like them to welcome them that welcome the Americans to our home for this occasion of soberest celebrations.'"

Now we're both laughing. It's so funny the way Sam is saying it, too, transcribing their uncle's facial expression onto his own ebony face.

"He's too ridiculous!" Sadie exclaims.

"You gotta love him, though," Sam says, smiling wide and warm. "Remember at Disney World? When you were so excited to see Snow White, Sadie? And when Uncle Drew was the first to find her, he ran at her so fast the poor woman in the costume got scared and screamed for security?"

"I remember that!" I say. The summer we were eleven. I was in this family then.

We all laugh for what feels like a full minute and then the food is in front of us. But before I can take a bite, Sam reaches over and pats my left hand where it is lying on the table. "I'm glad you're back, Coley," he says.

"Me, too," Sadie says, bumping her shoulder into mine.

"Me, too," I say. And at this moment everything is so fun and joyful and wonderful I'm not sure I want to know what last night was about. Or even what the last three years were about. I don't know how I ever considered not coming on this trip.

Εκπαίδευση (Education)

The strangeness of the countryside rolling by our window almost makes up for the fact that I'm still not surrounded by salt water. Almost.

We're all squished into a van. Sadie is sitting so close to me on the front bench it feels like we're kids again with no personal boundaries. Nikos, our sommelier (apparently that's a dude who knows a lot about wine), is speaking and his English is completely understandable, but I'm too distracted by the different-ness of the island outside the van to pay much attention to what he's saying about how they farm in Santorini and its crops and vineyards. We drive through another city, Fira, barely bigger than Oia, which can easily be walked twice over

in the course of one afternoon, and out onto a mostly aban-
doned road. To the left there are hills, layers of red rock piled
jagged on top of each other. To the right, the road drops off
suddenly and in the distance is flatland spotted with the
occasional house or two. It's farmland, we learn. Mostly
grapes. And beyond that is the sparkling sea.

We eventually descend the hill, zigzagging down the mountain at angles that make it seem impossible for the van to stay
on the road and not go tumbling down the rocky cliffs. We
cross into the flatlands and drive by stringy vines dripping
with bright-red and perfectly circular cherry tomatoes. "These
are in season," Nikos says.

"Yum," Sadie says to me, and I nod.

Then we turn another corner and we stop, and crawl out
of the van, and follow our guide into a dusty field dotted with
even rows of small bushes. Sadie walks right next to me, her
elbow almost touching mine, and Sam and Rose are close
behind us. I don't ever walk like this with anyone anymore,
even with Mark. We hold hands but there's always a few inches
between our bodies above our wrists. But I recognize this as
the way I used to walk with Sadie everywhere: the pool, the
mall, the hallways in middle school. I can't imagine walking
this close to anyone else really. Not Louisa, not my mom. Not
even Adam or Peter.

Does Sadie walk this close to everyone? Or is this just how little girls walk? Are we turning into little girls again because that's the only way for us to be best friends?

We follow Nikos about ten feet into the field. The ground is packed hard but puffs of white dust sprout around our feet, almost like chalk. It's not sand and it's not soil; it's something I've never seen before. When Nikos stops in front of one of the little bushes, Sadie says, "Coley!" and hip checks me so hard toward Sam he has to catch me, his palms seizing my shoulders before I fall over.

I laugh, though. This is another little-girl game we used to play everywhere all summer until our hips were covered in blue and purple bruises. It's another joke I forgot to miss. I wonder how much of Sadie I've been missing without knowing it. I wonder if I'll be aware of everything I miss about Mark when I get home, or if there are things I'll forget. I don't know which to wish for.

I give Sadie an "I'll get you later" look and Rose comes up to stand next to her on the other side.

"Oh, you two are so adorable," she says, but the look sliding from her dark eyes down her button nose is pure disgust.

Sadie and I both have to twist our necks to glance at her. She's so much taller than us, with thick hair that falls in perfectly smooth waves around her shoulders as if she's immune to the heat that's cooking the island for the rest of us. She wears a black sundress with flip-flops.

She tosses her hair to the side farthest from Sadie and Sadie says, "Shut up."

Rose laughs, a noise so clear and high and purposeful it is both beautiful and cruel. "Does she always dress like that?" Rose asks.

And I shrink to a feather inside my clothes. I'm in jean shorts, a pink T-shirt from Target, and sneakers because I thought we might be hiking or something. Yes, I always dress like this. There's nothing wrong with dressing like this for a daytime tour of an island approaching a hundred degrees.

Sadie takes a step away from me. I expect her to say "shut up" again or that I look fine, but she stares at her shoes and shakes her head and I wonder what it is about this cousin of Andrea's that can get to even my most self-assured friend. "No," Sadie says. "She doesn't."

I shrink even smaller.

"So these are the grapes." The guide's voice seems to boom over us, and I realize how quietly Rose has been talking even though her words are so powerful.

"No way," Edie says, stepping closer to the bush on the ground. It's barely as tall as my ankles. None of the bushes in this field are as high as my midshin. "Grapes grow on vines," she says. "We weren't all born yesterday, you know."

Everyone chuckles except for Rose and Sadie and me.

"It actually is a vine; take a closer look," the guide says.

I couldn't care less about vines or bushes or grapes or wine right now. All I want to do is change into some fabulous outfit and then crawl back into the bed in my cave.

But because it suddenly feels like we're on a field trip, and because I always follow the directions, and because now that Sadie isn't at my elbow I morph back into Little Miss Perfect, I take a step toward the bush and lean over it. It's a brown coil of a branch all twisted together, a doughnut of leaves.

"I think you look great." The words are slippery on the back of my neck. I didn't realize Sam had followed me, tilting his body right behind mine. Suddenly I'm covered in goose bumps and I don't know how that happened.

He straightens as I turn to smile at him, and I'm hoping he can't somehow see the bumps on my legs or the way my stomach dropped and turned to jelly. He's smiling that warm smile, those two beautiful dimples peeking at me. I cannot be thinking this way. He cannot possibly have meant those words like . . . *that*. This is Sam. Sadie's brother. Not Mark.

Somewhere over my shoulder I'm aware of the guide, and

Sadie and Edie comparing the shape of a twisted vine to a basket or a snake or a beat-up Slinky. But in my vision are only Sam's smile and dimples and happy, sincere brown eyes.

"You shouldn't listen to a thing Rose says. All week," he adds in a whisper not quite as close to my skin. Relief and embarrassment cause my heart to slow back to normal. He was protecting me. He's basically my big brother, too.

My hot big brother.

I glance across the crowd and see Rose whispering something to Sadie, Sadie smiling shyly at her flip-flops.

We hike the rest of the way through the vineyard and enter a wooden building. There is a wide open area, a concrete floor the same color as the wooden walls. Along the back wall is a counter and to the left a table is set with nine places, each with three wineglasses.

"And this," the guide says, "is where you finally get to taste some wine."

"Whoo!" Edie cheers. "It's about time for some wine in this crowd."

Mary Anne, Rose, and Aunt Kat laugh.

We take seats around the table. Me between Sadie and Sam. Sadie between me and Rose. It's beginning to feel like assigned seating. In the center of the table there are baskets filled with various kinds of cheese and bread and olives, so Sadie, Rose, Sam, and I at least have something to snack on while the adults sample the wine.

Our guide disappears for a second and I'm still thinking about my outfit, shrinking with embarrassment at Rose's comment (and burning with something slightly different at Sam's) and wondering why Sadie said no. Why couldn't she say I was fine in what I was wearing? Why couldn't she stand up for me?

And all of this thinking brings me back to the first question: Why does she need me here anyway?

I'm so involved in my own brain that I don't even notice Nikos circling the table with a bottle and filling up glasses, until he's leaning over my right shoulder, between Sadie and me, and a golden liquid is building up in my glass. I raise my eyebrows, but I don't say anything.

Nikos starts talking about how before you taste the wine you have to look at it against something white to see the color of the liquid versus the color of the surface. Then you do something called the sniff and slurp and you have to put your whole nose in the glass.

I go through the motions, tilting my wine to see the color change and shoving my nose all the way past the lip of the glass. But I couldn't care less. I've never tasted wine. Even my church uses grape juice instead. I've only seen wine on a handful of occasions since Mom and Dad don't drink it and the parties I go to only have beer. I can think of a million things I'd rather be doing than sitting at this table being totally embarrassed for two opposite reasons and learning all about a topic I've never even thought about before. Starting with swimming in the darn sea. And ending with making out with Mark in Sally's little brother's bedroom again.

"And without further ado," Nikos says, "drink!"

I put my glass back on the table politely but everyone else—everyone, everyone else—brings their glass to their lips and takes a sip.

"We're allowed to drink the wine?" I whisper into Sadie's ear. *In public? In front of your mother?*

Rose smirks so hard she almost spits her mouthful across the table. "Is she serious?" she asks.

Sadie turns her head away from me, toward Rose, and nods. "Yes, she is. That's really our Colette." They both start snickering and I stare wide-eyed at the back of Sadie's blond-and-purple head.

That's it. That's why she needed me. To be Rose's punching bag. To protect her from Rose's scorn by being an even more pathetic mess. Tears threaten to fill my eyes.

I imagine the two of them laughing in secret at how innocent and childish I've been acting. Trading notes on the stupidest things they've seen me do. I imagine Sadie telling Rose all about my church-basement first kiss, my breakup with Mark, my willingness to drop everything for a chance to be near her again.

"Colette." Edie rolls her eyes at me. It feels like knives going into my heart. I miss the old Edie almost as much as I've been missing Sadie. "The world doesn't end at the American border. You can drink here. The drinking age is eighteen."

She barely looks at me before she buries her face back in her own wineglass.

"But I'm—"

Sadie's fist comes down hard on my thigh and I suck in a breath to keep from yelping. *Seventeen.* Sadie turns from me to Rose.

"*Caramba,*" Rose breathes in almost silent relief. They share a smile before they both take another sip.

I shift my gaze from the back of Sadie's evil head to my wineglass and I wonder if Edie is basically telling me that I have to drink it. Yes, I've had alcohol, but never more than one drink at a time. Never at three in the afternoon. Never wine.

Despite all the warning speeches my parents and pastors have given me about peer pressure, I never imagined a situation like this.

Now everyone's staring at me, the freak who dresses in T-shirts and sticks her nose in glasses that she wasn't ever going to drink from. Even Charlie, Mary Anne, Martina, and Jorge look at me passively, like they want me to chug this liquid so they can get their next taste. Rose and Sadie look like they're about to burst with laughter if I don't take a sip. Sam looks worried and Edie looks plain annoyed and they all try to back me in a corner and drown me with wine.

I raise my glass to my lips and allow a tiny bit to enter my jaw. It's sour and acidic and surprisingly thin. It doesn't taste anything like honey or nuts or any of the other foods Nikos listed before we started peering through our glasses against the white tablecloths. But I swallow quickly and then it's gone and everyone starts paying attention to their own wine again. Nikos talks about flowers and apricots as he circles the table with a second bottle.

Sam leans into me and whispers again, and even though I'm sad and angry and almost crying and punching a wall, my stomach does that jelly thing and I turn some of the anger on myself. "A little wine might help you deal with everything today," he says. "You know, with Rose." He clinks his glass against mine.

So I take another sip.

Ω

Three vineyards and countless gulps later, we pull back into our dead-end parking lot and pile out of the van. The sun has only been down for about thirty minutes so the sky is hanging low, a deep purple, and the crowds have already thinned enough to see the storefronts.

I'm not sure what drunk is. But even though I'm stuck on an island where my purpose is to be a human bully-shield, and the snickering from Rose has not stopped, and my heart is still broken and it aches every time I think about going home to no Mark, I still feel like smiling.

Edie and the adults vanish as soon as the van is gone. Charlie and Mary Anne say they're off for a romantic dinner. Sam, Rose, Sadie, and I stand in a circle. Sadie and Rose are whispering to each other and giggling at nothing like they have been all day, Sam is looking at the people milling around, and I'm smiling like a clueless idiot.

"What are we supposed to do now?" I say finally.

"*Supposed* to do?" Rose mocks, eliminating the Spanish accent from her voice so that she sounds like me. "What do you think, there's, like, an assignment?"

I shrug because yes, that is what I thought. This entire trip is an assignment. I drank the wine today because Edie told me to. I went on the stupid wine tour because it was on the schedule she handed out. And I'm only on this island in the first place because Sadie told me I needed to be. So it is an assignment. I'm right and Rose still manages to make me sound stupid.

"Shut *up*, Rose," Sadie says, but she's smiling at her.

Sam rolls his eyes. "I wanted to get some dinner," he says. "Maybe test our knowledge with the Santorini wine list."

Now Rose nods, perky. "Okay!" she says.

But she's barely finished the second syllable before Sadie screams, "No!"

We all jolt backward at the force of her word.

She fakes a giggle, shifting from her right foot to her left. "I, um, I mean that you can't go," she says. Then she looks up at Rose. "It would be, like, weird . . . you know?"

I wonder if Sadie is drunk, too.

I look at Sam to see if he knows what's happening. He's staring wide-eyed at his short, blond little sister and her tall dark bully. He opens his mouth like he's going to say something, but then he turns to me and shakes his head. For a split second he looks surprised to find my eyes on his face and a small dimple flirts with his left cheek.

I tell my heart to slow down.

"Fine," Rose says finally. "It's nice to see you again, too, Sadie." She says it like it should hurt but I swear her face looks scorned.

She turns on a heel and marches up the parking lot, little clouds of gray dust erupting at her feet.

"Rose!" Sam calls, but she keeps walking.

I look at Sadie as she watches the dark shape disappear, and when she finally turns her face back to mine, I demand, "What's up?"

I mean it like, what's going on here? The wine has stopped the smiling effect, but it's still filling me up, making me bigger, reminding me that I count, I matter, even in the face of my complicated and dramatic and intriguing friend. Or ex-friend. Or whatever. She owes me answers.

But she says, "Let's go get some dinner. Sam?"

"Sadie . . ." He trails off for a second and she tries to stare him down. "She doesn't—"

"Shut up, Sam!" Sadie says, almost as fiercely as she just screamed at Rose.

"Sadie?" I say, but she's already wandering through the parking lot. The wine is pulling at the corners of my lips and sitting heavily on my eyelids, making me slow and sad instead of full and confident.

Sam gives me a melancholy smile and then follows his sister.

Even if I am confused by the goose bumps and the jelly-belly and the speeding heart, I'm glad he's here. It would be nearly impossible to deal with Sadie without him.

Ω

Sadie, Sam, and I are only halfway through the appetizers we ordered for our dinner at the next little cliffy restaurant we found when Sadie puts down her fork and announces, "I'm tired. I'm going back to Mom's room."

I stare at her in disbelief. Sure, Sam and I have been doing most of the talking—it turns out he's a walk-on on the track team at Rutgers and I've been drilling him about the tryouts and telling him about my own swimming aspirations. But I can't understand why anyone would leave this dinner. It's a rainbow spread before us. The tomatoes in the salad are absolutely red the same way the lemons on the calamari tray are completely yellow. The saganaki (fried cheese) we ordered came to the table literally on fire and now the bites of it melt in my mouth gooey and rich. The spinach pie is green-and-white layers of creamy goodness inside flaky phyllo dough, and the beef patties are like sliders, so delicious they don't require ketchup or a bun. Then, there's everything else. The sky is a dome above us, dotted with white stars. The moisture in the air kisses our skin and the cool breeze shifts through our hair. The sea cracks at the rocks below our feet and all around us conversations in Greek and English and French and Spanish and Russian intermingle. Plus, the wine is golden and it's starting to taste like flowers and honey, like Nikos said.

It's the best moment of the day. I can't believe she'd want to leave now.

"No, I'm not really hungry. All the wine made me tired. You guys finish, it's okay."

"It's only ten o'clock," Sam says.

Sadie shrugs.

Sam says, "I was going to finish dinner, then go find Charlie or Andrea or something and let you two hit the town. I didn't mean to get in the way."

You're not in the way, I think. *Please don't go.*

"I'm just tired," Sadie says again.

I open my mouth to throw in my own objections about the food and the sounds and the ambience. About the magic of this moment after a long and difficult day. But the wine must have loosened my jaw or something because what comes out is: "But we just got rid of her."

Both Sadie and Sam turn to stare at me.

"I mean—" I say, but they both know exactly what I mean. We finally got rid of Rose and we had to deal with her all day. We're finally back to the normal, easy people and we can joke around like we did at lunch or tell secrets like we did at my cave last night or finish eating and go sneak into the infinity pool. But still, I shouldn't have said that. I can almost hear my mother scolding me.

Sadie's shock turns into that new wide-eyed pathetic-ness that I'm so sick of and she shakes her head and stands to leave.

"Sadie," Sam says. She stays standing, but she looks at him. "Don't go."

"Sam! I'm . . . I have to . . ."

Once again I'm in that position: I have no idea what's going on. But, right now, I don't care. I take a sip of wine and feel it run warm through my veins. I take another bite of the gooey cheese. If Sadie is going to ruin tonight by going to bed early, that's fine. I don't need to join her.

"Have fun," she says and then she disappears into the multilingual crowd.

Sam sighs and picks up the calamari dish, spooning a few more breaded rings onto my plate before helping himself. I wonder why he did that. I tilt my head at him and he sighs again.

"The thing about Sadie is . . ."

Sam is about to tell me. He's going to give me the answers that Sadie won't. He'll tell me why she needs me and why I'm here and everything she's been hiding. A few days ago I would have stopped him; I would have said I wanted to hear it from Sadie herself, but now I don't care. Tomorrow I will be stuck all day with these people again and Sadie will have no chance to explain. We'll be on a boat. Unable to escape through either wine or running away. It's time for me to be clued in.

He trails off and stares into the black sea and the black night. His face is serious, the coffee-bean-colored edge of his jaw reflecting the golden lights lining the awning of the restaurant. He squints, concentrating or determining some-thing, and even though he's squinting his brown eyes look so deep and thoughtful and serious and kind.

And, oh, my gosh, I cannot have a crush on Sam. He's Sadie's brother. He thinks I'm a kid.

What would my mother say?

"The thing about my sister is . . ." He pauses again, sighs again. He shakes his head. "I think she'll have to tell you her-self," he concludes.

I nod, my eyes on my plate out of disappointment or fear that if I look at him my heart will go crazy.

I don't want to push him to tell her secrets, but I'm not ready to drop it completely. I want to keep him talking about Sadie, and then maybe some clues about whatever-this-is will slip out.

"What's it like . . . ," I ask. I think about how to finish it. I think about what he would actually answer. "To be Sadie's brother?"

Sam flashes me an enormous smile, lighting up the entire cliff. "Really?" he asks.

I squint at him. "Yeah. Why? Is it that different from being Charlie's brother?"

Sam laughs. "Uh, yeah," he says.

I roll my eyes at myself. "Obviously. I mean, I know that. But . . . how is it different? To be Sadie's brother, I mean?"

Sam shakes his head, his smile rotating back and forth. "You know, most people are never comfortable enough to ask us that," he says. "Me and Charlie. They act like we fit right in with the rest of the family."

I bite my lip. That wasn't what I meant. I wasn't even thinking about how Charlie and Sam look so different from the rest of the Peppers. When I spend enough time with them, I tend to forget. I'm tempted to flush, embarrassed, but I can see that the question somehow made Sam happy. So I smile.

"I mean, it's just as well," he's saying. "I wouldn't want to be explaining it all the time, you know? I'm black and Haitian and adopted and all of that, but I'm also more than that, you know? But still . . . it can be hard to look . . . to *be* something that your family isn't."

He trails off and I gaze over his shoulder into the Santorini stars, thinking of my own mother and father and little brothers. "Yeah," I say.

"Still," he says. Then his hand taps mine on the table. "I'm glad you noticed."

And we're smiling at each other.

He thinks you're just a kid, I remind myself.

But when we walk back to our hotel, he's standing closer to me than usual even though the sidewalk is empty without the swarms of daytime tourists. We're silent, like we don't know what to say now that we're alone. The night is so dark above us that it's hard to see anything but the white-marble sidewalk and the lit-up storefronts. I wonder what his life is like. That thing that I've been feeling, that thing that separates me from my family and my youth group friends, for Sam that difference is real. It's obvious. Even if you forget about it after you hang out with him for just a little while, that difference is still there. I bet he feels it every day, as much as I do, more. What's it like to be black here, on this vacation, in crowds of people who wear different clothes and speak different languages but who are still mostly white? What's it like to look so different from most of your family? I've never thought about it before. Sam is a Pepper, but he doesn't look like one. Edie and her parents and Sadie and Andrea and her parents, they all look like one family, while Sam and Charlie look like each other. I could look like a Pepper, though. I'm the right color and the right smallness. Sam sticks out—so dark and big and manly. But he's the one who belongs here. He knows exactly who he is in this crowd and where he's supposed to be.

And he's the one with the answers; he knows why I'm here.

I'm looking at him while I'm thinking this. His dimples have disappeared in favor of squints and he's swaying a little while he walks, his elbow bumping against my shoulder.

I don't know if it's the wine or the silence but I want to ask if he knows how to be a human bully-shield.

He bumps me again as we enter the gate for our hotel's set of stairs, and I realize that he's also had a lot of wine tonight.

When we get to my door I wave and say, "Thank you for dinner." It feels weird and awkward considering how he protected me today, how the conversation flowered over our meal. But he also protected Sadie today, and Rose. Sam smiles at everyone like that, talks to everyone like that. I can't let myself think it's anything more. That would be wrong to so many people. Mark. Sadie. Mom. Me.

He turns to go but then he's back. He puts his palm on my arm, directly below where my pink sleeve cuts off. His dark fingers wrap around my bicep and I love how they look there, in contrast to my own skin. But I can't think that. I can't think anything.

"I'm really glad you're back, Coley. You're good for my sister," he says.

He holds my arm tight and he looks right into my eyes, and his are so deep and open that if I look at them too long, I'll fall in.

I turn away and then he walks down the stairs and he's gone for now and thank God, because I'm crying. Because I miss Sadie. I miss my family. I miss Mark. Being broken up doesn't mean I stopped loving him, and being snickered at for an entire week won't make me stop loving her. Feeling separate and different won't mean I don't love my family either. Huge forces might disappear from my life forever, but they won't disappear from my heart, which means I need to make it grow and stretch to fit more people. And that's hard work.

Αμαρτία
(Sin)

Mark and I are in a pool. Some pool suspended somewhere in the universe.

The edges of my vision are flimsy.

I'm leaning against a wall, my feet on the smooth tile floor, my shoulder blades resting on the scratchy concrete. And he's several feet away, walking toward me quickly but not getting any closer.

I'm wearing a bikini, white with red and pink cherries printed all over it like Sadie's bedspread. It has ruffles in the angles that slash across my chest. The water laps at my breasts, the blue sagging between them and reflecting the dark freckles that dot the skin below my collarbone. My hair floats in the water in every direction, tickling my bare shoulders.

Mark moves toward me. I can't tell what he's wearing because all that I can see above the blue of the water is the expanse of his shoulders, the plane of his chest, the bump of his Adam's apple as he swallows, nervous, looking right at me.

Suddenly he's here, pressing into me, bracing my body against the wall of the pool, tilting my head back so he can kiss me, and running his hands down the length of my front. He grazes my stomach, my hips. I kiss him, and in my brain I follow the tracks of his hands, no longer feeling the water or the wall or the sun on my head, not feeling anything but the way he's finally touching me. My face gets hot as his hands move faster. Then he yanks at the top of my suit and it comes off in his hand and—*poof*—disappears. I stand there topless and watch him look at me, my breasts floating in the airlike water.

"We can't do this," he says.

I jolt upright, sucking in oxygen and whipping my head around to get my bearings. My face is burning hot but other than that nothing is like in the dream. I'm in my cave. In bed. I'm still wearing my cutoffs and T-shirt. And Mark is not my boyfriend. I say that out loud. "Mark is not my boyfriend."

It was so real, so vivid, that it seems impossible that he's not. Not mine, anymore.

I lie back, pull the extra pillow over my face, and try not to think about what my church or my mom might call that dream.

How can I still be having dreams like this?

I've never told anyone about them, for obvious reasons, but I've wondered. Is this normal? Is this wrong? In all of our purity workshops, even in the sex ed classes at school, they always talked about boys having dreams like this and how that was perfectly natural, blah blah blah. But no one ever said anything about girls. And it's not a question I can ask.

I turn over, trying at once to erase the dream from my memory and catch the last wisps of it, to hold them against my body before they disappear.

I don't know how I'm even able to dream like this. How is it that I have no idea what it feels like to have a half-naked body pressed against mine, and yet my brain makes it happen in my sleep?

And why am I still dreaming about Mark?

When the whole pool has gone away, vanished out of my window into the Santorini night so that I can remember only that I had a sex dream—the cherry bikini and Mark's face reflected in the water, but none of the elusive details about what it felt like—I roll out of bed to change into my pajamas and brush my teeth. The taste of wine coats my tongue and the roof of my mouth in an acidic film. I wonder where that taste was during the dream.

I'm too riled up to go back to sleep, so I flip on the

TV. Instead of some Greek soap opera or game show, it's a menu like on a tablet. One of the items says something about free Wi-Fi. Then I see, for the first time, the keyboard propped up on the table below it. It's not only a TV, it's a computer.

I'll check my e-mail and maybe play around on Facebook until I'm tired.

The nighttime sounds and the salty air waft through the open window about a foot to my left as my fingers fly across the keys. It feels weird to be doing something normal in such an exotic place.

I see his name in my inbox right away. Even though it's at the bottom of the screen, buried under a pile of junk and check-ins from my mom. I hesitate for a second before clicking on it, the mouse vibrating over the *a* in "Mark." It says he sent it the day we left. I must have barely missed it.

I'm so sorry. I was unfair and jealous and it's all my fault. But I've prayed about it and I realized that I was wrong. You need to do what you need to do, but that doesn't mean we have to break up, right, Colette? I'll miss you so much in Costa Rica. I'll think about your smile and your laugh and your kindness every day and I'll whisper how much I love you before I go to sleep each night in case the wind can carry

it the 6,142 miles to Santorini. I can't wait to see
you when you get back. Love, Mark

I shake my hazy head. I'm barely able to see the words, let
alone understand them. *Does Mark think we're still . . . ?
Didn't he say that . . . ? With the way I've been missing him,
why am I not happier about this?*

Bing! My chat window opens up.

Louisa: Are you really there? Is it really you?

Me: It's really me.

I type. I ignore the confusing message. The breakup that
wasn't. The promises that I've been breaking and he's been
making. The way I've yearned for him and missed him and
mourned losing him, and now I miss the missing.

Louisa: How is it? How's Sadie??

Me: Weird.

A few silent moments go by so I open the first of the three
Mom-mails. She sent it right as we were landing in Santorini.

Dear Colette, I was hoping to hear from you by now.
Please let me know you're safe. I'm worried about
you and so is your father. Remember: Ephesians 6:1
"Children, obey your parents in the Lord, for this is
right." Love, Mom

I bite my lip. Talk about an international guilt trip.

Louisa: Weird how? Weird mean?

Me: No, not really. There's this other girl here who is really mean. And Sadie is kinda using me to . . . block it? To shield her?

I don't know how to explain it to Louisa. I don't know how to explain the cliffs or the sea, or how fun it is to be with Sadie but how small she can make me feel, or how I miss Mark and also wish he would disappear. Instead, I click on the next e-mail. Mom sent it this morning, after she knew I was safe and all, so I'm holding out hope that there will be a layer of forgiveness, something that shows she'll still be talking to me (and Dad) when I get back.

Dear Colette, I wanted you to know that I just purchased tickets for us to see Peter's play. He is talking constantly about his solo. I know that you had shown interest in attending. I have purchased three tickets, one for the Friday night performance and two for the one on Saturday night (so that Peter will have someone there each night). You may attend with your father or with me. Please let me know which of us you would prefer as your chaperone on Saturday night, August 18. Also, perhaps you'd like to meditate on this verse in your prayers today: John 14:23-24 "Jesus answered and said to him, 'If anyone loves Me, he will keep My word; and My Father will love him, and We will come to him, and make our abode with him. He who does not love Me does not keep My words; and the word which you hear is not Mine, but the Father's who sent Me.'" Love, Mom.

I don't even know what that Bible verse means. And does all of that chaperone talk mean I'm grounded? Why can't she say that? Why can't she use her own words? How am I supposed to be honest with her when she's hiding behind Bible verses?

But beneath the anger, I feel stupid. If I took my twelve years of weekly Bible study more seriously, I would know these verses well enough to know what she means by now. I should know exactly what I'm doing wrong.

Louisa: That's messed up.

Louisa: So, how are you acting?

What does that mean?

Me: Huh?

She doesn't answer right away and my brain scrambles for something else to say. I want to keep talking to her; it feels so good to talk to someone who I know is my friend. But I don't feel like thinking about Sadie anymore. Or Mark.

What I want to talk about is Sam: how nice he's being, the

jokes he's telling, how he stared into my eyes last night. I shouldn't even think about that stuff. Turns out, I still have a boyfriend. A boyfriend who won't touch me.

Louisa: Okay, don't be mad. But I mean, like, be yourself, you know? Like Fun Colette. The way you are with me.

Fun Colette. Am I Fun Colette?

Me: What time is it there? What are you doing awake?

Louisa: Um, it's 8:30. Of course I'm awake. :-)

Louisa: I'm studying Japanese. Ugh. :-/ I have to leave in two and a half weeks.

I click on the final Mom-mail. She sent it a few hours ago, when she got home from swim practice with the boys, I guess.

Dear Colette, I hope that you are missing us by now as we are surely missing you. Yes, you would have been in Costa Rica this week anyway, but I believe we are all missing you more because we are not sure how your decision making and moral compass have led you so astray. If you are missing us, please call. We will attempt to help you fix the mistakes you have made. For today's prayer, think of this: Galatians 5:19 "When you follow the desires of a sinful nature, the results are very clear: sexual immorality, impurity, lustful pleasures."

My cheeks burn. With embarrassment, anger, humiliation, exposure. It's like she can read my mind even across the sea. How does she know my legs turned to jelly when Sam whispered on my neck today? How does she know I was naked in my dream with Mark? Does she know I've been having sex dreams since, like, eighth grade? And if she does, why didn't she talk to me about it?

Mortified, I turn away from the computer and take a deep breath. Enough of this weirdness. I have another rough day tomorrow.

I have a boyfriend, again. My mom is guilt-tripping me. I'm scared of my sex dreams. I'm worried about disappointing an entire list of people. I'm afraid of Sadie.

I'm totally back to being Miss Perfect, Miss Grecian Perfect.

I whip back to shut the computer down and a message from Louisa floats in the corner.

Louisa: Don't be mad, C. I just mean, have fun, you know?

Louisa: Do you think I can not go to Japan, though? The way you just didn't go to Costa Rica? Can I just skip it?

Louisa: Guess not. Anyway, I gotta go. Have a great day in Santorini!

Sorry, Louisa. I didn't change. You probably won't either.

Ω

"*Do you want to play the milk-bottle game?*" *I asked.*

Sadie and I were wandering the boardwalk after dinner. We were allowed to do that on our own that last summer, when we were thirteen. Every night I'd been trying to knock over all the milk bottles at the one game booth and win the stuffed frog. Before I was a swimmer exclusively, I was the pitcher on my little-girl softball team. Some of the skills must have stuck around because when I launched that softball at those milk bottles they all clanked and tipped back and forth, and all but one actually fell on the floor. My dad gave us five dollars to spend each night and if we didn't spend it all, we had to give it back to him. So far all of my money had gone to trying to rocket those milk bottles off the stand. I was determined to get that frog before our beach week was over.

"Nah," Sadie said. She looked around at the beach store-fronts and the whizzing rides and beeping games. The lights of the boardwalk reflected off her so-blond hair. "Sorry, Coley, I'm getting a little bored with that." She blinked her mascaraed eyelashes. She and my mom had gotten into this annoying habit of "getting ready for dinner" together. I was invited to join in, sometimes, but I found the whole thing even more tor-turous than watching cartoons with seven-year-old Adam and Peter.

I followed Sadie as she started wandering away from the main part of the boardwalk, away from my milk-bottle game.

I was getting bored with my mom painting Sadie's face with makeup every night, but I hadn't complained about that.

"Want to play a different game?" I asked, even though all the games were behind us now.

"Maybe later." Sadie sighed.

Something was wrong with her or me or us. I couldn't tell what she was thinking or what she wanted to do, and she obviously couldn't read my thoughts either because if she could we'd be back at the milk-bottle game, me shooting softballs and her cheering me on. It was lonely not knowing what she wanted.

We walked over a few more wooden boards in silence. I followed her gaze to a teenage boy and girl walking toward us hand in hand and I felt the old fear start to gnaw at me. I was afraid Sadie was growing up more quickly than I was. I'd seen her looking at boys so much this week and even earlier in the summer, at the pool. Boys who were with girls—holding hands, kissing, or lying on towels together. I looked at them, too, and registered how happy it seemed to have your hand in someone else's. But I saved it for later. One day I'd want a boyfriend. One day I'd want to giggle over crushes. But I knew I wasn't there yet. And if Sadie got boy-crazy without me I didn't know if I'd be honest and tell her how boring I found that for now, or if I'd change the entire plane of our relationship by faking it until I caught up. We didn't talk about boys too much, other than Jeremy Price who pulled our hair and whaled snowballs at us so hard they left welts on our cheeks.

"Let's go in here," Sadie said. We were almost at the end of the boardwalk, standing in front of a tiny drugstore. It was quiet and had the usual amount of lights. It didn't fit in with the screaming and beeping a few yards away.

I followed my friend into the store and watched her finger bright bottles of nail polish and shiny tubes of lip gloss. I wandered away from her into the candy aisle and contemplated a big bag of Reese's Pieces. If I wasn't going to have time to play the milk-bottle game anyway, I should buy them now. But if we were going from here to the game, I didn't want to waste my money.

"Coley!" I jumped when I heard Sadie squeal my name from across the store.

Beside me a woman with a toddler on her hip rolled her eyes at me like she somehow knew to look at me that I was Coley and that Coley was a no-good kid.

It was exciting to be looked at like that.

"Coley!" Sadie yelled again.

I found her in the hair-products aisle, clutching a small white cardboard box to her chest.

"Coley!" she said when she saw me. "I totally need to buy

this. I need it. But it's nine dollars. Will you lend me your money today and I'll give you mine tomorrow?"

I looked at my friend with her pink eyelids and sticky-looking eyelashes and out-of-place lips—she had chewed off most of her gloss at dinner. She was practically vibrating at the possibilities of the box in her hands.

"What is it?" I asked.

She turned the box around, holding it like an injured bird in the nest of her fingers.

"Hair dye?" Why were we standing under fluorescent lights discussing hair dye when we could be out in the salty air while I pelted milk bottles with a softball?

"Isn't she beautiful?" Sadie asked.

The woman on the cover of the box stood in a background of white. Her hair, blond, cascaded down her back and she stared at us over her shoulder with brown eyes that made you want to crawl into the box and find out what she was like. But the magenta streak down the back of her blond head was the least beautiful thing about her.

"Uh-huh," I said. "But your mom is never going to let you dye your hair a weird color."

"It's not weird," Sadie said. "It's original." She kept gazing at the box. "Besides, I'd never let my mom do it. She'd totally mess it up."

I lowered my eyebrows at her. I was not going to dye her hair behind her mother's back. Plus, I'd probably screw it up, too.

"Who will do it, then?"

"Your mom, silly," she said, looking at me and giggling. I hoped she couldn't see the way my cheeks suddenly burned with jealousy or embarrassment or possibly anger.

"Fat chance. She'd never let me dye my hair. She gets mad about the girls in church who go from brown to blond or blond to black."

"She dyes her own hair," Sadie said. She was looking at the box again.

Were we about to stand in a store and fight about hair dye during beach week?

"Just to get rid of the gray," I said, repeating my mother's line. "That's different."

"Nope," Sadie said, not looking at me. She didn't seem to realize how close we were treading to a fight. "She told me she's been highlighting her hair since she was sixteen."

Wrong.

Sadie was wrong about that. She had to be. It couldn't be that Sadie knew more about my own mother than I did. It couldn't be that she got my mother's first kiss yesterday morning and that my mom did her makeup before she'd ever done mine and that she told Sadie stuff she hadn't told me, stuff that was the opposite of everything she had told me. That couldn't be.

Sadie was still talking. "And she's so awesome. She could totally do my hair. Just look at my face. My mom never keeps the eye shadow inside the lines the way your mom can. Your mom is cool. You're so lucky, Coley."

I didn't want to think about the fact that what my mom shared with me was all about rules and doing what's right, and all of the cool stuff she apparently knew she chose to share with Sadie instead. And therefore even if my mom was the best and the smartest and the prettiest and all of that, that still didn't make me lucky.

"You can borrow my money," I said. "But there's no way you'll be allowed to dye your hair."

Sadie gave me a quick hug before she yanked the bill out of my front pocket and then rushed toward the counter.

Back on the boardwalk I asked, "Why do you want magenta hair anyway?"

She ripped the little box out of the plastic bag and stared at the woman on the cover so hard I was sure she'd walk right off the planks if I wasn't there to guide her. "I want to be noticed, you know?" she said finally.

"Noticed?" I said. I didn't know. What did that even mean?

"Yeah, you know. I want to make a splash. I want to be so obviously Sadie."

I giggled. "Who else would you be?"

She smiled back but she didn't say anything. She kept staring at the box.

"You mean noticed, like, boys and stuff?"

Now she looked at me, considering the question.

"Yeah, I guess. Boys, girls, adults. Whatever. Everyone."

I tried to hold in my relief that this wasn't some boy-crazy fascination budding.

"You mean like a movie star?"

She stopped walking and grabbed my upper arms to spin me around. "Ooh! Coley! Like a movie star! Can you imagine?"

Now we were both giggling and it felt good. She started strutting back and forth in front of me.

"Now on the red carpet," she said in her thick announcer voice, "Sadie Pepper. Bang! flash! go the cameras. No one can get enough of me." She struck several poses ahead of me on the boardwalk. The lights of the games in the distance glowed behind her and she suddenly looked beautiful and almost grown. But I laughed because she was still silly and I knew she always would be.

She stuck out a hip and jammed her fist into it. "Can't you see it, Coley? Wouldn't it be great?"

I nodded. It wouldn't be my dream, but I could see Sadie loving the red carpet.

"So this is your first step to stardom? Magenta hair dye?"

"Yup." Sadie clutched the box. "Just you wait. As soon as this sucker is in my hair the TV people and cameras are going to show up and I'll get magazine gigs and parts in movies. Just you wait. Till tomorrow."

We laughed and walked so close together our elbows touched.

"And what happens to your best friend when you're rich and famous?"

Sadie slung her arm around my neck. "You'll be right next to me on the red carpet. And everywhere. Always. Right?" she asked.

I nodded. "Right."

Somehow that last part of her dream became the least true.

Μυστήριο
(Mystery)

Sadie bursts in the front door of my cave with the first rays of the sun.

"Dude!" she says, way too loudly. "You left your door unlocked all night."

I roll onto my back and groan. My hair is twisted all around my upper body. My brain throbs in a techno-beat rhythm between the bones of my skull. My mouth tastes like I've been sucking on cotton.

"It's safe here," I croak.

But it's weird I didn't lock my door.

The wine made me forget, and I'm so glad my mother will never have to know about that.

Sadie sits on the edge of my bed and hands me a bottle of

water. It feels good even resting in my palm, like the condensation can rehydrate me through my skin cells. I scoot up on the bed and lean against the back wall. Only one drink a night from now on.

"Drink," she says.

"What time is it?" I ask.

"Nine," she says.

I drink and she watches. Why is she here? We don't have to be ready for this catamaran-ride thingy until one.

"Look, I'm sorry about yesterday," she says. And because I'm still too fuzzy to shrug it off, to nod seriously, to do anything that Perfect and Reasonable Colette would usually do, I say, "Ha!"

"I am. I'm sorry," Sadie repeats. "We're supposed to be acting like we didn't . . ." She pauses.

I freeze. How will she say it?

"Take a break," she concludes.

I roll my eyes.

"But it's hard. And Rose—"

I cut her off. "Why did you need a break from me?"

Her eyes go wide. "I didn't," she says. "I didn't need a break from *you*." She stands up and shoots one of those smiles at me, throwing the purple part of her hair over her shoulder. Then she grabs all the blankets and whips them to my feet. "This is boring. Let's go shopping."

The next thing I know we're showered and dressed and on the white-marble sidewalk. We're licking cones of gelato, our breakfast. We're having fun again. This trip is a seesaw between fun and awkward, fun and embarrassing, fun and terrifying. I know what my mom would say—fun is dangerous. But I don't want her to be right.

I'll be Fun Colette for now, like Louisa said.

We go into one of the more organized-looking stores in the maze of souvenir and clothing and art shops along the marble pathway. I pause at a display of magnets made of lava, thinking about a surfboard one for Adam, the owl for Peter. The wad of cash that my dad shoved into my hand feels like a hot coal in the pocket of my jean shorts, a burning lump pushing against my hip, and I know I shouldn't spend it, not even on my brothers.

Sadie appears beside me, her gelato gone and her limbs dripping with hangers bearing various Greek clothes.

"Come on!" she says. "They have dressing rooms in the back!"

She hands me a stack of hangers and disappears behind one of the two curtained-off changing areas. Looking at the clothes, I'm not sure if we're playing dress-up or shopping for real.

When I'm standing in the dressing room in just my white bra and jean shorts, I call, "Which should I try on first?"

"The one on the bottom," Sadie answers.

I pull out the bottom hanger and there it is. Bright pink and purple stripes broken up by an occasional line of brown. Shiny and precise, like it knows exactly how big it needs to be and where it needs to fall. Brown strings dangle in every direction, and I wonder how I didn't know there would be a bikini on one of these hangers.

I shouldn't put it on. Not even to see what I would look like on this boat today if I were a normal girl. I remember Mom's e-mail about temptation from yesterday.

I reach out and touch it and I'm surprised at the smooth surface against my fingers, the netting against my thumb. It feels like my racing suit.

"Ready?" Sadie calls.

"Almost," I say. I wiggle out of my shorts and my bra. I'll see what it looks like. I won't listen to my mom's international guilt trips anymore.

I yank the four strips of fabric onto my body quickly, before I can change my mind. When I look in the mirror, I can tell it should look good. I can see how the random brown stripes highlight my eyes, how the bright pink stands out against my tanned skin. But something isn't right. It's askew. It's more revealing than it means to be. I pull on the top corner of one of the triangles and my chest shakes. I pull on the other one and it reveals a little plop of white at the bottom of my breast. I quickly tug the top down again.

"Ready?" Sadie repeats.

I hesitate. But we're supposed to be acting like we're best friends. "Would you come in here?"

She slips behind my curtain and even though she's wearing the same suit as me, I see her eyes go wide in the mirror. "Colette! It was made for you!"

I turn to look at her. "Something's not . . . right."

She glances at my chest, then looks at my feet. She says, "You tied it too tight. Untie it at the top, then spread the bottom as far as it can go along the bottom strings. Then retie the top as tight as you can without bunching the bottom together."

She's gone before I can ask her to do it for me.

I do what she says and then . . . I can't help smiling. I know this is a prideful smile, an immodest smile, a just-plain-wrong smile, but I smile.

Oh, my gosh, am I actually thinking about wearing this? About spending Dad's money on a skimpy bikini?

"What do you think?" Sadie asks.

This time I open the curtain.

"You look amazing, Coley," she says. "You have to wear that today."

Can I wear this in front of Sadie's family? In front of Sam? I feel my face start to flush.

"Coley!" Sadie says, all eager and smiley. As usual her enthusiasm is catching. "Wear it!"

"I'll buy it," I say. "We'll see."

I tune out my guilt as I hand over the money. It's only fifteen euro, about twenty-two dollars. Dad probably won't ask what I did with twenty-two dollars. That could have easily gone to lunch or dinner or something. And Mom . . . does she even know Dad gave me a handful of cash? Either way, she'll know I did something wrong. So I might as well enjoy it.

If it even is sinful to think you look good in a bikini.

"We should head back and get ready," Sadie says as we leave the store. "Promise me you'll wear it."

I stop and face her on the sidewalk. "Do you promise you'll be nicer? Even when Rose is around?"

My words startle her and, for that moment, they startle me, too.

"I promise." She nods, biting her lip. "I promise I'll be nicer today no matter what you wear. But you look so good in that suit, I think you should wear it."

Ω

Back in the cave I stand naked in the bathroom in front of the mirror, looking for the difference between nude and bikini-ed. Somehow a few square inches of brightly colored fabric do make a difference in terms of decency.

I step into my black suit and wiggle it onto my body. The straps snap on my shoulders. The fabric clings to my skin, gluing it all close to my bones. My breasts look like pancakes encased in black Lycra. My butt is high and flat and totally visible. It's actually not modest, this suit. It's tight, so tight the skin next to my straps and under my arms has to puff out to accommodate it. It's completely immodest, I realize. It just doesn't seem that way because it's not flattering.

I hold the top of the bikini against the chest of my suit. Which thing should I wear? Which girl should I be today?

My watch says it's twelve forty-five. I have fifteen minutes to make up my mind and join the rest of the wedding party in the dusty parking lot.

How did this become such a big deal?

Before I know it, I've dropped my suit top and walked across my cave, my phone in my hand, dialed and ringing.

"Little lady!" Dad answers, hushed. I realize it's five forty-five a.m. at home. I imagine him sneaking his ringing cell phone out of the bedroom to take my call in a whisper. He must have sprinted out of there in order to answer as quickly as he did. Was a vacation worth tearing my family apart? Something else I'm not going to think about.

"Are you okay?" he asks.

"Dad?" I say quickly, guilty. "Can you not tell Mom it's me?"

"Don't worry," he says. "She's not . . . she didn't hear the phone."

That's weird. But I don't have time to ask.

"What's up?" he says.

"Okay, remember when you told me to remember everything I know and be myself?"

"Yeah." His whisper sounds worried.

"Well, I kind of hate when people say that."

"Oh?" he says. I half expect him to reprimand me like Mom would, but instead he answers like he wants to hear what else I have to say.

"It's the kind of thing that sounds so easy, just be yourself. Obvious. Like, you don't really have another choice but to be yourself."

"Yeah?" Dad says.

"But, sometimes I don't know who that is, really."

My mother would call this preposterous. My mother would say I'm exactly who God made me to be. That everything about me is made with a purpose.

My dad doesn't.

"Me either," he agrees, heavily.

I don't have time to wonder what he's thinking or what's not easy on his end or if he just gets it, so I keep talking. "So, tell me what you meant. Should I really be myself, as is and without thinking about it, you know? Or should I be myself like the self you and Mom want me to be? Or . . ." I trail off.

Dad says, "Uh-huh?"

So I keep talking. "Or should I be the other one . . . the self I want me to be?"

He sighs. "It's best when those three things are all the same, isn't it?"

I nod, and I think he can tell I'm nodding even though he can't see me.

"But, if it's that hard to figure out, it's probably best to be who *you* want you to be."

"Right." *Duh*. It makes so much sense that I wonder how it was even a question. I keep the phone to my ear and rush into the bathroom, pulling a strap of my racing suit down off my shoulder.

"I knew this vacation wasn't going to be all fun and games, kiddo. I knew there'd be some growing and decision making, too, but—"

"I gotta go, Dad," I say, barely hearing him.

"Okay, little lady, thanks for calling. I'm praying for you."

It's the thing we always say to each other. I've only been away from my family for, like, forty-eight hours, so I don't know why it seems like a line from ancient history, something from a faraway land. I don't know why it makes me roll my eyes.

But for some reason my dad keeps talking. "And I don't mean I'm praying for, you know, your soul or anything. I'm just praying for you to be happy and safe and have a good time."

"Thanks, Dad," I say. "Have a good day."

He laughs.

Ω

An hour later, when I'm lying on the netting on the front of the catamaran, with Sadie's chatter to my right and the ocean sloshing underneath me and the sun beating down on all of the exposed parts of my skin, the bikini doesn't seem that skimpy. It's like the environment itself covers me up, the sunshine clothes me where the bikini leaves off. Sadie's in a bright pink one of her own, her blond-and-purple hair spread out beneath her head, a gossip magazine propped up on her stomach and a stream of cheerful words coming out of her mouth. She is wearing a lot of makeup, too. I only have on a little lip gloss.

"Look at that." Sadie shakes the magazine and tilts it toward me so I can see some model in an angular black-and-silver dress.

"Are you still hoping to end up on the red carpet one day?" I ask. Sadie's dreams, like everything else, might have changed. We covered the past when we shared all those secrets two nights ago, but we still haven't updated each other on our futures.

She props herself on her elbow, facing me. "I forgot all about that," she says. Even though it's the whole reason she started putting those colors in her hair, and the colors are still there. And now, as we face each other smiling and remembering Sadie's boardwalk strut from almost half a decade ago, I'm not sure if she's changing back or if I'm stretching to meet her where she went.

Everyone else on the boat is behind us, behind the controls and the little indoor part, in the very back. They're sitting around a table sipping sodas and wine and eating snacks. But Sadie and I couldn't resist the water.

The catamaran is like a square-shaped platform between two canoes that prop it up and guide it through the sea. In the very front, where we are right now, nets sag between the two canoe pieces and we can lie on them like hammocks and be as close to the water as possible. It's saltier than any water I've ever been in; I can tell by the smell as the waves rush under my body. And it's so blue. I can't wait to get in, to feel it all over my skin.

Sadie puts the magazine down. "No red carpet anymore," she says. "I'm a little more logical now."

She smiles at me and I don't smile back because obviously she had to grow up, but it still feels sad.

"I've been asking Mom to get me voice lessons, actually. I could be a good singer, right? Maybe I'll be on *American Darling*. Or try out for *Star Challenge*. You know, something like that. Something that leads to a real career."

Now I smile because *American Darling* and *Star Challenge* arc TV shows, which means they aren't that much different from being a movie star and strutting your stuff on the red carpet. Sadie hasn't changed as much as she thinks.

"Okay, everyone," one of the crew members says, clapping her hands. The two of us look up at her and giggle because it's funny for two people to be called "everyone." "I was just explaining to the rest of the boat. First, we sail past the red beach, there." She points and I follow her finger to the side of the island. Sure enough, a rust-colored cliff rises out of the sea and at its base is a shoreline of bright-red sand. The people on the beach are only little specs from this distance, but I can see them, swimming and sunning themselves and reading under umbrellas as if they're on a beach that's any normal color. "Then the black beach. We break for lunch. Then we swim in the hot springs."

"The hot springs?" Sadie asks.

"By the volcano," the guide says. "The water is hot. You swim right into it."

I feel my heart race and Sadie looks at me with big excited little-girl eyes. We'll swim in water that's like none we've felt before.

The crew member disappears and Sam, Charlie, Mary Anne, and Rose come join us on the front part of the boat. Rose settles her body right next to Sadie's on the same net. Sadie scoots over a bit to make room for her.

"Hey," Rose says softly.

"Hi." Sadie studies her toes.

Rose is in a stylish one-piece, not the kind made for racing and not a skirted one like my mom's dorky suits. I've never seen one like this before. It's deep purple, which shows off the richness of her skin. It swoops low between her breasts and it cuts wide to show her whole back but it still covers her stomach. She's not fat exactly, but she's a big girl, tall and curvy. Her one-piece is somehow more sexy than my bikini.

She leans closer to Sadie and Sadie scoots away. Rose moves like an elephant, each muscle shifting with exact precision.

"How was your dinner?" Rose asks. It sounds like she's trying to be nice.

Sadie stares at me.

"Delicious," I say. But I'm not sure if Rose hears. She's looking at the back of Sadie's striped head while Sadie stares at me, and it feels like we freeze that way for too long.

"What? Does *novia* have a problem with me lying here?" Rose says. She's talking to Sadie and I don't know what that means, but I know it is about me by the way her eyes are challenging me.

My face burns when I realize I've been studying her.

Sadie shifts away from her, not saying anything.

"No," I say. "No problem."

I yank one of Sadie's magazines onto my knees and start turning pages even though what I want to do is smell the sea, watch the multicolored beaches go by, and wonder out loud with Sadie what it must be like to swim in volcanic waters.

I angle my head around to see where everyone else is. Charlie and Mary Anne have climbed up to the pads on top of the catamaran. Sam is still leaning against the pole like he doesn't know where to sit.

"What's her problem?" Rose says to Sadie again. "Did you guys have a fight?"

Not recently, I think.

I half hope Sam is going to settle his body next to mine even though I know I shouldn't hope that when I still have a boyfriend. Sam is Sadie's brother anyway and he's so much older than me. There's no way he'd ever think of me like that. Probably.

"She doesn't have a problem," Sadie says. I hate when she talks about me like I'm not there.

I twist back to Sam again. In a quick motion he rips his T-shirt over his head and then he's wearing only royal-blue board shorts. His abs contract under his skin and his chest expands as he takes a deep breath. I'm in trouble.

But I'm going to be the me I want to be.

That me does not have a crush on Sam.

And that me is not intimidated by Rose. Or by Sadie.

And that me is friendly.

"Have you ever swum in hot springs?" I ask both girls.

"No," Sadie says quietly. Her eyes are glued to her magazine.

"Oh, she's cute," Rose says again.

It's one too many times.

"I'm right here you know, Rose. I can hear you."

I say it calmly. I say it like I can be as intimidating as Rose is herself. But Sam, Charlie, and Mary Anne start whooping, and I realize they're laughing at what I said, at me. They can hear me.

I forget how water is tricky like that. How the splashing and crashing of little waves beneath my butt will make it difficult for the person next to me to hear something, while my voice will reflect off the water to be carried far away.

Rose's cheeks turn pink and it makes her look a little nicer. Almost pretty. She's beautiful all the time, in that scary way, but embarrassment suits her.

"Sorry," she says, softer. "But it's not like we're actually going in the hot springs, right, Sadie?"

"*What?*" I spit it.

Sadie sits up and so do I. Sitting on the nets we're almost eye level with Rose. We both stare at her.

"The sulfur will ruin my bathing suit. It will ruin all of our suits. And you girls don't want to ruin your bathing suits, do you?"

Who cares about this stupid bathing suit?

"Well, Coley," Rose says, and I wince. "You do what you want. We're not going in the hot springs, right, Sadie?" Rose gives her some meaningful look.

Sadie turns her head to me, but she doesn't say anything.

"We haven't been swimming the whole time. We have to get in the water," I say. *Plus yesterday, you promised. You promised we'd go swimming today.*

"How much did you spend on this suit?" Rose snaps one

of Sadie's straps and Sadie jumps away from her hand. "It's BCBG. It probably cost over a hundred dollars. You don't want to drown it in sulfur the first time you wear it, do you?"

Sadie turns to me.

"This is our chance to swim in a volcano!" I almost shout. "How many times in our lives are we going to get to do that?"

Somewhere on the boat I'm aware of the crew pointing out the black beach and somewhere in my brain I know that I probably won't get to see that ever again in my life and that I should be paying attention to the sea and the sky and the sun and the scenery rather than engaging in some twisted tug-of-war over my ex-ex–best friend.

"If you wanted to go swimming," Rose says, her eyes hard on me like black marbles, "you should have told her to wear a different suit." Now she's talking to me like Sadie isn't there and I'm no more comfortable on this side of one of these backward conversations than I was on the other one.

I sigh, trying to bring it down a notch. "You're going swimming, right?" I ask Sadie as quietly as I can.

She shrugs.

"She won't," Rose says, all confident and mean. She smiles smugly down at Sadie's blond head.

Before I can stop it the words tumble out of me, hot pelts of flame. "What's your problem with me anyway?"

Rose leans across Sadie, her mean eyes zeroing in on me like I'm the worst person in the world. She speaks slowly, her words as exact as her movements, and so quiet that even with the water there's no way anyone except Sadie and I can hear them. "You know damn well what my fucking problem is."

My eyebrows scrunch together and I tilt my head, more confused than angry.

"Don't curse," Sadie says quietly. "Colette doesn't curse."

But who cares about that right now?

Rose straightens up and looks at Sadie. All of her armor has fallen off and instead of being scary she's sad. "She doesn't know?"

Sadie doesn't say anything.

Rose speaks louder. "She doesn't even know about me?"

Sadie shakes her head.

"How can she not know?" Rose demands. Her cheeks are on fire and this time it's terrifying, not pretty.

"Okay, okay, okay!" Sam says, coming up behind us. "Everyone should decide whether or not she wants to go swimming regardless of whatever anyone else is doing." Sadie and I turn to look at him, but despite the proximity of his half-naked body I'm too angry and confused to register him standing there. "Rose, no one's going to make you go swimming. Colette, no one's going to stop you," he says, smiling directly at me. The small part of my brain that wishes I'd watched the black beach go by also wishes I could enjoy that smile.

"She doesn't even know about me?" Rose demands again, standing up and towering over my shrinking friend.

If Sadie brought me here to protect her from Rose, maybe that's what I need to do. I twist my torso across Sadie like a shield. "What's to know?"

Rose turns on her heel and storms down the boat with remarkable grace considering the way it's teetering back and forth. We feel each footstep shake the nets as she disappears.

Once she's gone, everything about what Rose just said clicks through the gears of my brain until it processes the truth. There's something I should know about Rose. There's something everyone on this boat knows except for me. Sadie has me on this boat and everyone knows something that has something to do with me and something to do with Rose and I don't know what it is.

I take a breath to stay calm. I try not to let the anger rushing through my veins flood out onto Sadie because I can hear my mother's voice in the back of my head telling me that yelling never solves anything. I ask her very quietly, "Sadie, what's to know?"

She opens her mouth. She closes it. "I really thought you knew . . ." She trails off.

"Thought I knew what?" I feel the heat in my veins building and building.

She whips her head around. Mary Anne and Charlie are still a few feet away from us. Two crew members are to our left anchoring the boat.

"I can't tell you in front of everyone," she says.

The crew calls us for lunch.

Mavia
(Fury)

There are two tables for lunch on the boat, each spread with platters of fresh fish, bread, vegetables, and Greek sauces and spreads. Edie, Sadie's aunt and uncle, and Rose's parents are already sitting at the smaller, outside table, so Sadie and I have to climb down the steps into the main cabin and squeeze around a table with Rose, Sam, Charlie, and Mary Anne. Throught the open boat door, I hear the adults make jokes about the kiddie table as they laugh and clink glasses together Inside it's stony and silent.

We chew. The boat rocks us back and forth.

Sam and Charlie manage a forced conversation about basketball. Mary Anne tries to ask the rest of us what we're wearing to the wedding tomorrow. No one answers.

I chew my cod, barely tasting its deliciousness. And I think. What could this entire boat know about Sadie and Rose that I wouldn't know? That Rose would be angry that I didn't know? That Sadie wouldn't want me to know?

And of course I can come up with a theory. But it can't be what I think it must be. Because there's no way that Sadie has been lying to me about something that huge for that long.

So, I don't talk. I won't talk. I'll sit here and turn into a human volcano, the hot angry words I want to yell sloshing in my stomach like lava.

When we all climb back outside, the sun is lower in the sky and the wind pummels our bodies, trying to knock them over. Goose bumps crop out across all of the inches of my very exposed skin so I wrap myself in one of the beige, catamaran-provided towels and attempt to keep balanced on my way back to the front of the boat. It's empty except for one member of the crew.

"That's the volcano," she says.

And there it is, rising up out of the sea directly in front of us, an angry black rock on the horizon. I sink onto the net, holding my knees in front of me to make myself as small as possible as we approach the volcanic monster.

Eventually the rest of the "kids" come out and watch the volcano, too. But they don't sit down on the nets. They stay behind me where I can't see if they're watching the mountain or staring at me, a tiny pebble on the edge of a catamaran, being sprayed by sea and blown around by wind.

"You're a quiet group," one of the crew teases.

Charlie and Mary Anne start talking about the volcano. But I hear Rose's smooth, round voice beneath them. "So . . . you aren't going in, right?"

I don't hear Sadie's answer.

The volcano gets closer. I can see that it's not in the shape I expected—perfectly round like a fourth-grade science-fair project. Instead it's full of bumps and planes, parts jutting out into the sky and parts that look like they fell away. It's like any mountain, except surrounded by waves. The sea has lines of pale, almost white water streaking through the blue and they get larger and gather together as the monster gets closer to us so I know it's changing the sea somehow. The smell of rotten eggs wafts around us, replacing salt and sunblock.

Then it's right next to us and I see that it's actually not a mountain at all. It's a desolate pile of black rocks, each the size of a giant's fist. They stick out at sharp haphazard angles, like a bunch of coal-black giants drowned reaching for the sky, then froze. It looks angry. It matches how I feel. The ship is now surrounded by whitish water chopping against us.

We stop.

"Okay!" the crew member says, too perky. "Who's going in?"

I'm terrified. I've never been afraid to swim before, but I can see that swimming in the hot springs is not the cheerful experiment I imagined. Instead, we have to jump off the side of this boat, drop four feet into the water, and swim our way into the crack on the side of an angry mountain.

My mother would absolutely tie me to the boat and refuse to let me move. But she's not here.

"When you first jump in, the sea will be cold," the guide is saying. "But as you get closer, it gets warmer. It's the sulfur. That's what smells, too."

It smells awful. The wind whips my hair around my face and the boat rocks jerkily with the force of the waves. But I have to go now. I can't back out after everything I said.

"I'm going!" I hear her voice behind me, and I watch as Sadie drops her towel, trips across the boat's surface, and propels her body, BCBG and all, into the sea.

"Me, too!" Sam cannonballs off the boat.

"Anyone else?" the guide asks. "It's best if you stay together!" She's still calling, but I'm already in the ice-cold water, propelling my arms and kicking my feet so I move like a dart toward the angry black hill.

I ignore how my bathing suit slides around on my skin, refusing to stay the way Sadie taught me to put it. I fling my body forward with the current, past Sam and coming up behind Sadie.

Sadie might be winning this vacation with her mysteries and her ability to make me do whatever she wants. She might be winning life with her hair colors and her oh-so-many friends and her family that laughs and keeps each other's secrets. But I'm winning this. The race. I'm beating her to the volcano.

Then I'm right beside her. She says, "Hi, Coley," like this is some sort of friendly game. With a few quick strokes I'm past her.

I'm not fast enough. It's an awkward freestyle with my head out of the water so that my torso is crooked and my kicking feet can't quite reach the skin of the sea. My body tilts back and forth like a metronome each time I take a stroke and the waves occasionally reach up to slap me in the face. Still, I'm ahead of her. Of course I am. I'm the faster swimmer because I'm the one who's still on the swim team. I stayed the same.

I will get inside the volcano first.

I glance at it looming over me, the entrance still fifty feet away. It feels like looking down at the grass when I've climbed a few branches too high on Sadie's backyard tree, and I quickly focus on the water.

The first wave of warmth envelops my body just as I hear Sadie yell, "Coley, wait!" Immediately it's ice-cold and her voice is gone again.

Now the mouth of the volcano is only about ten yards away. The patches of warmth come more and more often as my body rocks its way through the waves. First it's only moments of hot water that blast my chest or my thighs, but then it's like swimming in a hot tub. An angry white hot tub full of choppy waves.

When I reach the opening of the mountain, which is like a parted set of jaws ready to swallow me whole, I straighten out and tread water for a second and my feet get cold. There's a line of water at my ankles that divides the ninety-degree surface from the fifty-degree undercurrent. I know nothing about volcanoes. Is this opposite-temperature what makes them erupt?

Can I actually swim into a volcano? Alone?

I turn around. Sadie is only about fifteen feet behind me. "Coley!" she yells.

And *bam*, I'm off again.

Between the angry walls, it's immediately silent. The shouts of the swimmers behind me, the waves breaking against the black rock, the wind howling toward the island, all stop. Ahead of me is a tunnel, made of the same dark bumpy walls as the outside of the volcano and filled with warm water.

I wish I could slow down and enjoy this. I wish I could let myself feel the fear that will turn slowly to excitement because I am inside a volcano.

But instead I move forward. My feet are still cold if I let them dangle straight down. I want to get to the spot where it's hot everywhere. Even if it burns me.

I move deeper inside the monster, the water getting incrementally warmer with each stroke, my tiny spot on God's map getting incrementally farther from Sadie's, even though I know I'm heading toward a dead end.

The tunnel twists to the left and then it opens up. I'm completely alone in the middle of a volcano. The water is hot. The walls are black. But the water at my feet is still cold.

If it erupts, I'll be the first one killed. And maybe that will count for something. Maybe the fact that I'll be the first body thrown toward Heaven will help me get in after the number of times I've broken the fourth commandment recently.

I spin around slowly. There's orange writing all along the rocks closest to the water. NESTOR WAS HERE. EAC+WJC. EILEEN AND ERIN, BESTIES 4EVAH. DANNO ROCKS. Proof that other people have come this far and survived.

I doggy-paddle over to the edge and reach my hand out to touch the stone just beneath the surface. My fingertip turns orange immediately. I wonder if that's happening to my bathing suit, like Rose said it would.

I write my name on a rock. I write "Sadie?" underneath it. Where is she? I thought she'd come into this area right behind me but maybe she gave up. Maybe she's hurt.

No, I'm not going to think that. I'm not going to worry about her when she clearly hasn't been worrying about me.

I go back to what I estimate is the exact center of the opening. I float on my back. The black walls of the volcano form the shape of a C with the blue sky framed between them.

This is incredible, I think. I'm in the middle of a volcano, surrounded by naturally warm water. I feel my heart slow as I calm down. I picture what I would look like from above, a body suspended in the middle of a black mountain. It's inconceivable that all of this is on the same earth with my square bedroom and our tiny kitchenette and the hill at the town pool. I'm not angry anymore. I'm not sad or mad or confused. Instead, I'm suddenly close to grateful, close to prayer.

"Coley!" I turn and there's my old friend, her blond-and-purple hair streaking out behind her body.

I almost get angry, but we're in a volcano. I have a week to get angry. I have eight more hours today to get all of the secrets out of her. I only have a few minutes in this place.

"Isn't this . . . ?" I can't think of how to finish.

She old-lady-breaststrokes over to me, nodding. "Yeah." She tilts her own head back to look at the sky.

"Where is everyone?" I ask.

"They all gave up and turned back about halfway in." She laughs. "That was a hard swim."

She's right. I feel my arm and leg muscles twitching with the effort of it.

Sadie gives me her inside-joke smile. "We're the only swimmers strong enough to make it all the way in here."

I smile back, enjoying the quiet, the black walls, the sky, and the presence of my friend who I will be mad at later.

"Coley . . ."

I look at her, floating on her back. She talks to the sky.

"I have to tell you . . . I thought you knew that . . . I should have . . . I needed you to come here . . . with my family . . ."

"Yes?" I say. My heart rushes. Finally, the answer.

"I needed you to be my . . ." She's taking so long I'm sure the eruption will begin beneath us before I know what she's going to say. "Date."

"What?" I ask. My voice bounces off the angry walls and back into the warm water. "Your date?"

"Remember my broken heart?" Sadie says. She's talking fast now, words flying from her mouth like she didn't want them to be kept inside all this time. Like keeping them in wasn't her own fault, her own choice. "Well, until the other night, I really thought you knew. I thought you knew I was a . . . It wasn't broken by a boy. I mean, no one at school knows. It's not like you're the last to know. It's not . . . It wasn't broken by a boy because it was broken by . . . her. And I couldn't stand to see her again. She was supposed to have some hot girlfriend here, too. You know, some girl from her school where everything's perfect and she can be out and no one cares about it. But everyone cares about beautiful Rose. She's always talking like she can have any girl she wants, and so I was sure she'd have some hot girl here and I'd be all alone and I needed someone and . . . well, you were just . . . perfect."

She lets out a huge breath like she's relieved or something, like all the words were keeping her from breathing. Like that was all the answers and none of the questions.

I stare at her and I think four words. *Sadie is a liar.*

She mumbles toward my face, "I thought you knew."

She's been lying. For so long.

Probably since we were little kids.

Forever.

"Coley?" she says. "What are you thinking?"

I stare at her. I'm thinking about her lying because it's the part I can think about, the part I know is wrong. Because I can't even try to think about everything else yet.

"Oh, yeah," she says suddenly. Her breath is short as her arms and legs move around to keep her upright in the water and I don't know if it's because she's nervous or because she's not in as good shape as me since she quit the swim team. "I'm supposed to say that I know this will take some getting used to for you and stuff, so I don't need you to say anything about that right now. I just need you to say that you still care about me. That you'll still . . ." She swallows. "Love me."

Something flinches in my face. She needs me to say I care about her? After she used me? After she dragged me to another country with a lie?

She needs me to *love* her?

And because I can't look at her lying, begging face anymore, I dive, my whole head, my whole body, submerged in the burning hot water where it's quiet and angry just like me, and then I open my jaws and I don't care that the eggy sulfur runs into my mouth and ears and up my nose. I let out the loudest silent scream I possibly can right into the bottom of the volcano and if it causes the cold water to mix up with the hot water and if that's what causes an explosion, then that's okay with me. The thought of being flung into the sky, far away from Sadie's flailing limbs, is a good one.

Because then I won't have to deal with what this means about Sadie or our friendship or me.

When nothing happens I launch my own body up out of the water and pound and kick my way toward the mouth of the volcano. "Coley!" Sadie yells behind me. But I don't care. I don't care if she's not a good enough swimmer and she's stuck in here forever. I don't.

I freestyle my way down the tunnel. The current is against me now, and even though the water is warm around my body, the splashes that hit my face and ears and climb, salty, into my nose are cold.

"Coley!" she calls again, and because my own muscles and joints are aching now with all of this effort, I turn around and find her clinging to the side of the rock wall.

I want to leave her here, screaming and helpless and not ever knowing if I would have forgiven her. But I don't want to be the me who's angry enough for that. I tread water until she catches up.

"You're still going to the wedding with me tomorrow, right?" she asks quietly.

I shake my head. How can she even ask me that?

I swim back to the boat. But I make myself be the girl who keeps her close enough to ensure she's not drowning.

Ω

I sit in the same position on the catamaran's nets, shivering and watching the monster disappear. I can't believe I swam into a volcano. And I can't believe that every time I think about that now for the rest of my life, it will be an angry memory instead of an adventurous, magical one.

I'm glad I'm by myself. Either everyone took one look at my angry face and decided to leave me alone, or they're too cold to sit out here in the shade, exposed to the wind and the spray.

I can't believe I'm stuck on a boat with her. A girl who lied to me my whole life. A girl who twisted a childhood promise into a messed-up bribe.

A girl who is gay.

All I want is to be back in my cave. Alone. I hate that I'm on a boat, trapped with the liar and her family in some alternate world where there are no rules. I know it's my fault that I'm here. I talked about missing Sadie until my dad felt he had to sneak me out in the middle of the afternoon. But life was so much easier when I did everything my mom said and I was the girl who loved Mark.

I feel a warm body lower itself next to me on the net.

I turn. It's Sam. Someone else who has been keeping me clueless.

"If you sit here, you'll get sprayed," I say.

"I can see that," he says. He gently tugs the soaking wet towel off my shoulders and wraps a dry one around me. "My sister is bawling her eyes out in the bedroom with my mom."

I don't know what to say. What I feel is jealous—that Sadie

has someone to turn to and I don't, even though she's the one who did something wrong. Sadie has a mom who will let her cry instead of reminding her to count her blessings and walking away. Edie loves Sadie so much she can be this mad at me without even talking to me about it.

Finally I say, "There's a bedroom?"

"What happened?" Sam asks.

I shrug.

"She finally told you, didn't she? About Rose?"

I look at him and something in my heart softens. I don't want it to happen, but when I see his eyes, they're like velvet. Like all the flecks of brown in them can shift around so they look so many different ways and I want to crawl inside them and use that velvet as a blanket and sleep until I feel better.

I nod. I try not to cry.

He puts his arm around me and I can't help collapsing into his chest. I try not to feel the way the towel has slithered away from my hip so that a little of the skin on his side is pressed warm against me. I try not to feel the warmth at all even as the boat slides back into the sunny waters. I try not to feel the way his breathing is measured and gentle. I try only to feel the protective brotherliness. But I fail.

"You know, she really thought you knew. She thought you'd known for a long time that she's a lesbian."

He says the word so easily, like he's calling her a blonde or a teenager or something benign. I can barely hear that word related to my Sadie without choking.

It's not that I think she's wrong. But every other time I've heard that word, it's been an insult, not a fact.

"It's always hard to hear at first," he says.

And I realize that once upon a time he also found out that his sister . . . liked girls.

"She really thought you knew, though. You know that, right?"

I shake my head again. "How would I know?" I say quietly.

Everyone knew but me. It was such a trap.

"I kept telling her she had to tell you about Rose. Rose is . . . challenging. But she didn't know you didn't know—"

"Why didn't you tell me?" I interrupt, my voice muffled.

I feel his shoulder rise and fall. "I couldn't." He shakes his head.

I snort.

"I wanted to, I really did. But it was her business, you know? She owed it to you to tell you. And I didn't want to mess up your relationship with her, or mine."

I fake a laugh.

"She's still your best friend," Sam says.

"I feel like I barely know her," I say.

He shakes his head. "She was wrong, but you still know her."

I snort again. The me I want to be does not snort sarcastically, but I can't stop.

"But there are a lot of things you don't know about her. A lot of things you never knew about her, and she was still your best friend."

"Like what?"

He laughs. "Everything. No one knows anything about us. No one even asks us. Like why my mom has black sons and a white daughter. Why my mom never works but sends us on these lavish vacations. Why Sadie looks exactly like Mom. And who Sadie's dad is."

Sadie's dad is dead. That's what she told me when we were little and my mother always told me not to ask anything else about that. But who was he? What was he like? How could I never have wondered about that before? And why did he and Edie put their family together like this?

"Look," Sam says. "I love my sister, but she can be selfish. That's what you get to be in our family. You get love and presents and time and vacations. You get everything. You know that, Coley. You used to be a part of our family, and if you hadn't disappeared you'd still know that." He smiles and his dimple shows up again. He tightens his arm, pulling me with it in an almost-hug.

"I'm not the one who disappeared," I say.

"Huh," Sam says, tilting his head at me. "Really?"

"Why would I disappear?"

"You know," Sam says, "I always thought it was because Sadie was a lesbian. That you couldn't accept her, or that you weren't allowed to or something stupid like that. That's why we all assumed you knew. But clearly you didn't."

I shake my head.

He squeezes me again and I'm confused by how happy that makes me, right when I'm so sad.

"So, you weren't a close-minded little jerk of a kid, huh? You wouldn't have ditched her anyway, huh?"

I don't answer. I store the question in the back of my mind for later.

And then, since he's shirtless and warm and Sadie is so selfish that it seems like me being a little bit selfish isn't too big a deal, I lean my head on his shoulder.

Φιλία
(Friendship)

"So, where are you going now?"

I turn around at the first step to my cave, and I see Sam standing behind me. He must have followed me as I huffed off the bus and charged back here. Sadie sat on the bus with her head on Edie's shoulder while Rose sat next to her own mother and snickered at us. I was the only one sitting alone.

Back to my cave to sleep? To my balcony to call my parents to ask them to send me home like this is some sleepover where I got scared? Down the three hundred steps for an actual swim?

I shrug.

Sam looks at me with those eyes. They're almost sad.

"I was thinking about grabbing some dinner," he says,

nodding toward the northern tip of the island. "The sun will be setting soon."

He squints.

"But Sadie . . ." I trail off.

He nods and bites his cheek.

An image lights up my brain, a fantasy. I'm crushed against Sam's chest in a slow dance and he leans down and gives me a deep kiss. I shake my head. I have a boyfriend.

"I know. I'm not taking sides. It's just that she has my mom and Charlie and even Andrea. And . . . I thought maybe you could use a friend."

My heart hammers in my chest. There are a million reasons I should turn around and go into my cave. I can't help that he's cute and warm and being with him makes me say whatever is on my mind, but I can shut this crush down. I have a boyfriend. And apparently a soon-to-be ex-girlfriend. Sadie, Rose, Mom, Edie . . . too many people are already mad at me.

But despite all of that, I find myself nodding.

I only have so much longer to make the wrong decisions.

"Get changed," he says. "I'll be back in fifteen minutes. We gotta hurry to catch the sunset."

I shower quickly, tie my wet hair into a knot, and pull on my nicest shorts and top. Since Sam still isn't back when

I'm ready, I decide to reread that last e-mail from Mom. When she said she'd help me fix things, did that mean that if I can't handle this she and Dad will bring me back home? Did that mean I can disappear back into my old perfect life? Do I want that?

There's a new one.

> Dear Colette, how are you doing? Please do write back to me, or call. You have not called or written during your entire trip and I am quite worried about you.

That's how she opens, even though I called Dad yesterday.

> Remember that if you are confused or you realize you have stepped astray, we will scrape the money together to bring you home. When you think about friendship, consider this: 1 Corinthians 15:33 "Do not be deceived: Bad company ruins good morals."

How does she always know what I'm doing?

The mouse hovers over the reply button. My mind seesaws between telling her I'm ready to get out of here and telling her I'm fine and I can make my own decisions. I open the new e-mail but I can't type anything. Both of those notes would be a lie. And I'm so sick of being trapped into lies.

Louisa: You there?

Just as the chat window dings open, there's a knock on my door and I have to close out of everything.

Sam stands on my balcony in a maroon polo shirt. I haven't seen him wear anything with a collar the entire time we've been here and I let the hope flutter through my heart that he's trying to impress me, too.

Once we're on the marble sidewalk heading toward the very tip of Oia, he says, "So, are you going to the wedding tomorrow?" And I know that he's trying to get me there for Sadie.

I open my mouth to say no. There's no way I'm going to let myself be used by my secret-sometimes-not-secret-other-times lesbian ex–best friend. But Sam is looking at me hopefully and his smile is impossible to resist.

I should not be here.

But I don't feel like getting a speech about why I should go. "I haven't figured it out yet," I say as we climb the stairs of a restaurant advertising a great view of the sun.

The Greek waiter pulls out my chair and he only gives one menu to Sam. To anyone looking, it seems like we're on a date.

I wish, I want to tell the waiter. *My real date is his sister.*

I should not be here, sitting across from this cute boy. I should be holed up in my cave, chatting with Louisa, figuring out what to say to my mother.

"I never knew you were such a thinker," Sam says. I want to ask him what he means but the waiter is there. Sam orders wine and food. He didn't even ask me what I wanted but he orders the saganaki, salad, and seafood pasta that I definitely would have ordered.

The waiter pours us each a glass of wine and leaves.

"What do you mean, a thinker?" I ask. And even though I remember how my brain was pounding this morning, I take a sip because the cute boy ordered it and now he's looking at me. One glass won't hurt.

Sam says, "I remember you as Sadie's giggly friend. I don't remember your eyes being so thoughtful."

I take another sip to hide the way I flush.

We have a direct view of the sun where it hangs in the sky, a burning orange ball. It sinks slowly closer to our little balcony table and the sea below us. We're high above the marble pathways and the clay sets of stairs. People begin to line them and stare into the sky even though it looks like any other sky. I'm more interested in the view of Oia from up here, the pathways, caves, and colors.

"So, what have you been up to?" Sam asks.

I look at him, questions in my eyes.

"I mean, besides swim team. What have you been doing since you disappeared from our lives?"

"I didn't disappear," I remind him.

"Well, whatever happened. What do you do besides swim?"

"I wish I didn't have to do anything but swim."

He laughs.

Our food arrives and he starts to dish some onto my plate. I don't want to enjoy being treated like this, like a lady on a date with someone who is going to take care of her. But I do.

How do you keep yourself from liking things that are wrong? How does my mom keep herself so within the rules?

"Do you have any new friends or . . . you know . . . a boyfriend?"

I smile to mask the guilt that starts thudding in my pulse. *Mark. Mark. Mark.* He's somewhere in Costa Rica pounding a hammer with the same beat. Here I am on the other side of the world sitting across from a hot guy who called my eyes thoughtful and wants to know what I'm like. Will the Perfect Rule-Following, Straight-A-Getting, Churchgoing Colette come crashing back into my body? Soon, I'll fly home. I'll be Mark's girlfriend and Mom's daughter. Dad will be silent with me. Sadie won't be my friend. Louisa will be gone.

"My best friend is moving away," I say. It's wrong, definitely wrong, not to tell Sam about Mark when he specifically asked if I have a boyfriend.

I talk about Louisa and how much I'll miss her. Sam asks the right questions. He tells me about his own friend who is studying abroad next year and how he'll miss her at Rutgers. We talk. And the more we talk, the less I think about what I'm saying.

"It's different, though," I say about his Rutgers friend. "Because I don't really have other friends."

My eyes go wide as soon as the words leave my mouth. It's not something I usually admit out loud.

"I mean . . . I do, kinda, but Louisa . . ."

"Coley?" he prompts. I love how he calls me that.

"You know how you were talking about feeling so different from your family?" I say.

He nods.

"Well, I know it's not the same thing. But sometimes I feel different from everyone around me. Like I'm the only one who thinks about things, asks questions. Like I'm the only one who's bored with our town and our school and our church. And my family. And Louisa is . . . not the same as me, but not the same as everyone else either."

"Yeah, I get it," he says, those eyes trying to bore their way through mine. "I do. At least in my family it's not so different to be different." He laughs. "We're all a bunch of weirdos."

Honest. "I miss your family. A lot. I miss Sadie."

"You have Sadie," Sam interrupts.

I can't help rolling my eyes.

"Look," he says. At first I think he's making a point, but then he nods out at the sea and the sky and I turn my head. I forget all about Sadie, Rose, Louisa, everything. The sun hovers above the horizon and paints the sky in deep oranges and purples and pinks and maroons—all the colors of Sadie's fake hair. I smile to myself. Below us, the pathways and sidewalks and stairways are jammed with people reverently watching as the sun kisses the horizon and sinks slowly into the sea.

I can't believe the colors. The volcano is a black silhouette on a molten rainbow canvas.

The restaurant hushes, the crowds below are still. Everyone is holding her breath at the beauty and grace of the moment. The energy buzzes around us, silent but excited, happy, joyful.

Then the sun is just a sliver of brightness, a neon line peeking out from over the sea, saying good-bye until tomorrow. And then it's gone.

To my surprise, the entire island erupts in applause for the sun and the sea and the energy and one another and I know my mom is somewhere calling this vacation lavish and unnecessary and dangerously fun, but to me *this* is a God moment.

I turn back to Sam. He's not looking at the spot where the sky just swallowed a burning star. He's looking at me.

"All the colors reflected off your skin," he says. "I've never seen that before."

My breath catches. I see his dimples and the light in his eyes and it's impossible that I have a boyfriend in another country and a disapproving mother and an ex-friend who is his sister and who thinks she can pretend to be dating me. It's impossible because we are the only two people in the world, staring at each other with a background of orange sky.

"Anything else?" The waiter bursts the moment. When he's gone Sam says, "I'm not going to try to convince you to go to this wedding tomorrow. But I do know that Sadie invited you, Colette, instead of any of her other friends, for a reason."

Did she? I guess I still don't have the full reason.

"And I know that Rose put her through the ringer last summer. She could use your help with whatever is on her mind."

I sigh. The bigger person would go. But how can I be the bigger person when Sadie makes me feel so small?

Besides, I came here to stop doing the right thing all the time. To do what I want to do. To be selfish for once. So, I shouldn't have to feel small and do something for someone else. I came here for a break from my mom's constant reminders to be the bigger person.

Then again, my mom wouldn't tell me to go. She wouldn't be able to get past the gay part.

And I am past the gay part. Aren't I?

"What are you thinking?" Sam asks.

"I . . . I don't know," I say.

He nods. "If you're uncomfortable, you're uncomfortable. I don't think you should be, but she should have checked it out before she dragged you all the way to a foreign country."

I'm not uncomfortable, I'm angry.

He puts his hand on the table, right on top of mine. "But if you're there tomorrow night, will you save a dance for me?"

And then I'm smiling.

Ω

I see her blond head from the top of the hotel steps as Sam walks me home. She's sitting on the stoop outside my cave, her face propped up on her knees. She's staring at the black sea.

All of the fantasies of the good-night kiss Sam might give me that I shouldn't want vanish out my ears when I see my "date." I can't believe she's sitting there. I can't believe she thinks I want to talk to her after what she did to me today.

Sam must see her, too, because he says, "I better let you go." And with nothing more than a pat on the shoulder, he's gone.

Sadie hasn't seen me, so I take a minute to think about the me I want to be. That me isn't afraid of a girl who uses people and lies to her friends. That me isn't afraid to stand up for herself.

I walk right past Sadie on the steps and calmly shut the door to my cave behind me.

"Coley!" I can hear her yelling as she charges up the steps after me. She starts banging on the door. "Coley!"

"I'm going to bed," I say.

"Coley!" she yells. "I have to talk to you!"

I stick my head out of the window next to the door. "We'll talk later," I say. "I'm tired."

The only thing I want to do is crawl into my bed, cover myself with the blanket, and replay the evening in my head. Sam telling me I have thoughtful eyes. Sam staring at me instead of watching the sunset. Sam asking me to save him a dance.

"Please, Coley," she's saying.

"You could always come to my room."

I hear the wavy and intimidating words float across the Santorini air and onto my doorstep.

"I'm staying right next door to your precious *novia*."

I don't know if it's pity for Sadie or being sick of Rose or anger at both of them, but I open my door and pull Sadie in.

She stands with her back to the front wall, looking shell-shocked. She stays there, still and silent, as I get my pajamas out of my bag and act like I have a million more important things to do than listen to her.

Finally I look at her. "What are you doing here?"

"My mom was snoring and I couldn't sleep."

I stare at her.

"I have to talk to you," she says.

"So, talk."

"Look, I'm sorry, Coley," she says, crossing the cave to sit down on the little bench. I'm running out of fake chores so I start rearranging the clothes in my suitcase. "I shouldn't have done that."

I look at her. "Done what?"

Some of her actual spunk comes back into her body, like she's distracted from her apology. "Do you like my brother?" she asks.

I narrow my eyes at her. "No." I try to stop there, but I can't. "Why would you even say that?"

She shrugs.

"Of course I don't."

She nods, but I can tell she's not buying.

"Besides, I have a boyfriend."

Sadie squints. "I thought you and Mark broke up," she says.

I forgot I told her that.

"I thought so, too. It didn't stick."

She chuckles. "Didn't stick? Isn't it up to you if you're dating him or not?"

I roll my eyes. This is not the time for her to have a point. "I can't like your brother. I'm dating you, remember. Are you here for an actual reason?"

She gets quiet again. She looks at her hands folded in her lap. "Are you going to the wedding tomorrow?"

If I do, it's to dance with Sam. Not with you. I don't answer.

"I . . . I really thought you knew. I'm sorry."

"You thought I knew that you dragged me here to go on a girl-date?" I say.

She shakes her head, vehemently. "No, no, no. I thought you knew that I'm . . . you know . . . a lesbian."

I sit down on the edge of the bed, refolding a pile of already-folded clothes in my lap. Can I make myself get used to that word?

I stare at her as she perches on the edge of the bench in my cave. How would I know something like that? I feel so dumb for not figuring it out, but I'm not sure how I was supposed to.

She follows my movements with her blue eyes, and I know that she's beautiful but I'm not gay. I didn't know she was gay. Am I stupid? I've never known a gay person before. Most of what I've heard about gay people has been from my church, and I know they aren't the best source on the subject. Why would she think I would know?

"Coley," she's saying, "I really don't think I'm going to hell or any of that stuff. I'm really just myself. I can't help—"

"Stop!" I say. I can't think about hell and choice versus instinct and all the stuff I've heard within the walls of my church. "I'm not saying . . . any of that."

She shuts her mouth, like she's surprised that I'm more concerned with everything else than with the gay-ness.

"You don't think I'm going to hell?"

"No," I say. I think of my mom, my church, and everyone I know who are all the same, who think the same way and who are so different from everyone here. And how much better it feels to be with the Peppers than all those other people. "No," I say again.

"Then why are you angry?" she asks.

"Because you used me!" I exclaim. "You knew I wouldn't want to come here to pretend to be your date, so you made it some big secret. You made me pretend everything was back to normal when you were lying to me. Everything is your fault."

She stares at me, wide-eyed, and I pant and go over the words I just said and know that there are still some missing.

"Oh," she says quietly.

"And I'm mad because"—my voice is small now, my blood full of pathetic-ness like I'm about to use that word "need" even though I'm not—"you didn't tell me."

"Oh," she says. "Oh. I'm sorry."

We freeze like that for minutes until I'm sure we'll sit like this forever, silent, across the room from each other, suspended somewhere between friendship and loneliness. But then she says, "It's so hard. I never tell anyone."

I nod, feeling numb.

"The first person I told . . . she made it really hard on me. She's the only . . . Well, until you, I've only told one person . . . It was so long ago and so . . . awful . . ."

I nod again. Her words keep humming around my ears.

"It kind of ruined everything when I told her . . ." Sadie stumbles. She's crying now, tears running over her perfect cheekbones and down her tanned face. "My family knows but

I didn't . . . I didn't have to say it. The first person . . . Since then I've been so afraid . . . Can you try to understand?"

"I'll try," I say. *But it still hurts you chose Lynn or one of those other girls to tell instead of me. It still hurts that you let us splinter apart before giving me a chance.*

Sadie stands. "That part," I whisper. "That part I'll try to understand. But will you try to understand the other part?"

"What's the other part?" Sadie asks.

I can't go to this wedding, I decide. I can't be that manipulated.

"I thought you invited me here for me. I thought I was important to you. After waiting for years and years to figure out what happened to us, I flew to another country just to be with you and then it turns out . . ."

She sits on the edge of my bed next to me, her eyes wide and pleading. "I do need you, Coley," she insists. "I do."

I bite my lip.

She straightens. "I'm sorry, Coley. I really am. But will you please come to this wedding with me? If you don't Rose will know that it was all fake and I'll look even more pathetic. See? I still need you."

Forget how pathetic you're making me look. Feel. Forget that I thought we were going to be real friends, not fake dates.

"It hurts every time I see her," she says.

Forget that I left my own boyfriend and I'm having to rewrite my own life so you can have revenge on some ex-girlfriend.

"It won't mean anything. It won't be real. I just need to prove to Rose that I'm over her."

"But you aren't," I say.

Her eyes stay wide and pleading.

It hurts every time I see you.

"It's not like it's a real date, Coley. It's fake."

Everything has been fake.

"You see Rose, Coley. You see how awful she is to me. Can you try to understand how bad it will be if I show up without you tomorrow? How she'll stomp on my heart and squash it all over again?"

I hate that she looks so sad, even if I am angry.

"Imagine it was Mark somewhere with some other girl. Imagine having to see him flirt and cuddle and kiss other girls right in front of you."

The thought makes my heart clench in my rib cage.

"She did that to you?"

Sadie nods. "Worse," she says.

I sigh.

"Will you think about it, Coley?" Sadie pleads. She sounds like she's a kid again, begging me to loan her my best shirt for school, to lend her my five dollars on the boardwalk, to ask my parents if we can stay up a little later at a sleepover. "I'll be your best friend."

That last part's a joke. I know it. She says it with the inside-joke smile. But it still melts me.

"I'll think about it," I say.

Ανακούφιση
(Relief)

Relief comes in the form of sleep and by the grace of God or the universe or whatever is out there after all, my dreams drift away from Sadie and my parents and Rose and the volcano. But I am in the sea.

I do a perfect freestyle away from the cliffs of Santorini, though I can feel their beautiful presence behind me. The salty waves slide along my skin, tickling my arms, my sides, my butt, my legs. I feel the sun baking the top half of my body as my feet kick and I move forward and my face is surrounded by cobalt blue.

Still, I hear the rustling of waves behind me and then I feel strong, warm hands slide up my calves. I know it's Sam, but I don't turn right away. I float suspended and enjoy his palms as they make their way up the back of my legs, and despite the sun, goose bumps form on my spine.

When his fingertips reach my butt I realize that I'm naked in the water and, embarrassed, I turn to see him.

He treads water, smiling at me like he expected me to be unclothed, like it's natural. His own naked shoulders and chest are suspended above the blue and I reach out to touch his wet skin.

And then I'm awake.

There's a banging on my door.

I sit up, rubbing the sleep out of my eyes. The sun is streaming through my open windows at such a harsh angle that I can tell it's so early there's no way I should be awake yet.

And because at the moment I'm too tired to try to figure anything out and I'm too lonely to have any sort of conversation I yell, "Go away, Sadie."

I crash back into my pillow and meditate on Sam's smile, his skin, eyes, muscles, trying to use him to chase away all the other thoughts that are taking my brain by force.

I know I can't do anything about Sam. It wouldn't be fair to Mark. As confused as I am about my mom and even my dad right now, there are some things that are just wrong, like cheating. Plus, Sam is Sadie's brother and his mother hates me.

But I'm too tired to stop myself from thinking about him. He's the only good thing about this trip.

And for some reason the typical guilty feelings don't follow this naked dream.

Why did Sadie have to come back? Thirty seconds ago I was in the sea, about to have a guilt-free moment with Sam. Instead, here I am, lonely and confused in my cave.

I hear a click and I sit up in bed. Sadie is standing against the inside of my blue door. She freezes wide-eyed. "Sorry," she says. "The door was open."

Why did I do that again?

I lie back down.

She comes over and sits on the side of my bed. I curl away from her.

"I have to tell you something else," she says.

I pause. I want to tell her to leave so I can go back to sleep. But I'm also thinking about what Sam said last night—that Sadie needed me, specifically me, for a reason. I still don't know everything that happened.

"What?" I say, but I make my voice all bratty.

"I missed you."

I roll onto my back to look up at her.

"I still miss you. I hate it," she says. And she crumples, speaking through sobs. "I hated leaving you on that bench when I knew you just wanted a milk shake. I hated when we got to school freshman year and you waved at me in the hallway without saying anything. I hated being so mad at you when I saw you in the bathroom that time." I kept waiting for you to come to me and tell me it was okay that I'm gay, that you accept me, but you never did. I thought you knew and I thought you hated me for it."

"How would I know? You didn't tell me."

She shakes her head. She's crying harder now.

"I always thought you knew. I thought I wasn't good enough for you. I realized—just a minute ago when I was lying next to my mom, staring at my ceiling trying to make sense of everything—I realized that if you didn't know, it makes me the bad guy."

I sit up and put my hand on her shoulder. "I didn't know," I say.

I pray she doesn't ask me what I would have done if I did know. I pray she won't ask me if I would have followed my church's rules and turned away from Sadie if I had found out before this island pried my mind open. Because I don't know.

"I can't help who I love, Coley," she says. And it makes sense, so I nod.

"Sadie," I say.

She twists her neck so she can look at me.

"I'm really tired."

She laughs. I roll over and she lies down next to me on the bed. "Me, too," she says.

My mom would hate this. My mom would call this bad company, the web of sin, me curled up under the covers and Sadie spread out on top of them two feet away from me. My mom would call this against God, just because of who Sadie is.

My mom would be wrong.

And with that thought, I fall back to sleep.

Ω

The next day, Sadie had a magenta streak zigzagging through her hair.

I was just out of the outdoor shower, dressing for dinner in the back bedroom. Sadie burst in the door, smelling like soap with her head wrapped in a towel.

"Coley!" she said. "Ta-da!"

She whipped the towel away and shook out her dry hair. Sure enough, the very back of her head was streaked magenta.

"My mom did that?" I asked. "My mom?"

Sadie nodded and I watched the streak bounce up and down. "Doesn't it rock?"

I shrugged. It didn't rock. It looked like she'd colored in her hair with a highlighter. The line was in the exact middle of her head, dividing the hemispheres of her brain. And it zigzagged back and forth like the stripe on Charlie Brown's T-shirt.

But I didn't say any of that because you don't say anything if you don't have anything nice to say.

Sadie walked toward the wall and twisted around, trying to study herself in the little mirror that hung on it.

"It is so cool. I can't believe how amazing I look," she said. "Your mom is awesome, Coley."

My mom was a lot of things. She was righteous and knowledgeable and occasionally fun. She was a good mom, I thought, because we never went hungry and we always went to the beach. But she wasn't awesome-mom. In my opinion, awesome-mom was Edie, who always seemed more concerned with hugs than rules.

Sadie collapsed on the bottom bunk and watched me comb my own long wet hair.

"I want to be like your mom when I grow up," Sadie said.

It was the opposite of what she'd told me the day before.

"I thought you wanted to walk the red carpet."

Sadie flipped over and propped herself on her elbows. "Oh,

I do!" she said. "But I mean at home. At home, I want to be like your mom. I'll have dinner on the table for my kids at the same time every night. And if they're shouting at each other, I won't let it keep going. I'll make sure they stop and say 'I'm sorry.'"

I turned around and looked at my friend sprawled out on the bed, fantasies running through her brain.

When I grew up, I would probably be like my mom, too, because it was the right way to be. But I'd want to be like Edie—I'd want to still have my own friends and be more concerned with what my kids were saying when they argued than with making them stop.

"That's what makes my mom awesome?"

"No," Sadie said, snapping out of whatever daydream was forming in her eyes. "That's what makes her a good mom. What makes her awesome is that she does my makeup and dyes my hair." She gave me that smile and said, "You'll probably be just like her, too, right? So you can totally be the best person to watch my kids while I'm on the red carpet."

And we laughed.

Later that evening, after dinner and the boardwalk, after the boys were put to bed and while Dad was outside shaking sand out of the towels and Sadie was in the bathroom, I found my mom in the kitchen and asked her the question that had been bugging me all day. The one that was code for everything that had been bothering me for days and weeks and months.

"Why did you dye Sadie's hair?"

She laughed. "I don't know. I was feeling spontaneous. Don't tell me you want yours dyed, too?"

I shook my head. Like she'd ever even consider it.

"Good. It's a bit vain, I think. Dyeing your hair like that."

"Sadie said you dye your hair," I said.

My mom leaned toward me and pressed her finger to her lips. "Shh!" she whispered. "That's a girl-secret." She winked at me and it made me feel good. At least she told me, too.

"Why did you tell Sadie your secret?" I asked.

Mom laughed. "Don't be jealous now, Colette. Jealousy doesn't suit anyone."

My cheeks burned and I shook my head.

"Anyway, you're my little girl, but I've been having fun with your friend, you know? It's been nice to have a little woman around who wants to learn about all of the womanly things. You were always such a tomboy."

I swallowed. Was I a tomboy?

"It's just some harmless fun, okay, baby?" Mom tweaked my chin. "And you know what our church always says: if you want to catch a fish, you have to go up the right stream.

I know it might look weird for me to bond with Sadie over trivial things like hair and makeup. But that's just a starting point."

My face was twisted as I tried to work out what she was saying.

"And Sadie . . . she needs it."

"What do you mean?"

Mom paused and thought before she answered that part. "You know, Colette, I'm trying to do the right thing. Sadie is so . . . sweet and . . . feminine and . . . she lives in that house. That crazy family . . ."

Mom didn't see my eyes getting wider with each word she said.

"It's not natural. Sadie needs some good mothering." Now she looked at me, but she still didn't see how shocked I was that my own mother couldn't tell how wonderful and sparkly and warm Edie was. "Don't get jealous, Colette, okay? You have a good mom. You were lucky enough to get that by birth, but not everyone is."

And even though deep down in my heart I knew Edie was a great mother, I nodded. Because my mother always knew all the rules and so she always did the right thing.

Ω

When I wake up a few hours later, I'm smiling. The Santorini sun is now streaming in my window and my ex-now-new– best friend is snoring lightly by my side. I smile at the ceiling, thinking about our old sleepovers, the ones at my house, when we always shared my queen-size bed. Away from the beach, I was always awake first and I would lie next to Sadie hoping she would wake up soon so we could start our day of imaginary play and games and laughter and swimming in the pool.

But now we're here, across the world in a cave on Santorini where the sun is so strong it almost has a smell and the stairs carved into the sides of cliffs allow you to see everything at once and yet have a million surprises a day.

I'm also thinking about something Sadie said this morning. Something that made sense. "I can't help who I love."

I don't think I love Mark anymore. And even if it feels wrong to break his heart, I can't help who I love. Of course I love him for being a good person, for being kind to me for so many years, for being my first boyfriend, but I don't think I love him like that anymore. And if I don't love him, we have to break up. We did break up.

I don't have to accept him as a boyfriend again just because he said so.

And that's what makes me smile the most. Because . . . *Sam.*

Sadie is suddenly upright next to me.

"Sorry!" she says, too loudly.

I sit up and turn to her. "For what?"

"I didn't mean to fall asleep here," she says. "I was so tired and we were talking and—"

"Uh-oh," I say. "Will your mom be mad?"

"I don't think so." She's talking fast. "But I thought you—"

"No," I say firmly, smiling. "I don't care." *You're my best friend.*

"You don't?" she says. The pleading in her blue eyes is almost electric. "About anything?"

I laugh. "I care about some things. But I'm on vacation."

"I mean . . . you forgive me?" She closes her eyes like she's afraid of the answer.

"I forgive you. Mostly," I say. "Let's go get breakfast before it's too late."

I disappear into the bathroom, and when I come out Sadie wraps her arms around me in a bear hug. And then we're hugging and laughing. Relief dances around our heads in almost visible music notes. We never meant to be ex-besties. It was all a mistake.

Forgiveness makes me feel light, like I'm swimming. We walk out of the cave, arms around each other, laughing.

"Sadie?"

We both turn. Rose stands in a red bathing suit on the

balcony next door, a Greek coffee in one hand, a bottle of sun-block in the other. Her brown eyes are wide as saucers and her strong face looks broken open.

I watch Sadie stare at her.

"Seriously, Sadie?" she says.

Sadie looks at her feet. I can almost feel her heart beat through my arm, which is still draped over her shoulders.

Rose shakes her head, looking right at me. "I really thought this was fake," she says. And I know she means me—a fake date, a fake lesbian.

I wait for Sadie to say it.

But Sadie shakes her head. "Sorry, Rose," she says, like she's trying to sound mean.

Rose's face hardens. "Your mom is going to kill you when she finds out you snuck out last night," she says calmly with a slow, phony smile.

Sadie walks away and I follow her down to the breakfast level, a disturbing smile spreading on my own face. Why do I want to beat Rose? Why do I like it that Sadie chose me?

"I always thought that would feel better," Sadie says, lean-ing into me once we're sitting.

"What happened with her?" I ask.

She shakes her head, stuffs a bite of eggs into her mouth. We eat quietly, but in solidarity.

Then Sadie starts talking. "It was so hard. She didn't . . . she hated that I wouldn't tell anyone. She kept threatening to break up with me if I didn't come out at school."

I chew my eggs and listen. She's talking about another girl. She was in love with another girl. Why doesn't this seem weirder?

"She hated that I'd, like, flirt and stuff . . . with guys . . . you know, so no one suspected."

I nod.

"She didn't get it. She goes to high school in New York, the city. People are more open-minded there. There are other, like, out-and-gay kids in her school. There's even a gay-straight alliance and a lesbian volleyball club at the community center. She didn't get how strange the way I am would make me at our school."

I try to imagine Sadie being an out-and-gay kid at our high school. I can't.

"She cheated on me finally. She texted me a picture of her half-naked with some gorgeous girl from her school."

My eyes go wide. Two naked girls . . . it's so confusing.

"You're coming to the wedding now, right?" Sadie asks quietly. Her broken heart is clearly reflected in her eyes.

"Yes," I say. *Please don't get more specific. Please let me come as your friend.*

"You'll come . . . as my date?" she asks.

At this moment I feel closer to Sadie than I have in three years, or maybe ever. It's like our blood is running through the same veins. Her frown is piercing my own heart, her hurt is weighing on my own limbs and she is mine. All I want is to protect her. But what she's asking makes me feel off-kilter. There's something weirdly familiar about it.

"Do I have to do anything differently than I've done all week?" I ask.

She shakes her head no.

I glance up toward Rose's balcony. I imagine her telling Sadie she loved her one minute, then cheating on her the next. It makes me want to punch her.

I take a deep breath.

"I'm in," I say.

Εκδίκηση
(Revenge)

Standing naked in the shower, my fingertips rubbing the shampoo suds through my hair, I think for the first time about what it means that Sadie is gay. She fell in love with another girl and a girl broke her heart. When she has fantasies and sex dreams (if she does) they look a lot different from mine.

I can't keep the images Sadie has planted in my brain over the past few hours from running through my mind in a constant stream. Sadie kissing Rose. Rose and some other girl half-naked on a cell-phone screen. Rose's eyes, jealous over me.

The girl I was closest to throughout my entire childhood, who I played with every day, who I sat next to every chance I got, who I loved. She's gay. I'm not.

I know I'm not a lesbian. I think Sadie's beautiful, but

I have the chest-crushing fantasies, the sex dreams, the jelly-legs with her brother, not her. But I'll pretend to be gay for one night for her. The thought is so terrifying it's exciting.

All my life the whole gay thing was about a bunch of anonymous sinners. I never thought of it in relation to anyone I knew, to myself.

I'm curious.

And I know what I'm about to do is wrong. I know it's wrong for any version of Colette—Fun Colette or Perfect Colette, Responsible Colette or Spontaneous Colette, even the Colette I Want to Be. It's wrong to hurt someone purposefully, even if she almost destroyed your best friend. But given the way the layers of anger and curiosity are building up in the steam, I'm going to do it anyway.

$$\Omega$$

An hour or so later, I stand next to Sadie in my skintight, bright-red strapless dress and watch as Andrea and Ivan say the words that will change their lives forever. I'm Sadie's date, I keep reminding myself, an internal mantra. I'm a lesbian for the next twelve hours. In the small crowd of spectators, I stand so close to Sadie the backs of our hands brush against each other. Pinpricks of excitement light up my skin.

Now I know how I fit into this crazy Pepper family: I'm the date.

"Ivan," Andrea says deeply and with such emotion that I'm jolted into remembering that this is not about me or Sadie or Rose. It's about Andrea and Ivan. But it feels like my life must be changing more than theirs, like my risk is the greater one.

Andrea takes a shaky breath, sucking in tears and tightening her grip on Ivan's hands. They face each other on a bit of earth that juts out over the sea. A woman stands with them to officiate, but she's not a minister or even a judge or anything. She's a friend of Ivan's.

Where will I have my wedding? I wonder as Andrea lists the promises she's making to the man in front of her. Will it be in a church or on some beautiful island? Or neither? Will my pastor or a judge be standing in front of me? All of the things that I always thought were predetermined about my future are up for debate.

And Sadie . . . what kind of wedding will she have? I remember all of her dreams about the kind of mom she would be. I think about her heartbreak over Rose and how real it feels. At every wedding I've been to, I've wondered about my own someday in the future. I turn to look at my friend-date. Does she imagine this day for herself? Who does she see waiting for her at the end of the aisle? Or walking down the aisle toward her?

No matter what it looks like, I want to be there that day.

$$\Omega$$

After the ceremony, we march in a short parade to the same cliffy restaurant where this roller coaster started.

Back then, only three days ago, the world was black and white and I was simply choosing black. Now, sunset, the sky explodes beyond the restaurant in a flurry of color and even though it's beautiful, it's complicated. I can't figure out if what I've agreed to do for Sadie is good or bad, right or wrong. The crowd stands at the edge of the restaurant while the sun paints all the colors across the sky. They watch with the same kind of hushed enthusiasm I saw last night. But today I don't watch the sun. I stare at the backs of their heads. I see Sam. I see Sadie, a smaller version of Edie, who is standing next to her. I see Rose a few people down the row. I take a deep breath and tell myself I'm ready.

When the last edge of the sun disappears, the island claps and cheers, and the band behind me begins to play soft elevator music.

Food is spread out around the tables on the perimeter of the restaurant and a bar is set up kitty-corner in the back. Sam catches my eye and smiles.

I try not to let my heart speed up.

I scan for my date. She's talking to Charlie and Mary Anne, and Rose is right behind them, definitely within earshot. I take a deep breath: here we go.

I walk over and put my palm on her elbow. "Can I get you a drink?" I ask.

She smiles at me. It's the inside-joke smile and it feels so good to know what she's thinking, to know that we're on the same side, that I almost cry.

"Sure," she says. "Maybe a mojito?"

I don't know what that is, but I walk up to the bar like I've ordered drinks a million times before and I ask for two of them. I'm a lesbian tonight, one who is old enough to order drinks. The mojitos are green and served in triangular glasses with stringy leaves streaking through them and a pile of black sugar settling at the bottom. Delicious.

I cross the patio to Sadie and let my fingers rest on her lower back when I hand her her drink. I make sure to catch Rose's eye and smile. Rose chews her cheek.

The music swells into an actual song and we form a ring around Andrea and Ivan as they dance to "At Last." I'm flanked by Sadie in a bright-yellow dress with a poofy skirt and Rose in a simple black dress that hugs all of her intimidating curves.

I imagine the two of them dancing, Rose dipping Sadie

the way Ivan dips Andrea. It's easy to picture. Me dipping Sadie, not so easy.

I fake-whisper in Sadie's ear, "You look great."

I try not to sound nervous.

Is this even how gay women talk to each other?

She looks up at me, inside-joke-smiling again. She clinks her green glass against mine and we both take another sip. I leave my hand on her shoulder and try to enjoy feeling Rose's eyes drilling into the top of my head.

Sadie squeezes my hand and my heart bounces.

Rose is clearly buying this. Why do I feel so jittery?

"All guests are now invited to join the bride and groom," the band guy says. They start to play a Stevie Wonder song.

We watch Ivan's nephew jump up and down on the dance floor before some of the adults begin to join in. Am I supposed to ask Sadie to dance? How would we even dance together?

Rose walks toward the bar. Sadie breathes a sigh of relief and takes a step away from me. "This is exhausting," she whispers. "But thanks."

I'm wishing, even though I'm sure it's not how lesbian couples dance, that we could dance like us, like we did in middle school, twirling each other around and around the dance floor, goofily acting out the lyrics, singing too loudly. Then, to my surprise, Sadie puts down her drink, grabs my hand, and spins me at arm's length. We lose ourselves in song after song of twirling goofy silliness. And in this moment I know what to do. I'm being myself. It's so . . . fun.

After the fourth song the band descends into a slow melody and Sadie and I smile at each other, each catching our breaths. "Being your date is easier than I thought," I whisper. "It's kind of the same thing as—"

Suddenly there's a sharp elbow in my rib cage. "Shh!" Sadie says.

I follow her eyes to the edge of the dance floor, through the pairs of swaying couples, to where Rose is approaching. "Shh!" Sadie says again. I wasn't even talking. I shrink about six inches.

Rose is standing in front of us, her eyelashes black and curving perfectly as she lowers her eyes right on Sadie. "Will you please dance with me?" she asks.

Sadie looks at her sparkly pink toenails. "Well, I . . ."

I can feel her eyes shift to my own black heels. We're close enough again that we can talk without words. I can feel what she's thinking. *Say no, Coley. Say you're going to dance with me. Say Rose can't interrupt our date like that.*

Part of me wants to freeze, to refuse. It's not that I don't want to dance with Sadie. I'm not sure what it is.

Instead, I put my fingers on Sadie's pointy elbow and lead her back onto the dance floor.

"Maybe later," she calls in a snotty voice over her shoulder.

I see Rose's face fall.

When I stop walking, Sadie presses herself against me, her hand pushed into the skin on my shoulder, her cheek close to my neck, her other hand squeezing my palm insistently. I keep her braced against me, my arm against her lower back, even as inside me my personality shakes and retches.

Not at the touch, though. At what?

"Thank you," Sadie whispers. "Thank you so much for saving me, Coley."

I smile because those words should feel good, and they kind of do, but everything else feels so bad. We turn and Rose comes into focus on the edge of the dance floor. She stands there alone, the toes of her flat shoes lined up with the edge of the wood paneling as if the floor is a pool and she's trying to decide whether to jump in.

Rose deserves this.

But as I think that, Edie's face comes into focus behind Rose's. She's not watching us. She's sitting at a table laughing with Sadie's aunt and uncle. Smiling the welcoming smile that everyone but me gets to enjoy these days.

And it hits me: I don't know if Rose deserves the punishment I'm doling out.

What happened between Sadie and Rose doesn't have

anything to do with me. And what does have to do with me is what happened between Sadie and me. Somehow we managed to tangle all of those problems together.

But can I ever have Sadie back if I don't come between her and Rose?

The song ends and Sadie's face is twisted into a ball of stress and exhaustion. "I'm going to the bathroom," she announces.

As soon as she's out of my sight, Sam is at my side. "Can I collect that dance now?"

He leans so close to me his lips almost touch my ear. His words slip smooth into my head before I remember that there are a million reasons I should say no. Sadie, Rose. Mark.

"Thinking again?" He laughs.

His eyes are on mine, like they're hugging me from the inside out. Being Sadie's date doesn't mean I can't dance with anyone else, right?

I want to dance with him.

I nod at Sam and then I'm in his arms. His hand is firm on the small of my back, his chest pressing into mine. My head fits just over his shoulder, so I can feel the heat coming off his cheek, the electrons popping between us. My heart hammers so hard I'm sure he can feel it through his own skin.

"You decided my sister's all right?" he says, so quietly I can barely hear it above the music even though his mouth is level with my ear.

I nod. "She needed me. You know," I say, almost apologetically. *We'll have the rest of the vacation to hang out after tonight.*

He spins me to the right and I'm dizzy and light-headed and floating even though I also know that he must still see me as a little kid. He must be glad I'm sticking up for Sadie like everyone else does. He must want to be my friend.

But I don't know why he's holding me so tight, ignoring the way my heart hammers into his chest, the way my cheeks flush because he's so close.

"It's good you're here for her then," he says.

I nod, my chin almost touching his shoulder. I want to memorize this moment, his hand against my palm, his shirt against my bare arm.

It's so . . . honest.

Then his lips are almost on my ear. "You look so damn hot in that dress," he whispers.

My heart jumps to my throat and my stomach tilts and wobbles and I curse Sadie for making it impossible for him to kiss me tonight.

I have to put a stop to this, this passion, this desire, this thing that is so real. I say, "You know Sadie wants me to—"

Sam jumps away from me. Sadie is standing right behind him. "Can I cut in?" she asks curtly.

He looks at me and it's the three of us figuring out this puzzle and I feel the same way I did before when it was Rose and Sadie and me and only one song. I should dance with Sadie. I should stop the pretending and dance with Sam. Why is everyone looking at me like I know what to do?

Then Sam shrugs sheepishly and his sister wraps herself back around me. My cells are still charged from being pressed so closely to her brother. My mind and my body are confused.

"Rose was watching you," Sadie hisses.

"Sadie," I say. "Maybe we shouldn't—"

She cuts me off. "You can't like my brother."

My jaw snaps shut. Did she really just say that?

I try, "You mean, tonight—"

"No!" Sadie says. She squeezes me tighter. She speaks to me through a forced smile. "I mean you can't like my brother. That's too strange. And Rose will totally be able to tell."

"Don't worry." I sigh. "I'm here with you, tonight. I'm your date, Sadie. And besides," I say with a weird smile, "I have a boyfriend."

I win a giggle out of her before I notice her squint over my shoulder and I can tell she's looking at Rose watching us and my insides feel icky and sticky like leftover scrambled eggs.

"You can't say that too loudly either," Sadie whispers. She plants a kiss on my cheek for good measure.

After a moment or two, Sadie adds, "You should probably break up with Mark anyway."

And for a second I think she's going to stop there. Even though I don't know if I agree with her or not, I'm happy to hear her say that. Because it seems like she's actually thinking about me, just me, not the way I fit into her twisted love life.

But she keeps talking. "Either way, you have to stop flirting with Sam, okay? If that goes on for the rest of the week, Rose will notice."

The rest of the week?

The scrambled eggs inside of me shake and multiply.

"Sadie," I say. "I don't think I can do this all week . . ."

"Yes, you can," she says. But she's distracted. She's focused on something behind me again. "You have to. Besides, you can't like my brother anyway."

I try to pull back but she presses her palm into my shoulder, asking me to stay this close, so close I can't see her. "What do you mean?" I say.

"Sam. You can't like Sam. I could not handle that," she

says lightly, without even paying attention, like whatever she's saying is no big deal, like she's telling me something as simple as don't smoke cigarettes or don't wear white pants after Labor Day.

Then I hear that wavy, snotty voice behind me again. "Well, Colette, aren't you the miracle worker," Rose says.

She sidles up beside us, dancing with Ivan's nephew on her hip.

"All I ever wanted from you, Sadie, is this. Just to dance with me, like this, in public."

Sadie turns her face away, her cheek now solidly pressed into my neck.

I face forward, trying to shield myself from the words Rose is saying.

I can feel Sadie's energy pulling toward Rose, Rose's pushing back at Sadie. I feel like a rock in the middle of a river, their love and their hate swirling all around while I can't move. I want to disappear.

How did Sadie do this to me? After years of not talking to me, after never even giving me a chance to accept her, how did she convince me that I owe her this favor? How did she manage to plant me in the middle of her love life without telling me about it?

And how could she try to derail mine?

I feel so gross with her pressed against me. I feel like my entire body is a lie.

I push her shoulder, trying to put a little space between us.

Rose is still talking, getting under her skin.

"I guess you must have found the perfect woman to act like this. I guess you never loved me enough to hold *my* hand in public."

I shove Sadie, not to end the charade but to put a pin in the intensity, to cool it off a little. She won't let me move.

Rose lowers her voice even more.

"She must be really good in bed," Rose says.

Now Sadie looks at her. And she winks.

That's it. It's too much.

I can't make myself into Perfect Colette for my mom anymore, and I also can't be Gay Colette or whoever else Sadie wants me to be.

I yank away from her and dodge between the spinning couples, around the food tables, and up the stairs onto the Santorini sidewalk.

My heels slip and slide over the marble planks of the main walk, and the restaurants and stairs and cliffs and stars go sailing by me as I sprint my way down the island. I can hear her fabulous heels pounding after me but I know she won't catch me. I'm faster because I'm the swimmer. I'm the one who stayed.

I step right out of my shoes and I turn past where the hundreds of stairs lead down to the sea, going farther north than I have before. The cool marble on the soles of my feet, the salty breeze on my cheeks, the island moisture in my hair, the breath rushing in and out of my lungs, all start to feel good, like maybe I can be myself and not worry about right and wrong, or fun and perfect, or Sam and Sadie—if I never stop moving.

But then, *bang*.

The sidewalk dead-ends into a sudden cliff and I slow my steps before my body goes tumbling over it. I stare down at the churning sea below and imagine if I had kept running, fabulous red dress and all. If the end of this road had been the end of mine, what would people have said about me?

I hear the *clang, clang, clang* of high heels behind me and I know I'm caught.

We stare at each other, two bright dresses in the dark of the island. Sadie's chest expands in her dress as she works to catch her breath.

Finally she says, "What the hell? What the hell, Colette?"

"Are you really asking me that?" I answer.

"After all this time," she says. "I wanted you to do one thing for me. Just one thing."

"What do you mean, after all this time?" I shout the words into the Santorini air, imagining they hit Sadie's ears and then poof away. "After all this time when you've been ignoring me, you ask me to do you some really screwed-up favor? After all this time of you proving how much better you are, you ask me to sink that far beneath you?"

"No, *you*," she screams back, the force of her words almost sending me over the cliff. "You're the one who thinks you're so much better. You're the one who can't handle who I am."

"You didn't give me a chance!"

"I did," she answers.

"When?"

Sadie sighs. She looks at the stars. She doesn't know what to say. I wish I could get back to my cave without finishing this fight. I wish I could get into the hotel without having to cross her path. I'm trapped.

"Tonight," she says finally. "I gave you a chance tonight and you ruined everything. Everything. You know how stupid I look for bringing you here?"

It's like she's punching me in the heart.

"Why didn't you get a real date then?"

"You think I didn't try? You think I haven't tried for the past year, the past *year*, to find a girl who would help me get over Rose, even just a little? To find another girl to hold hands with, to kiss? You think I like looking at Rose's Facebook page every night, watching it fill up with more and more girlfriends while I've only kissed one girl in my life? You think I didn't want a real date to show her I'm over her? You think I *wanted* to bring you?"

"Sadie," I say quietly.

"You think you're so much better than me because you can dump one guy and move right on to the next—to my *brother*—while I can't even find a second girl to kiss me."

"No," I say.

"You think I'm so pathetic because my heart stayed broken for a whole year."

"I don't think that!" I shout it, but not out of anger. Just to try to get her to hear me.

"If you had only done what I wanted tonight, she would like me again. She would have kissed me again. You know how long it's been since I've been kissed?"

"Sadie," I try again. She's talking crazy.

But then she says, "It's our town, our school, full of people like you who make it impossible for me to get over Rose."

"People like me?" I ask.

"Yeah," she spits back. She takes a step closer to me. "People like you."

"Like me?" I say louder.

She nods. "Crazy. Christian. Homophobes."

I cannot believe this. I take a step toward her now. "You think that's me?"

She nods.

"You think I ran away tonight because you're gay?"

She freezes.

"You think all of this is because you're a lesbian?"

Sadie considers for a second. Her face is a flash-card book of emotions: sad, pensive, frightened, angry. She settles on angry. "I think you're a hateful, homophobic loser who hopes I never get kissed again."

I cannot say anything. I cannot swallow such undeserved hate. I cannot try to arrange the pieces of this girl in front of me back into my best friend.

Instead, I prove her wrong. I step the final distance between us, I put my hand on the back of her head, I pull her toward my face, and then *wham*, my lips are against hers in a gooey, sloppy kiss and she's bracing against my palm but I won't let her go anywhere, not until I've proved my point, not until she realizes that there are many other reasons for me to be mad at her.

"Coley!"

But it's not Sadie. My lips are still pressed to hers.

I yank my head around and there's Sam, only ten feet from us down the marble sidewalk. "Sam . . ." I whisper it.

"Coley?" he says. "Sadie?" He shakes his head. "What the hell . . ."

Sadie stands next to me and cries.

"Sam?" I say.

"I was following . . . I thought you were upset, and I thought . . ." He pauses for a second, shakes his head again. "You kissed my sister!" he yells.

Since I don't know what else to do, I continue the charade. "What's wrong? I'm Sadie's date, aren't I?"

"Sadie's date?" he says. "I thought . . . holy shit . . ."

He turns and walks back down the sidewalk. I start to run after him but Sadie reaches for my wrist. I spin to face her. "What are you doing?" she demands through her tears. "I thought you were helping me. You stole my second kiss. I've been waiting for a year to be kissed again and you just stole it for something . . . fake. What's wrong with you?"

I open my mouth. "What's wrong with you?" I ask.

She shakes her head, sucking in huge sobs that rock her body back and forth.

"You tell me in one breath that you can't help who you like but that I'm not allowed to like Sam. Well, guess what? I do. I like your brother. I'm a real person who has real feelings, too, and I was just trying . . ."

She's still crying, but she nods. "You're messed up, Coley." The words are like knives slashing the little-girl part of my heart.

I've never been messed up. Not until I got here.

"So are you," I say.

I turn back to find Sam but he's gone, a shadow far down the sidewalk like he's been running.

I leave Sadie crying behind me, and I sprint after him. But when he veers to the right and descends back into the party, I keep going. He wouldn't want to talk to me anyway. Not now. I'm guilty and stupid and vengeful and messed up. Tears stream down my face. Sweat stains my dress, and the mess I made messier writhes behind me. I run and I run and I run until I collapse on the sidewalk in a heap and sob.

I messed everything up for everyone.

I kissed a girl.

I ran away from my mother.

I tried to hurt Rose.

I hurt Sam. I hurt Sadie. I hurt myself.

I don't know how long I sit in a red-minidress heap on that dark sidewalk, my legs kicked out in front of me, my heels thrown down at my feet, my hands constantly wiping my face. Santorini is still around me. The wind has stopped carrying the smells of feasts and the music of parties and the multilingual conversations. The heat has been sucked from the air so it rubs raw on my face and legs. The passersby have all gone to their hotels or their homes and it's just me, a big mess on a pristine sidewalk on a cliffy island on the other side of the world from everything I understand.

Συγχώρεση
(Forgiveness)

"I've been looking all over for you!"

I don't realize right away that the voice is talking to me. It comes from far away. It doesn't penetrate my shell of depression.

"All over!"

It's not Sadie and it's not Sam. It's not Mom or Dad.

I bring my hands away from my face and I see big pale fleshy feet being tickled by the bottom of a flowing peach dress. I look up. Edie.

I know she's going to yell at me. The realization pumps through my blood like cool relief.

"Sorry." I sniffle.

And then, even though she's in a dress that probably cost as much as my college savings, even though she's big, an adult, and so graceful she must be eons beyond this, she lowers herself to the ground and drops beside me, right on the dusty sidewalk.

"What's going on, Colette?" she asks. "What are you doing out here?"

I wipe tears from my cheeks and turn. She looks more like the Edie I remember right now than she has the entire trip. Her face is open in a half smile, her blue eyes look like they want to hug me while she sits next to me, not touching.

"This whole trip it has seemed like you've been having a grand old time with my kids," she says.

I nod. "I have," I say. "Thank you."

My face flushes. I can't believe I haven't thanked her yet. I know better than that.

I know better than a lot of things.

"So, what happened tonight? Why are you crying?"

She puts her thumb against my cheek and catches a tear and that only makes me cry harder because at once I'm wishing it was my own mother sitting next to me and knowing that my own mother would never catch a tear like that. She would tell me I'm being selfish by crying on this kind of a vacation.

"You don't know what happened?"

She shakes her head. "I haven't seen most of you kids for most of the night."

I take a shaky breath. "Then why were you looking for me?"

"Because you weren't there at the end of the reception and I—" She pauses and stares down into my face like I'm the most important thing in her existence at this moment. "I have to talk to you, Coley. I owe you an apology."

I blink, rearranging the salt across my pupils. *She* owes *me* an apology?

"Sadie told me today that you never knew that she was—"

"I didn't!" I cut her off. "I swear."

Edie laughs, but it's a sad kind of noise. "I know," she says. She cups her hand against my cheek. "I know. I believe you. I never should have doubted you, Colette."

I hiccup, praying the tears won't come back.

"I was so angry when Sadie decided to bring you on this trip. She kept saying, 'Mom, I have to bring Coley. She's the only one who knows about me. It's Coley or it's no one.'

"And I kept encouraging her to tell another one of her friends; I kept telling her that anyone would be better."

I gulp.

"She kept saying, 'Coley owes me this, Mom.' Then she took my credit card and bought your ticket—and I grounded her for that, believe me—but it was basically out of my hands at that point."

"Why are you telling me this?" I ask.

"Because I never should have held the way you were raised against you, Colette. I never even spoke to you about it. I'm disgusted with myself."

I raise my eyebrows. Is this the first time I'm receiving an apology from an adult?

"And because for the Peppers, forgiveness is our religion. We don't get too focused on all the details, but I always tell my kids that forgiveness is a divine act. So I should have forgiven you, a long time ago," she says. "Instead I held it against you. I didn't try to work it out with you; I didn't reach out to teach you another way. I've been angry at you for hurting my little girl for years and years and now, finally, she takes the time to listen to you and it turns out you never hurt her at all. I'm sorry."

"I did," I mumble.

She puts her arm around me now, and I sink into her warmth even though I know she'll pull it away as soon as I tell her. "You did what?"

"I did hurt Sadie. Tonight."

Edie's eyes go wide, and I see her trying to make them un-angry. "What do you mean? What did you do?"

"I kissed her."

Now she smiles. "Come again?"

"I kissed Sadie," I say. "I don't know why. I was mad and trying to prove something. I didn't want to be her date, and it didn't seem fair for her to tell me that I had to accept her but I wasn't allowed to be myself, so . . . I kissed her."

Edie is laughing, belly-laughing out of the huge crescent of her smile. *Her smile looks like Sam's*, I think, before I remember that he's adopted so that wouldn't make sense.

"What?" I say, but I'm smiling now.

"You mean to tell me that the worst thing you've done to Sadie in all these years is that you kissed her?"

I nod.

"Well, she probably deserved that," Edie says, glee dancing on her words. "That girl of mine will never learn, will she?"

Edie stands, and I stare up at her. What is she talking about?

"I told her, 'You can bring a friend for support, but you can't try to use her to get back at Rose.' I told her, 'That won't get you anywhere.'"

She's saying that stuff, but she's still almost laughing.

"You mean I wasn't supposed to be her date?" I ask.

"No!" Edie squeals. "No, you were not. You were supposed to be her friend." She reaches down, and I put my hand in hers so she can pull me to my feet. "Don't worry, I won't laugh when I talk to her about it. I'll use my most stern mom-voice," Edie says, turning on a gruff impression of an old man. "I won't tell her how much I laughed until years from now. But, boy, do I love watching my little girl learn from her mistakes."

She shakes her head at me, still smiling, then swoops down to gather my shoes.

"Let's go to bed now, shall we?" she says. "I'll make sure to have a chat with Sadie in the morning, and then I'll send her to you. We'll have this all straightened out before Crete."

I know that's impossible but my eyes are stinging from all the tears and my eyelids are heavy and at least if I've lost Sam and Sadie, I still have Edie. So I follow her.

On the way back I say, "Hey, Edie?"

"Hm?" She glances at me.

I'm nervous to ask, but the me I want to be wouldn't be nervous, so I do anyway. "How come I've never met Sadie's dad?"

Edie laughs. "I used to wonder why you weren't more curious about that. You had such a great relationship with your father as a little girl and all."

She knew that?

"But the answer is pretty simple. You haven't met him because Sadie hasn't met him because we have no idea who he is."

I flush pink. I've never thought of Edie like that, like sexual, like making babies and not knowing where they come from. I don't want to be thinking it now.

She laughs again. "Not like that, girl," she says. "I had a husband once."

My eyebrows jump. I had no idea.

"He was so . . . perfect. We were in love. And when he passed away, before we got a chance to make a family, I knew I'd never love again. But I inherited some money, enough for me and a few others to live on. He'd always wanted a son, so I thought I'd give him two, the only way I knew how. I went to Haiti, where I adopted the boys and I love them. Oh, do I love them." She smiles. "And I know it's only in my head that he's their father, it's not legal and it's certainly not biological, but they remind me of him. Boy, do they." She chuckles to herself then, shaking her head. "After a few years, though, I wanted a little girl. I wanted another child, one who wouldn't constantly remind me of the life I'd lost. One who looked like me. So I went through the steps and I got my girl. Her father's an anonymous donor."

Edie squeezes my shoulders.

"I've three beautiful kids. I'm a lucky lady."

We start descending the stairs to our hotel. My eyelids are heavy but I'm curious. "How did I never know that?" I ask.

"I don't know," Edie says. "There's something about our family. No one ever thinks to ask how we got to be the way we are."

I nod, but I know why. Because the Peppers are so clearly a family. No matter what my mother used to say.

Ω

The first thought that pops into my head the next morning: *I kissed a girl.* I stretch in my bed and rub the sleep out of my tired eyes. It's our free day.

No more pretending comes right after it. Today, I won't try to be anyone, not Perfect Colette, certainly not Gay Colette. I'll be myself. Today, I will go swimming.

I wander into the Santorini sunshine in my boxers and my T-shirt. I watch the light glittering on the water. I want to be me in that water, pure, honest me. So there's something I need to do first.

It's not necessarily the rightest thing to do, but I log onto the TV-computer and write Mark an e-mail. It's the only way I can contact him, and I have to do it today. It's not fair to me that he breaks up with me and then goes back on it while he's unreachable and I can't discuss it with him. I have to be honest with him, with me. And honestly, it's over.

> Mark, I love you, but I think that you were right about us the first time. We've grown apart. We hid too much from each other. We tried to be too perfect and now we're broken. I don't want to hold you back when you go off to Princeton. I want you to be happy and have a great life and not worry about what your girlfriend would think all the time, and I want that for me, too. I'm sorry that I had to tell you this way, but it's the only way to reach you.
> Love, Coley

Then I delete "Coley" and put "Colette" because I don't want to purposefully upset him. When I hit send, I'm feeling a little taller already.

There's an e-mail from Mom but I leave it unread. I'll call her. There's also one from Louisa.

> Colette, I'm so sorry I said that thing about being fun. I wasn't trying to tell you how to be. I thought it was only advice. I don't know if I'm overreacting but

> I haven't heard from you since I said that so I'm afraid you're mad at me.

I laugh out loud and type a quick reply. At least this is one problem I know how to fix.

> I'm not mad! It was great advice. I've been trying to be as fun as possible, like you said, but this whole trip is full of drama. I can't wait to tell you all about it when I get back. We'll have to go get pedicures before you leave, okay? And by the way, I'm glad I came here, drama and all.

Finally, I call Mom. Not to apologize exactly. Not to apologize for everything, anyway. But to try to be honest. To tell her that sometimes I disagree with her and I don't know how to handle it. I check my watch as the phone rings. It's three a.m. there; I can't get used to this time difference. I hang up before I wake her.

I take a shower and after determining that the little balcony-restaurant is empty, I sit for a quick breakfast all to myself.

But I'm only sitting for a moment before Sadie is beside me. My head jerks up. I thought for sure that this time she'd never talk to me again.

"I'm still learning how to do this," she says quietly.

"How to do what?" I ask.

"How to be a lesbian," she says. "I'm still figuring it out. It feels like I'm always going to be figuring it out."

I don't say anything.

"My mom said I have to talk to you today. She said I had to forgive you. She's suddenly all Team Coley."

I want to smile to myself, but I don't.

"And she's right . . . That kiss . . . felt like a huge deal. I've been waiting so long for another girl to kiss me and I hate that it was fake. But she's right. You couldn't know that."

"I'm sorry I kissed you," I say.

She nods. "And I believe you that you never knew, so I'm sorry. I shouldn't have called you all of those names. My mom says there's a lot of space between being a homophobe and not wanting to be my date." She chuckles but it's not friendly.

I nod. "I didn't want to pretend to be someone I'm not. I have to do that too much already, for my parents."

Is this going to be it? Is all the fighting going to be over? Now that all of the cards are on the table, can we go swimming?

But Sadie keeps talking. "I get it. So, I'll forgive you. I

won't stay mad at you like I have been for so long. Because that was wrong of me. But . . . look, it was wrong to bring you here. I see that now . . ." She trails off and I'm shaking my head, back and forth, back and forth, because I know what she's going to say and I don't want to hear it today, I can't hear it, it will hurt so badly. "I guess we were only meant to be little-girl friends."

My heart breaks so fast I'm sure she can hear it shatter.

"No," I say. It's quiet, but it's there.

She looks at me.

"I could have been there for you. I could have been the friend you needed on this vacation. But you should have told me. A long, long time ago." I say it gently. We're both in the wrong. We can admit that, forgive each other, and go swimming.

"I couldn't!" Sadie says loudly. "It wasn't about you, don't you get that? I tried to tell you, but after—"

"You tried?" I interrupt. "When?"

Sadie sighs. "Remember that last time we got milk shakes? A few days after I ditched you to hang out with the swim-team girls?"

I close my eyes and it starts coming back to me.

Ω

I sucked down a huge mouthful of sugary vanilla-and-peanut-butter and watched fourteen-year-old Sadie scroll through Facebook on her phone. It was four days after our final home swim meet, the summer before freshman year. She had promised me the milk shakes would happen the next day but she'd been so busy with Lynn and all of those new girls that it didn't happen for one day, two days, three days, four days. It took so long my muscles weren't even sore by the time we finally met up.

Sadie sighed and pushed the phone away before taking another sip.

She glanced at me. She wasn't saying anything.

Ω

"You were so bored that day," I say.

Sadie shakes her head. "I was distracted."

Ω

I was taking tiny sips, trying to make the milk-shake date last as long as possible. But Sadie slurped down her treat, looked at me, and finally spoke. "You ready to go?"

I hadn't even finished half of my milk shake. I stood up to toss it, though. This wasn't fun anyway.

Then, she surprised me. "Can I come over, do you think?"
she asked. "For dinner?"

Ω

"That was the day I tried to tell you," Sadie is saying. "I was going to . . . but I got so nervous . . . I kept putting it off . . ."

"Why?" I press. "Or why didn't you tell me after that?"

"Because of what she said to me . . . the first person . . ." Sadie is playing with her fingers, then raking them through her hair, then playing with them again.

Ω

On the walk back to my house, Sadie kept cracking her knuckles, then pulling her fingers through her hair. Her blue eyes stayed straight ahead as we took step after silent step. I could see her brain churning a million thoughts but I couldn't read one of them.

I didn't know what else to do to cheer her up. I lunged toward her and bashed my bruised hip into hers so that she went tripping into the street.

"Coley!" she yelped. But she was smiling. Finally.

Ω

I put my hand on Sadie's shoulder, even though she just said we aren't friends anymore. I put it there to keep her here. I need her to stay until I have the answers. I feel like this is my last chance to get them.

"When?" I whisper. "When did you tell that first person?"

"Then," Sadie says. "That day."

My heart jumps.

Ω

After a few giggly steps, her hip was suddenly against mine and I was flying, my right foot across my left, my left foot landing on the side, the road moving too fast beneath me. She got me good. Wham, I fell into a patch of muddy grass.

"Whoa! Coley!" Sadie squealed.

She bent over to haul me up. We smiled. My heart shifted out of the panic it had been in for the past four days. We were still best friends.

Ω

I take a deep breath to try to stay calm. I can't let her know I'm starting to panic because then she'll leave. And then I won't know. I have to know.

"Sadie?" I say.

She turns to me.

"What did she say? That person who you first told?"

Ω

We were still laughing when we got to my street. My mother spotted us through the window of the kitchenette, where she was starting dinner.

"Right in the shower with you, Colette," she called through the screen. "Don't go dragging that mud in here."

But she sounded happy. She was always happy when Sadie was around.

Ω

Sadie looks back at her feet and shakes her head. This entire breakfast patio is less sunny than it has been since we first got here, like Sadie's mood has the power to cloud it over.

"You don't get it," she says. "We weren't meant to be friends." It's barely audible, but it's there.

My heart hammers. I can't let her go.

I don't have to be her best friend. I don't need her to need me. I don't have to be everything to her. But I can't let us go back to nothing.

"Sadie," I say. She looks at me and I feel like this is the last time she'll ever look at me like that, like she's ready to be honest, like we mean something to each other. I feel like I have to get the answer to every single question I'll ever have right now. "Tell me what she said."

Ω

I streaked through the kitchen in my socks and pounded up the stairs toward my room. I expected Sadie to follow and wait for me there. But she didn't.

She stayed in the kitchen.

Ω

Sadie's eyes level into mine like she's trying to tell me more than her words will ever be able to.

"She said . . ." Sadie swallows.

I hold my breath.

"She said I was going to hell."

I keep my face steady but my pulse pounds in my ears, my heart becomes a gong in my chest, almost rocking me forward and face-planting me into the balcony.

Ω

"Sadie?" I called at the top of the steps.

But my heart fell when I heard their voices floating softly up the stairs.

"Want some iced tea, sugar?" Mom said. She never called me "sugar."

I was starting to think they liked each other more than they liked me.

Ω

"Who was it?" I ask quietly. Even though now I know. I already know. It explains everything. But it can't be.

Sadie shakes her head. "I . . . I shouldn't have brought you here. I'm sorry, Colette."

"Who was it?" I ask a little louder.

She stands and stares out at the sea.

Ω

"Sure," Sadie said.

I stood with my toes lined up on those steps, cursing the fact that I had to take a shower. Was it possible that Sadie knocked me in the mud just to get rid of me?

"Um . . . Mrs. Jacobs?" Sadie said. "I . . . Can I tell you something?"

Her voice was tiny, young, like we had gone back in time to before everything got so confusing, before their relationship with each other made me jealous of each of them.

". . . something I've never told anyone?"

Oh, that's it, *I thought. First my mom told Sadie her secrets. Now, Sadie was telling my mom her secrets. I couldn't take it.*

I got in the shower where I couldn't hear.

Ω

"Please," I say to the back of Sadie's head, to the sea and sun, to the universe. "Please tell me, and then I'll leave you alone."

Sadie doesn't move.

"Please, say it. I need to hear you say it."

Ω

When I got out of the shower, Mom said, "Edie called. Sadie had to go home."

I felt guilty for being a little relieved.

Ω

Finally, she looks over her shoulder. "Your mom," she says.

Then she's gone and I'm back in bed because there are some days you need to start over or skip altogether.

(Faith)

I lie in bed, ignoring the cheerful sun shining through my cave windows. I turn questions over and over in my brain as I turn my body over and over in the sheets.

What if my mom really knew?

What if she knew the whole time and said nothing to me?

Could she have let me think I lost Sadie, when *she* chased her away?

I jump out of bed to reread the e-mails my mom has sent me. I open the new one.

Dear Colette, your father tells me that you have called but that we simply keep missing each other.

If you need me, please call my cell. Also, I imagine you have all of the information by now. Let me remind you what we believe on the subject: Leviticus 18:22 "Thou shall not lie with mankind as with womankind. It is an abomination." Love, Mom

My hands shake as I click through her other e-mails: "bad company," "sexual immorality," "temptation" . . . none of it was about me.

She didn't know about the sex dreams or my crush on Sam or the way I've been trying to be the opposite of perfect. She didn't know anything about me. All of these e-mails are about Sadie. All of this has always been about Sadie.

I pick up the phone and call home. It's only about six a.m. there, so I call the house phone to wake her up. I imagine it ringing into the dark, my parents rattling awake thinking there's some sort of emergency. But there is an emergency. My body might be safe, but my soul is being thrown back into the erupting volcano.

"Hello?" Dad's groggy voice croaks.

"I need to talk to Mom," I say.

"Oh, baby," he says, suddenly alert. "Talk to me first, okay? I think—"

"I need to talk to Mom." I cut him off. He's been silent for way too long. He can't start calling the shots now.

"Your mom's going to say some things—"

"Dad! I need to talk to Mom! Now!" I shout it.

He sighs and then it's so quiet it's like the line has gone dead. I wonder if he's hung up on me. I wonder if he agrees with Mom. I wonder what the hell he was doing throwing me on an airplane and dropping me into this chaos without telling me anything.

"She's not here," he says finally.

"What?" I say. "Where is she?"

"She . . . Call her cell."

I pull the phone away from my ear and stare at it, my mouth hanging open. She left? My mom?

"Daddy," I whisper, wishing I were an eight-year-old with a voice this small and a body to match so that I could curl up next to him and lay my head on his chest, wishing he was still big and strong and fun and not completely broken like he sounds now. "Did she really tell Sadie that?"

Dad sighs, and I realize that he's not just fun or quiet, big or weak, right or wrong. He's a person. "She did."

"Where did she go?" I ask.

"She . . . I don't want you to worry about this, little lady," he says. "We're going to work this all out when you get back, okay?"

"Okay." My voice repeats his.

"We'll work this out when you get back, baby. But tell Sadie . . . tell her I'm sorry."

I nod and even though he's halfway around the world, I know somehow he sees me.

I call her cell.

"Colette?" she whispers.

Her voice sounds different, cracked, quieter, like my few days away from home could have changed her as much as they've changed me. A million questions rain in my skull: Where are you? Where are the boys? Why did you leave? Why did you say that to my best friend?

"What did you tell her?" I ask. "What did you say to her?"

And I know there's a part of her that's guilty or confused or a little bit unsure of all the rules because that's all I ask and somehow, even half-asleep, she knows exactly what I'm talking about.

"Sweetie," she says. "I said what I had to in order to protect you."

"What did you say?" I ask.

I hear her shift around and I imagine her prop herself up on whatever mystery-bed she's sleeping in, the faded orange nightgown she wears in the summertime slipping off a shoulder, her fake straw-colored hair sticking up behind her head. "I didn't say anything bad," she says. There's a highness to her voice that I'm not used to.

"Mom," I say, more quietly, "what did you say?"

She sighs. "I told her to repent. I told her she didn't have to be that way. I told her I would help. I invited her to church."

I nod. I can see how Sadie would misinterpret all of that.

But Mom keeps talking. "She refused and then . . ."

"Then, what?"

"Honey, you have to come home, okay?" she says. "We'll talk this over once you get home. I always knew I'd have to tell you this stuff, eventually, once you grew up, but an international phone call is hardly—"

"You should have told me a long time ago," I say.

"Maybe," she says. "I didn't know."

My jaw drops. She doesn't cite a rule or recite a Bible verse or call on a commandment. She says "maybe." Like she cracked. Like there's some room for what she should have done versus what she did.

She's still talking about why she didn't tell me. About how I was too young to deal with something so grave. About how she was protecting me. It's all complete nonsense. No. It's bullshit.

"What happened next?" I demand.

"I asked her to leave our house," Mom says. "I told her she was no longer welcome in our home. I told her—"

I'm so angry my face is on fire and my hand is clutching the phone so hard I'm sure it's about to burst into pieces in my fist. All this time they let me believe that Sadie ditched me. That Sadie walked away and chose other friends because they were cooler or more fun or had more money. They let me think that Sadie gave up on me. All this time my mother and father knew that wasn't true.

My mom was wrong. Wrong. So wrong.

And I want her voice to stop. I want her e-mails and her guilt trips and her self-righteousness to stop. But I know I might never get the details if I don't ask the last question, so I interrupt.

"What did you tell her?"

"I told her I would not let her take my daughter with her where she was going."

"Mom?" I squeak.

"I told her she was going to hell."

My heart slows and my brain spins like a top, trying to replay my entire childhood, every time my mom's voice has invaded my brain, every rule she's written for me, everything Perfect Colette lived by.

The way I was taught, that's the worst thing you can say to anyone.

I press Cancel on the pleading voice, the voice saying that she did what was right, the voice that's begging me not to get tempted into Sadie's web of sin. I press Cancel on the voice, and I reject the call when the phone buzzes.

I have too much of that voice in my brain already.

I lie back down, sad and out of breath and utterly exhausted at the thought that after all of this, I'm going to have to figure it out myself. What's right? What's wrong? Who do I want to be?

A second later the phone rings again and I almost fling it against a wall. But then I see Louisa's name on the screen.

"Hello?" I say.

I didn't think she'd be able to call me. Did my mom lie about the cell-phone thing? Is there even a phone plan like the one she told me about? Why didn't she just tell me not to call anyone?

"I didn't think you'd pick up!" Louisa squeals. "How are you?"

I shake the cobwebs out of my brain. I need to tell Louisa about all of this. But I can't do it for a dollar a minute.

"I've been better. How are you?"

"I'm great! I'm fun!" she exclaims.

I can't help but laugh. Thirty seconds ago I thought I'd never laugh again. "What do you mean?" I ask.

"I thought I'd get your voice mail," she says. "I wanted to thank you. Listen. That whole time I thought you were mad at me for telling you to be fun, I was, like, of course she's mad at me. How can I tell her to be fun when I'm never fun?"

"I wasn't mad at you," I say. It's so funny that she would think that. I've never been mad at Louisa.

"So, look. I did it."

"Did what?"

"I turned it down. I told the Japanese school I'm not going. I told my parents I want to have fun. I figured if Colette can do it, so can I."

"Wow!" I say.

"Let's have a great senior year, okay, Colette? Let's go get pedicures as soon as you get home and plan the whole thing."

I agree and when we hang up, I decide to follow her example and do something I would never have had the courage to do before.

Ω

I knock on the door.

At first, there's nothing but the yelling of Greek TV falling out her open window. It's totally possible that she's not here. She could have gotten up and gone swimming or shopping or exploring or anything else. Or she could be here. She could be sitting inside that cave, knowing I'm out here and pleading in a whisper for me to go away.

I'm going to chicken out. She has no reason to believe me anyway.

I knock one more time and the door swings open. Rose stands in the dark, her hair matted at the side of her head, her plum-colored silk pajamas askew, her eyes wild.

"Oh," she says. I see her shoulders deflate, her eyes focus. "It's you. Come in."

I step inside and she slams the door closed and I freeze. I guess in my imagination I thought we'd have this conversation outside on the porch in the sunshine with the smell of Santorini around us.

But now I'm standing in a warm cave that smells too much like Rose's tangy perfume. Her stuff is everywhere—clothes strewn across the bench, towels hanging off the edge of her bed, an exploding suitcase sitting on the floor, and bottles of products on each surface. Her TV is blaring—some news anchor screaming headlines in Greek. What am I doing here?

She walks over to her bed and flops on her back, throws a hand over her eyes.

"Look, I'm sorry," she says. "I give up. I'll leave you guys alone, okay?"

I stand on a clean patch of floor near the door and stare at her. She's not so scary when she's broken.

"I didn't mean to mess up your life. I wasn't trying to screw up a real thing. I didn't think it was real. I was hoping—" She stops abruptly. I see her shaking her head underneath her arm.

We coexist in a charged silence for too many seconds. "Did I wake you up?" I ask finally.

I don't know what I'm doing here. I don't know anything about her. I don't know how to apologize for pretending to steal her girlfriend because I don't know anything about that life.

But I have to forgive her, I think. Edie says forgiveness is a divine act. That sounds about right to me.

She curls her full body onto her side and pushes her thick hair out of her large brown eyes so she can look at me.

"It's exhausting being that mean all the time," she says. She smiles.

"Huh?" I ask her, smiling back.

She laughs. "You probably think Sadie was crazy to date me. You probably think she was totally desperate or . . . I don't know." She shudders. "And now she sent you here to shut down her big bad ex-girlfriend." She doesn't see me shaking my head. "But I'm not usually that mean."

"You're not?"

She laughs again. It's fake and forced but not snotty. Just awkward. "No!" she says. "I had to be. I was . . . when I found out you were . . . I couldn't . . ."

She curls her body tighter with each word. What I'm looking at is suffering and I'm responsible.

"All I ever wanted was to be like that with her. To hold her hand in public. To meet her friends. To brag about my beautiful, fun girlfriend. She wouldn't do that for me but . . . when I found out you were . . ."

"We're not," I say.

She freezes. "What?" she asks.

"It was fake," I say.

Rose props herself up, half sitting. "What was fake?"

"Everything," I say. "Everything was about Sadie . . . Sadie missing you."

Like this, I think, looking around at the mess in the room, which is as cluttered as Sadie's brain has seemed for the past few days. No wonder she needed me.

"What about you?" Rose says.

I nod. "She missed me, too," I say. "But in a different way."

Rose pops up. "You're not gay, are you?" she says, standing right in front of me. Her face is open and friendly. "You're not?"

I shake my head, smile.

"You're not gay! So you're here because—"

"Because you hurt Sadie too badly," I say, and I watch her face fall. But it's true. And I'm not going to take all the blame. "She needed some protection against you and she used me. But last night . . . I was trying to hurt you. It was this big show to hurt your feelings, and that's not me. I'm sorry."

"Sadie does that?" Rose asks slowly, her voice full of wonder.

"Sadie does what?" I say.

It's almost like she's not talking to me though. She's talking to herself. "I'm the one who does that."

"Who does what?" I ask.

She looks at me finally. "I'm the one who puts on a show to try to get back at people. At Sadie. I somehow always think that hurting her, that proving how great I am, will win her back." She pauses. "But it never works."

I squint. "You want her back?" I ask.

Rose deflates and drapes herself across her bed. "Yes!" she says. "I've been so lonely this whole year without her. Do you know what it's like to miss someone like that?"

I sit down next to her and manage a small laugh. "I know what it's like to miss Sadie," I say. "But not like that."

Rose nods, rolls onto her side. "She misses you, too, you know," she tells me. "She always thought you were mad at her for being gay."

I shake my head.

"Yeah," Rose says. "Based on all of those stories of the two of you, I never bought it."

Oh, my gosh, could I actually like Rose?

I take a deep breath of her perfumey air. Should I do this? For Sadie? After what she said to me earlier today?

"You really want her back?" I ask again.

"Yes!" Rose practically shouts it this time.

"Then why tell her about other girlfriends? Why act like you have the perfect life full of beautiful girls on Facebook?"

Rose gives me a half smile. "Sadie and I have our plots in common."

"What about the girl you cheated with? The cell-phone picture?" I ask.

Rose closes her eyes, swallows in pain. "Photoshop," she says.

My eyes widen. "What?"

She nods. "Photoshop. I'm awful."

I pull her arm so that she's sitting up next to me on the bed. "You aren't awful," I say. "But listen. Before I came on this trip, I had a boyfriend."

She nods.

"I loved him. I really did. But I lied to him all the time."

Rose raises her eyebrows at me.

"Not the same way. I, like, pretended to be perfect. Like, I'd drink at parties but not if he was there."

She nods again.

"But the thing is, he was drinking at parties, too. We were like that for two years. Now, we're so . . . disconnected, it's over. But it's not over between you and Sadie. You are connected. I could feel it when I was standing between you last night."

Rose's eyes go wide. "Really?"

"You have to be honest with her, okay? You have to tell her about all of the crap you pulled before she brought me here. And then you have to be nice to her."

Rose nods. "I will. I will. I love her," she says.

I smile. "I know."

I feel the sunshine streaming through the open window dance across my legs. I want to be swimming.

I stand to go.

"Coley?" Rose says. I don't hate her for saying it this time.

"Yeah?"

"Thank you. I hope I work everything out with Sadie and then I get to hang out with you a whole lot after this trip."

I sigh. "That won't happen," I say. "You have a chance with Sadie, I think. But this morning she dumped me forever."

Ω

An hour later, I'm the only place where I know who I am: in the water. I make it down the manure-strewn stairs myself, snuck past the scary donkeys, navigated my way through the crowded fish market at the bottom, and flung my body off the little dock. I'm in my black Speedo, not because of modesty or doing what's right, but because I want to go fast. And I am. I'm flying through the water, zipping back and forth past the little dock. I swim one way until I run out of breath and then I straighten up and feel the sand between my toes. I dip my head under the water and watch through my goggles as the fish circle my ankles. Then I dart back in the opposite direction.

The water is blue and warm and salty and pure. The sun bakes the top of my head as my fingers and toes turn to prunes. The island towers over me, reaches past where I can see and rises straight into the sky.

I'm finally in the water where everything should be perfect. Of course, nothing is ever perfect. Not even me. Not even Mom.

Why did she leave? Did I break my family apart? Do I even care when my family has been so wrong?

Can I ever forgive her?

When my muscles are twitching from exhaustion, I stand and tilt back to look at the sky. The wet sand massages the soles of my feet. The water shifts around my armpits. The sky is baby-blue without a single cloud and I am here and it is beautiful. I am by myself where I don't have to worry for a little while. I close my eyes.

Then *wham!* The world tilts, my foot goes shooting toward the sky and my face slaps into the water. There's a hand on my ankle.

I come up, startled and sputtering.

"You're It," says a smooth deep voice. "Thank God! I've been It for over three years!" I turn and there's Sam—wide smile, velvet eyes, broad shoulders, dimples. *Sam.*

My heart speeds up, pumping nervous blood to every part of my body, but I smile as soon as I see his face.

"Hi," he says. He takes a step toward me.

"Hi . . . ," I manage.

He stares at me and smiles and I stare back. He's surrounded by sea and topped by sky. The volcano is a miracle behind his shoulders. Everything is so beautiful but I can only look at him.

My face is caught between emotions like Sadie's, my cheeks burning with embarrassment remembering last night, my lips stretching with joy at seeing him here, in front of me.

He's mad at me. I kissed his sister.

I tell myself this logically, but my thoughts don't match his face.

He reaches under the water and pulls my pruney hand into his.

I let him.

"I thought you were . . ."

I think of how to finish as we stand hand in hand and shoulder-deep in the water. The current sways our arms back and forth like empty tree branches in the wind and we fight to hold on to each other, to keep our feet planted in the sand.

"Yes?" Sam says.

"I thought I screwed everything up," I say.

He smiles. "You're only one person. In the whole universe. You can't screw *everything* up."

"But I—"

I try to speak but then there's a finger on my lips and he's standing so close to me the water works around us instead of between us.

"Shh," he says. "My mom filled me in."

He puts his free hand on the small of my back.

"I'm sorry," I say. "Sadie—"

He shakes his head and pulls me closer, so that my body is just barely pressed against his. "I don't want to talk about my sister," he says. "That's over."

"I didn't know what . . . this . . . was," I say finally.

Sam nods. "I know. I know you didn't."

I feel my heart relax into my rib cage. It's wonderful to be forgiven like that, easily, readily.

"But I knew," Sam says.

"What?" I say.

"I knew what this was," he says. "Still do."

"What—" I say.

"Shh," he says again.

I shut my mouth and tilt my head up to look at him and then we're kissing. His arms squeeze me into his chest, his mouth plays music on mine, his hands press into my shoulders, and the water makes it impossible to stand. I'm floating.

I don't deserve this. I did everything wrong. I come from a messed-up family. I didn't even see that until today. I don't deserve this.

But that doesn't mean it's not happening. Regardless of what I deserve, it is happening. He's kissing me. Sam is kissing me. And I feel . . . right.

He pulls away from me and says, "Well, that's a first."

"What?" I ask, my head still full of clouds.

"First time I've kissed a woman who has also kissed my sister," he says with a laugh, and kisses my forehead. It tingles.

Without even thinking about it, I pull him into me again. "I shouldn't have done that," I say.

He laughs. "I know, I know." He pretends to trap me with a noogie. "If I had known you were her date, I never would have spent the whole week hitting on you. That sister of mine and her kooky plots. But it's over now, right?"

I nod. He smiles. Then he envelops me in his arms again, pretending to try to dunk me. I shake my head and fake a fight against his muscles even though I'm loving the way they are holding me in, anchoring my back against his side. Then his arms are gone. "Come on!" he says. "I'll race you to the dock!"

"Now?" I say. I start to freestyle after him.

"We have so much to do today," he calls back over his shoulder.

"All I want to do is swim," I yell.

He turns back to look at me, a flirtatious smile crossing his face. "Well, I was thinking we'd start with the white beach," he says. "But if you're afraid I'm going to kick your butt to the dock . . ."

"Oh, it's on!" I say. Then my head is in the water and I'm powering my way past his kicking feet and his propelling arms. If this were Mark, I'd let him win, I'd be afraid of hurting his feelings. But that's not me anymore. This time, from the start, I'm going to be all of me.

Χαρά
(Joy)

We spend the day exploring. We take a water taxi to the white beach, the one that you can't get to by the roads. We take another one to the red beach. We explore the archaeological site that may be the lost city of Atlantis. And we wind up back at the restaurant where we first watched the sunset.

This time, we hold hands across the table as Sam orders the same delicious meal.

This time, we kiss when the island applauds the sun's final ray.

This time, we walk back to my cave with his arm over my shoulders. This time, Sadie isn't sitting there. This time, Sam comes inside.

We're making out on my bed, his body spread out beside mine, his hands warm on top of my clothes, his smile popping up every time we stop kissing.

"I should go," he says finally, pushing my hair out of my eyes.

I realize that I haven't been thinking at all. I don't know what time it is. I don't know how long he's been here. I haven't tried to figure out if all of this kissing and hand holding means I have a new boyfriend. I'm not worried that I was talking too much or being too quiet or too forward or too shy. Who cares what my mom would think or what Sadie would say. I haven't thought about anything. It's been so nice.

"Don't go," I say, still not thinking.

He sinks his lips into mine again. "Believe me, I don't want to," he says. His body shudders against my side and my smile is so huge.

"Don't go," I say again. This time I kiss him.

He laughs. "I have to! Mom can be cool but if she finds out I shacked up with my sister's date, it won't be pretty."

We sit. Sam straightens his clothes. I look down at my own twisted T-shirt and try to chase the pesky bit of leftover shame out of my brain. The magic is going away already.

He puts a cushy palm on my cheek. "There you go thinking again," he says. "I'll tell her about us, don't worry."

I shake my head against his skin. "You're lucky to have your mom."

He stands. "In a second-chance kind of way, I guess."

I look up at him.

"I mean, my first mom gave me away. It's not always easy being where you're not supposed to be."

My eyes go wide. "I didn't mean—"

"Yeah, yeah," he says. "I know I'm not supposed to think about it like that. But sometimes I can't help the way my brain twists everything up." He shrugs his broad shoulders. After hours and hours of running my hands over them, I can see the way his muscles contract and expand underneath his shirt. "I know your family's not perfect either, but I always used to think you were the lucky one, you know, to be able to have two parents and no questions."

I think about that. "Sometimes I was. Maybe."

He smiles at me. "Sometimes I was, too. Maybe," he says. "I guess we're both a couple of oddballs."

We kiss good night and he's gone, and even though I know he likes me and even though I'm so excited to learn everything about him, too, and even though we had so much fun all day, everything isn't magically okay.

I lie in bed, watching the ceiling turn to inky black. This morning, if someone had told me that after the way I messed everything up last night, I'd still get to spend the whole day with Sam, that he'd forgive me before I asked, that we'd make out late into the evening, I would have thought it was going to be a perfect day.

But it turns out even the perfect boy can't guarantee a perfect day.

I lost too much today. Sadie. Sadie said good-bye forever. She didn't include an "I'll need you one day" clause this time. Sadie disappeared.

Mom. Mom told a little girl she was going to hell. Mom's voice can no longer be the compass for my life.

My family. It's splintered into two or three or four different places. I don't even know what's going on. It's only been a week—how can so much have changed? Is it all my fault?

As soon as I think that, "Octopus's Garden" rings electronically through my cave.

This time I answer.

"Did I wake you up?" she asks. Her voice is quiet and reserved, only a shadow of the voice she usually uses.

"Hi, Mom," I say.

"Colette," she says. "Are you having a good time?"

Yes. No. Yes, but it hurts. "Where are you, Mom?"

"I need to explain, I think. Do I need to explain?" she says.

I nod. She keeps talking.

"You know, Colette, I have this recurring dream. I've never told anyone about it before, but here you go. In it, it's the end of my life, okay? And I'm meeting my maker. It's God, okay? Sometimes it's a man and sometimes it's a woman and sometimes I can't tell. Sometimes it almost looks like a ghost and sometimes it looks like an angel and sometimes it looks like a stranger you'd meet on the street. But I always know that this is God, that it's the end of my life, that I'm a step away from Heaven, okay?"

"Okay," I say because she keeps asking over and over.

"And do you know what God says? The same thing, every time. Know what God says?"

"What?" I ask.

" 'That's not exactly what I meant,' " she says.

"What?" I ask.

"That's what God says. To me. Every time. 'That's not exactly what I meant.' "

"Oh," I say. I lie back down on the pillow. What is she talking about?

"Where are you, Mom?" I ask. "Why aren't you at home?"

"I'm going home now. Right now. I'm in the car, okay?" I've never heard her ask for my approval. Now it's like she can't stop. "I've been at Aunt Liza's, but I'm going home now, okay?"

"Are you getting divorced?"

It's a whisper. I don't know what to think. My parents don't fight. My mom yells and my dad shuts up. No one ever stands up to my mom. Now I did and the whole family falls apart.

I feel guilty about that but . . . she was wrong.

"No!" she says emphatically. "No. I love your father."

"Then why—"

"Colette, you might not have noticed this, but I have a hard time being wrong."

I almost laugh.

"I didn't want to admit it. I had to get away from everyone who was right to see how wrong I was. Your dad has been . . . trying . . . to tell me this for a long time. I had to get away from him to listen."

"You're going home now? To stay?" I ask. "Are Adam and Peter all right?"

And what if one of them is gay? What will you do then?

"They're fine. They think I've been away for work." She sighs. "Look, I probably shouldn't have said that to Sadie. And maybe I was wrong. Maybe your father has finally gotten that through my thick skull by sending you away from me. I've been thinking and thinking about you and Sadie, and about how that thing I said to her all those years ago was probably the worst thing I've done in my life."

"Why do you keep sending me those e-mails then?" I ask. I hear a car door slam and wonder if she's gotten home already.

"I was trying to explain myself!" Mom says. "I was trying to tell you where I'm coming from, that I had a reason to say that to her, that it didn't come from nowhere." She sighs. "Or maybe it would have been easier if you agreed with me when you found out Sadie is a . . . if you didn't run away and make me question everything. I hate being wrong." After a long pause she continues. "But it doesn't matter. I should say this: I was wrong. I was wrong a whole lot and I will be again."

"Sadie is a lesbian," I say. To be better than my mother. To use her example to make myself a good person in a whole different way.

She sucks in a sharp breath.

"It's just a word, Mom. It's just a fact."

"I don't . . . agree with Sadie's . . . lifestyle. Or with Edie's parenting. I can't. But . . ."

She's wrong. I'm going to have to live with a mother who is very wrong about my childhood best friend. It's going to take some divine forgiveness to figure this one out.

"But what?" I ask.

Mom sighs. "I don't know what to say."

"I always thought you had all the answers to everything."

"I know," she says. "I thought you were safer that way."

I shake my head because she'll always be my mom. She'll always say things like that when you want her to tell you she loves you. But I'm going to have to summon up the courage to forgive her when I get home. She's still my mom.

"You're home now?" I ask.

"Listen, Colette. In that dream, God tells me I'm not perfect, not on target but . . . I was always trying. I think God knows that, too. In the dream, I mean. I was always trying to do the right thing. I love you, okay? I was trying to protect you. I just . . . did it the wrong way."

"Trying doesn't count for everything," I say.

She sighs. "No, it doesn't. I'm sorry."

"I think you're wrong, Mom," I say. "You're going to have to let me disagree with you sometimes."

"Look, I don't know what's happening with your father. After all these years, I'm finally going to apologize and I hope he'll hear me. But no matter what happens, you're my kid, my daughter, okay? And when you get home, the first thing I'm going to do is listen to you."

Ω

The next day I'm thinking a lot about my mom's words when we pile into the big boat we're taking to Crete. My mom was not always right, but she wasn't always wrong either. That's probably true about everyone.

Sadie's sitting by herself in one of the cushy chairs by the window. I plop down next to her but she doesn't turn to me. Beside her the sea rushes by, Santorini disappears behind our heads. *Good-bye, island,* I think. *Good-bye, cave and volcano and wineries and mountain stairs and fish markets and sunsets and magical first kisses.*

I wait until the island has disappeared behind us to open my mouth. Then I say, "I love you."

Now she looks at me.

"That's what you said you needed to hear," I say. "In the volcano. It took me too long to say it, but you're my friend and I love you."

Sadie shakes her head. She looks back out at the sea.

"You can't get rid of me that easily, Sadie," I say. "We wasted too much time already."

"It doesn't matter," she mumbles into the glass.

"What?" I say.

"It doesn't matter. If I told you back then, you wouldn't have been friends with me anyway."

"Maybe not," I admit.

"You would have listened to your mom."

"I guess," I say.

She can't help turning to glance at me then.

"But you can't blame the whole thing on Mom either. You and I grew up a little differently. We went through different kinds of loneliness. You didn't want the milk shake."

"Huh?" Sadie's eyebrows crinkle together and I know that I get to have this conversation. I at least get to try to do the right thing.

"My mom was wrong. My mom was awful," I say.

Sadie nods. "I couldn't . . . tell you . . . You had to live with her. I couldn't let you . . ."

"I know," I say. "But it wasn't only my mom. You didn't want that milk shake anyway."

Sadie frowns, chews the inside of her cheek.

"It was me. I was holding on to you too tightly. I wasn't ready to grow up and you were, and that scared me. I didn't push you away. I held on tight, white-knuckled, until you were squeezed out of my life."

Sadie nods. But then she shakes her head. "It was me," she says. "I didn't give you a chance to stand by me. I didn't talk to you about how I needed to grow, different experiences, different people."

I shrug. "It was a lot of things. It probably had to happen. But it's over."

She stares at me.

"You don't have to be my friend," I say. "But I think I can still choose to be yours."

I stand to leave. Her face doesn't move.

"I'm going to go sit by Sam now. I like him, and you can't tell me not to. And Rose," I say. I watch Sadie's breathing quicken. "You should talk to her."

Ω

The next day, I'm back in my red minidress and black heels. We ride in a van from our regular old hotel on the Sea of Crete over winding hills and past countless olive trees, grapevines, and apple orchards to the site of the wedding reception. The van takes the bumpy dirt streets with a vengeance, throwing me into Sam's body every time the road curves right.

Sadie hasn't said anything to me since yesterday, but she gave me a little smile when I passed her and Edie sitting on the front bench of the van.

"That dress," Sam whispers in my ear, "is so hot."

He squeezes my hip and I nuzzle into the crook of his warm neck and I know that he's my boyfriend, that his heart is speeding like mine. There are a million things we don't have to talk about because we know. And that doesn't make everything hunky-dory, but it might make each piece of the mess a little bit easier to take.

The van stops and we climb out. We walk up a narrow road on a small hill. There is a red-brick patio lined with rows and rows of tables and smelling of fresh running water and savory sauces and so much food. There are hundreds of mostly Cretan people mingling around the tables. And in the middle of the patio is the largest tree I've ever seen. Its trunk is so thick it would take me and Sam and Sadie and Rose and Edie and my parents working together to hug all the way around it. It's bumpy like a child made it out of clay and couldn't be bothered to flatten out the knobs and indentations. It looks like a series of Santorini steps are carved into its side, for the little feet of garden gnomes to climb. The branches above are as thick as the average tree trunk and the sun shines through the green leaves, casting the entire patio in a jade light.

Sam and I stand hand in hand staring up at the monstrous tree and then I hear a voice behind us. "Ivan's mom invited over five hundred people. Can you believe it?" I turn. Andrea is smiling at us. It's not until then that I realize we are standing next to Sadie and Rose. "This is actually small for a Greek wedding. Most of them have thousands of guests!"

I try to smile at Sadie but she looks away.

"I'm so glad you guys are here," Andrea is saying. "I'm grateful to have at least a few familiar faces."

Then she's called away.

"Welcome!" Ivan's father stands on the other side of the tree with a microphone. "We want to welcome everyone to our party to celebrate the wedding of our son, Ivan, and his new wife, Andrea."

I join in as the Greek crowd whoops and applauds. It's nice to be in a crowd where I am actually one of the different ones. Where my difference is obvious and not hidden. Here, it's no big deal to be Haitian or lesbian or just me because we'll all be singled out as the Americans.

I turn to smile at Sadie again, but she's gone somewhere else. I try not to be disappointed.

"We are so pleased to be hosting this party at the Tree of Life," Ivan's father says. "Because this wedding represents the expanding of our family. Now, for our American family and friends, let me briefly tell the story."

There's a good-natured groan from the Greek crowd. Sam puts his arm around my shoulders and squeezes.

"We all know Zeus was quite a ladies' man," Ivan's father starts. People chuckle around us. "So once Zeus had been married to his sister Hera for a while, his wandering eye got the best of him and he disguised himself as a bull and kidnapped the beautiful Europa. Europa was an interesting choice because, while she was a privileged young lady of some royalty, she was still human. So Zeus the flying bull flew Europa to this tree and this is where they, ahem, created the first of Zeus's illegitimate children, King Minos and King Rhadamanthus."

Everyone else shifts around but I'm drawn in. This was the religion years and years ago? A god who was married to his sister? Who disguised himself to create illegitimate children? This was a story they told, a god they prayed to?

"Now, I don't know too many who believe in Zeus anymore," Ivan's father is saying. "But Zeus doesn't care. Because look at this tree."

I can feel everyone studying its beauty and nature right along with me.

"This is how it looks all year long. In the wind the leaves stay put. In the snow the tree stays warm. It never drops a leaf. You never see red or green or orange even when all of the trees around it turn to the colors of autumn. This tree always thinks it's summer. It always thinks it is time for new life. It has molded itself to fit the little feet of the many children who have climbed it. It has grown extra branches so that the heaviest ones will not fall. This is truly the Tree of Family, the Tree of Fertility, the Tree of Life. And likewise, we hope that the marriage of our son, Ivan, and our new daughter, Andrea, will always be full of life. Now let's dance!"

Sam pulls me to the dance floor and we do our best to copy the Greeks' graceful movements, but I keep my eyes on the tree umbrella-ing above our heads. There are a lot of things in this world that won't make sense, I decide. A lot of things maybe religion can't explain. And maybe we're supposed to live in a world of mystery.

The music slows down and I spend a song pressed tight to Sam, laughing at his jokes, whispering to him that he looks smashing, and only blushing a little. When the next song begins and it's still slow, I feel a tapping on my shoulder.

I turn.

There's Sadie, smiling at me. "Can I cut in?" she asks.

I step aside to give her to her brother. She'll yell at him for dancing with me. She'll demand he doesn't date me. I don't know what he'll say.

"No!" she says. "I want to dance with you, Coley."

Now Sam walks away. Sadie holds both my hands and starts twirling me like we're little kids and I follow but I can't bring myself to giggle.

"I'm not sorry I brought you here," she says.

"I'm not sorry I came."

"Because you like my brother," she says. She's looking at me out of the corner of her eye like she thinks it's funny, like she's harmlessly teasing me, but it might be a trap.

"How about this tree?" I change the subject. "What a story, huh?"

"What story?" Sadie asks, ducking to spin herself under my arm.

I stop dancing. "The one Ivan's dad just told," I say.

Sadie turns a little pink. "I missed it." She sways and swings her arms around, dancing in front of me like it doesn't matter if anyone joins her. "I wasn't here."

"Where—"

"I was with Rose!" she says, happy and quiet and whispering and all best-friendish. And even if I'm not her best friend anymore, my face lights up for her. "Over there!" She points past the tree. "Kissing!" she says, lowering her voice.

"That's good?" I say, but I can tell it is.

"Thanks to you," she says. "You did it, Coley."

Now I start dancing.

I shrug. "I talked to her. That's all."

"No," Sadie says, finishing a twirl. "That's not all. I realized that if I could be that wrong about you for so long, you who I knew better than anyone, I could also be wrong about Rose." She smiles at me. "And I realized that if you could find a way to hold on to me, even after so many years of me pushing you away, then I better find a way to hold on to Rose."

"Good," I say. "I'm happy for you."

I try to mean it. I try not to be jealous that at the end of this Rose gets the forgiveness and I only get the thank-you.

"You know," Sadie says, "you're right that it wasn't all your mom and it wasn't all me being gay and you being all Christian. It wasn't all one thing. But you're wrong also."

I raise my eyebrows.

"You're wrong that it had to happen. It never had to happen," she says. "If it had to happen, if we were supposed to not be friends, even for a little while . . . it wouldn't have hurt so much."

And now, even though we're both smiling, we're also crying and we're hugging and it doesn't matter that Sadie is gay or that she's Sam's sister or that she was mean to me three years ago or any of the things that always seemed to matter so much. It matters that she's mine. My friend. My fish. My Sadie.

Ω

I don't invite Sam into my hotel room that night. There will be so many nights in the future for making out, for enjoying my hands on his skin, marveling at the way my heart beats into his. Nights for the kind of completely self-assured belly-laughing that comes with Sam's jokes, for the puffed-up feeling in my chest that comes from making him laugh. There will be lots and lots of moments and days and years for that. But there won't be lots and lots of mornings in Greece.

So I curl into my bed and I let the memories of summers past, of squealing-girl laughter, of pretend-games and board-walk milk bottles and jumping waves and yanking ankles dance in my brain all night. And in the morning, like I knew she would be, she's there as soon as the sun is rising.

She's taken my air-dried Speedo off my unlocked door-knob and even though I'm awake as soon as she opens the door, I stay still until she whips it across my body.

Then we're up and we're outside. The two of us, Sadie and Coley, run barefoot in our one-pieces through the sprawling green campus of the resort. We run and run until we splash directly into the frigid Cretan sea as if it were the Jersey shore, and we dive underneath, squealing and laughing. We swim as far as we can, then we stop and jump a wave and splash each other and dive for ankles, and I know that today, just for today, we are not getting out of the water.

Because we had to grow up. We had to deal with hor-mones, with broken hearts, with boyfriends and girlfriends, with parents who make mistakes, with loneliness, and with finding new friends to fill it. And we'll have to grow up even more. We'll have to deal with college, with moving away, with making up our own minds, choosing our own faiths, creating our own families, and finding so many more friends.

But we don't have to be grown-ups today.

Today is a summer day. And there's nothing in any part of the world as fun as a summer day with Sadie Pepper.

Acknowledgments

Michelle Nagler, thank you for starting this revision like an editing rock star, and Caroline Abbey, thank you for finishing it like an editing maestro. Heartfelt thanks to Laura Whitaker and everyone at Bloomsbury for all of the polishing, support, publicity, and on and on.

Kate McKean, thank you for your help with the idea and the early drafts, and for fielding my endless questions. And especially for your pep talks!

To the people of Santorini and Crete, thank you for being so welcoming, informative, and proud of your islands and culture. What a way to research!

Jessica Verdi, Corey Ann Haydu, Dhonielle Clayton,

Mary G. Thompson, Alyson Gerber, Sona Charaipotra, Amy Ewing, and Riddhi Parekh, your encouragement in the early drafts and your vision in the later ones were priceless. Thank you.

Nestor Alvarado, thank you for consistently answering my questions in Spanish.

Deep and heartfelt thanks to all my friends for supporting my dream with such enthusiasm. I'm more grateful to you than I could describe. Katherine Aragon, Kate Beck, Rebecca Beers, Megan Burke, Molly and Mike Colonna, Kathy Davidson, Melissa Heinold, Linda Hu, Leslie Marchese, Jenn Meyers, Tommy Obst, and Betsy Schroeder, thank you for the steps you took to support book one (*Me, Him, Them, and It*) and to help set up this one for success!

I am so grateful to my entire family. Aunt Catherine and Brittany, thank you for the support of your book clubs. Sarah, Mary Lou, Bridget, Ali, Greg, Kelly, and Kelly, thank you for your e-mails, discussions, and consistent checking-in. And to all of my aunts, uncles, and cousins, thank you. I don't know where I would be without your support.

Ronnie, Eric, Eileen, Eric, Tommy, and Erin Larsson, thank you for welcoming me, and my books, into your family. Your enthusiasm, reading, spreading the word, celebrating, and general awesomeness are more than I could ask for.

Dan Carter, brother, your support of the first book blew me away. Thank you for standing behind my dream and for reading my books . . . even if they aren't comedies.

Beth and Bill Carter, Mom and Dad . . . this is the hardest sentence to write. There's no way to thank you for being the kind of parents you are and always have been. I am immensely grateful for everything you've taught me, for the support you've given me, and, especially, for the way you've loved me.

And finally, endless, bottomless, boundless thanks to my favorite travel buddy, my life partner, my love. Greg Larsson, I love you.